"YOU LIKE MAKING IT DIFFICULT FOR A MAN, DON'T YOU?"

Annie didn't respond but moved into the next room. A four-poster bed draped in white netting. The bridal suite, of course.

Ryan's touch on her bare skin sent a little spasm through her. "You won't let any male past your wall where you keep your feelings locked."

He was so close she could feel his breath on her face.

"It has been the only way I could survive in a man's world."

His hands cupped her shoulders, bared by the cut of the red gown. "Let yourself surrender, Annie. Only in surrender do you really win."

At these words she felt a curious weakness. "I don't know how to do that. Surrender."

"Tonight I am going to show you."

Also by Parris Afton Bonds

For All Time
Dream Time

Available from
HarperPaperbacks

Dream Keeper

PARRIS AFTON BONDS

HarperPaperbacks
A Division of HarperCollinsPublishers

This is a work of fiction. The characters, incidents, and dialogues are products of the author's imagination and are not to be construed as real. Any resemblance to actual events or persons, living or dead, is entirely coincidental.

HarperPaperbacks *A Division of* HarperCollins*Publishers*
10 East 53rd Street, New York, N.Y. 10022

Cover illustration by Pino Daeni

First printing: January 1994

Printed in the United States of America

HarperPaperbacks, HarperMonogram, and colophon are trademarks of HarperCollins*Publishers*

❖ 10 9 8 7 6 5 4 3 2 1

For Lou Todd

You are that golden thread that
makes the fabric of life brighter and better.
How blessed I was when our threads
interwove twenty years ago.

According to the aboriginal people's "Dreamtime" legends, Australia was once a vast featureless land inhabited by giant spirit creatures. Over time, the spirits made epic journeys across the land, creating mountains, rivers, rocks, animals, and plants.

To eighteen-year-old Annie Tremayne, her late father and mother were such spirit creatures—larger than life. Over time, Annie's parents and her grandmother, the renowned old lady, Nan Livingston, had changed the face of Australia with their epic deeds.

They were the Dream Keepers. People who pushed back the boundaries of possibility. Each in search of his or her own Dreamtime.

BOOK ONE

Once a jolly swagman camped by a billabong,
Under the shade of a coolibah tree;
And he sang as he watched and he waited
till his billy boiled,
"Who'll come a-waltzing Matilda with me?"

1

1870

"*I don't know who I am* or what I want to be!" Daniel Tremayne said.

Annie's backbone slumped lower in her grandmother's settee, about the only comfortable piece of furniture in the old lady's office. Annie watched her brother pace before the large leather-top desk. She knew exactly what was going through her twin's mind.

As much as her brother loved their grandmother, he was weary of being groomed by her to be heir to the powerful New South Wales Traders, Ltd.

"Of course, you do, my pet." With a veined and liver-spotted hand, the eighty-six-year-old grande dame of Australia patted his arm. "You want to be premier of New South Wales. When the timing is right, naturally."

Daniel's boyish mouth drooping like a mournful hound's, he stepped away from her desk and her clasping hand to move closer to the windows of the New South Wales Traders' office that overlooked Argyle Street below and the harbor beyond.

Too often, Annie had looked out upon the same scene. Throughout their childhoods, she and Dan had alternated between the wonderful wide spaces of the Dream Time station and the confines of the NSW Traders office in Sydney. Occasionally, they had roamed its wharfs and warehouses. Nan Livingston's magnificent house overlooking Elizabeth Bay had been merely a showplace to sleep and sometimes eat. Life for Nan Livingston began and ended here at NSW Traders.

Iron-clad ships jostled for space in Sydney Cove with the wool clippers, their masts looking like a leafless forest. Many of those ships carried NSW Traders' registry. July had brought a wintry storm screeching in from the Pacific, and the ships bobbed liked corks on the turbulent gray water.

Today, the initials C.O. on the post office flag signaled that a telegraph had been received stating that the mail packet had been sighted off Cape Ottway, forty-four days away.

"Aren't the ships lovely, Daniel?" Nana said. "Look at all their brasswork glinting in the sun.

Their fantasy figureheads and crows nests. Where have all those square-rigged sails been blown? How I wish I hadn't been born a woman. I would have shimmied up those foremasts to the crow's nests with the ease of any buccaneer."

This was one area that Annie could agree with Nan. To have been born a man would have been ever so much more fun. Perhaps that was why Annie loved Dream Time. There in its untamed expanse she was free to be.

Simply . . . to be.

Why couldn't she derive pleasure, as did Nan Livingston, from watching NSW Traders' vessels arrive, putting in from far-flung places? The old woman knew every rivet and every meter of wire rig and wooden mast and spar.

Daniel jammed his hands in the pockets of his tweed jacket. Staring out at the symbols of his family's wealth, he asked quietly in a voice that occasionally still drifted upward into the soprano range, "Lately, Nana, I have wondered what price my parents paid in sharing your dreams for Australia."

"Their lives," Annie said softly. She rose and crossed to Dan in that silent feline tread peculiar to her. Just another example of the differences between her twin and her. Dan had confided once that he felt cursed by his small frame—that it was short, delicate, and awkward like a girl's. Her own rangy frame had the agility of an aborigine experienced in shimmying up trees and treading their limbs with the precision balance of a tightrope walker.

Unlike her twin, the shy Annie had been saddened but not diminished by their parents' deaths. Annie's strength was renewed by her occasional visits to the desolate beauty of the outback, which Daniel could only detest. Australia's people, not its land, fascinated her brother.

When everything was considered, she and Daniel weren't alike at all. In looks, there was only the vaguest similarity, with Annie inheriting her parents' extraordinary height. Rebellious red hair framed her square face with its soft hazel-green eyes, whereas his eyes and hair were "boringly brown," as he had once complained.

Annie knew who she was and what she wanted. Life at Dream Time.

"I don't want death," he muttered now. "I want life. My life."

Behind them, Nan said, "You talk as if I don't want you to have a life of your own. I only want you to have the best life possible. That's why I've been preparing you for a successful takeover at NSW Traders's helm when I'm gone."

Preparing?

More like maneuvering and manipulating, Annie thought. She put an encouraging hand on Dan's shoulder. He turned his head to look at her, and she saw the flicker of a memory they both shared. A beastly painful memory.

Her brother's gaze moved past her to Nan. It seemed to Annie that he forced himself to turn and face his grandmother. Annie knew her grandmother loved him best. Her biased affection had become overt after her daughter's and son-in-law's deaths in an explosion that had ripped apart a paddle steamer on which they had been journeying.

"You called me back from Oxford for some reason. What is it, Nana?"

She shifted her diminutive, mummylike frame in the wing chair. "Hartford College had let out for the summer, Daniel. It's not as if I'm taking you away from your studies."

Annie saw her brother's hands knot in his pockets. She knew that feeling when trying to hold her own with their grandmother. Sometimes Annie felt as if there wasn't enough air to breathe. Especially here in NSW Traders' offices.

Right now, she had the uneasy feeling that her twin was going to be giving up something if he surrendered one more time to the irascible old woman. And, God, they both loved her so much. Owed her so much.

Nana was a tough disciplinarian. She knew the meaning of the word in its fullest sense, because she had been transported to Australia as a convict, sentenced in England for collaborating with the French.

Since Annie and Daniel were nine, when their parents had died, their grandmother had taken over raising them. She had given unstintingly of herself . . . and had demanded everything of Daniel. Annie knew Daniel feared his best was not enough, would never be enough.

"Nana has found a wife for you," she said. Yesterday morning she had espied him crossing the common between the stock trader's market and the entry to George Street. He had been with the daughter of a grazier, the holder of a small selection a few miles from Sydney, and so she had avoided them, though she knew he had seen her.

Sensing the showdown that was coming, Annie returned to the settee to sit out the coming scene. She plopped down and stretched out her long legs. Her lean, lithe body was clad with a Dolly Varden dress, named after the heroine in Dickens's *Barnaby Rudge*. The dress was too frilly and did not become her. The printed cashmere material gathered over a bustle in the back accented her slouching position.

"Annie, sit up straight like a lady!" Nan turned her piercing hazel eyes back on Daniel. "I've met a charming girl I thought you might have some interest in, Daniel. She is the daughter of the owner of the Broken Hill Silver Mines."

Daniel visibly shuddered.

Another intrusion in his life, Annie thought.

His gaze flew to her, and she knew he thought she must have gone to their grandmother and told her about sighting him with a mere grazier's daughter yesterday. Why wouldn't he think his sister a tattler after that horrible episode with the letter years before?

Her eyes returned to her grandmother's implacable expression. Nan would never countenance an alliance with a grazier's daughter. Was this one more of his grandmother's machinations, a diversionary tactic?

To Daniel's credit, he managed to keep his voice calm and level. "Really? Why would I be interested in her?"

The old woman's fingertips pressed against each other and released and pressed again much like the childhood game of spider and mirror. "She is lovely, refined, educated—a graduate of Vassar College in the United States."

"A graduate? How old is she?"

"Only two years older than you."

The way her hand waved, as if dismissing the statistic, triggered an alarm clanging in Annie's ears. Surely Daniel had heard it, too. "Tell him, Nana. He's going to find out anyway."

"Tell me what?"

Nan Livingston sighed. "Yesterday's *Sydney Dispatch* announced your betrothal to Caroline Balzaretti."

"What?"

"I had nothing to do with that leak. James Balzaretti and I had merely discussed the possibility and had agreed not to pursue it any further until you and Caroline met."

"My God!"

"Daniel, the Balzarettis are pure merino sires and dams."

Annie hated that term, merino. It implied that their blood was not tainted by convict ancestry. She watched Daniel run a finger under his stock collar and knew her brother was, at last, fast reaching his own explosion point. Often, she had felt that same rage coming before she even knew what it was. She and Daniel had never been allowed to be angry openly.

"My God, Nana!"

"Control your temper, young man, or you will be sent to your room."

"Damn your interfering, dominating soul, Nana! If you want connections, marry off Annie to some lord. After all, Annie is *your* watchdog!"

With tears in her eyes, Annie sprang to her feet. "You're all too ready to spend the income from NSW Traders, but you're not willing to give up your style of living. You're not the one who has to come second!" Was that her shouting? It must have been.

"I never wanted to be first!"

Their grandmother looked as startled as Annie felt.

Daniel stepped forward, as if he had made a decision. Never before had either her brother or she made a decision. Not one that wasn't influenced by their grandmother. Or maybe even this one was influenced by her, because Daniel looked as though he were finished with letting her control his life.

Did her brother, like herself, need desperately to find himself? To prove himself?

With her heart afire with fear, she saw her twin silently, coldly, turn and walk out the door, out of the mansion, out of her grandmother's and her lives.

"Where do you think Daniel's gone? This isn't like him."

Annie watched her grandmother pacing the parlor. No one would have guessed she was eighty-six, such vitality emanated from her. "You don't know that. He hasn't lived here since he was twelve. Why did you send him to Harrow, Nana, when he only wanted to stay here in Australia?"

"I had his destiny to consider. Our colonial prep schools could never provide the kind of education needed for a country's leader."

Destiny? Did she think she was a divine force shaping human beings? "Then why couldn't you have just sent him to a smaller boarding school in England?"

The old lady stopped pacing, and her black alpaca skirt swirled about her high-buttoned boots. "Trust me. I know what's best for my grandson."

Annie wondered why Nana didn't remember often enough that she was her granddaughter. An education in the colony had been good enough for Annie.

"Don't you think Daniel's old enough to make the decision about what's best for himself, Nana?"

Nan Livingston waved a hand in a dismissing gesture. "Daniel is immature for his age." She resumed her pacing. "Where could that child be? Annie, tell Wright to get the phaeton and drive down to The Rocks. I want him to check out all the pubs and dives. Tell him not to forget the brothels on Pitt Street. Daniel could have taken it in that young male's brain of his to go on a bender in order to assert his independence."

Annie pivoted and headed for the servants' quarters, on the lower floor at the rear of the three-story Georgian mansion. She got no farther than halfway down the long corridor with its frames of Romney portraits and marble busts. Her footsteps slowed, faltered, then stopped.

After all, Annie is your watchdog.

That remark hurt. Yet in a sense, she supposed it was true. In her mind's eye she saw the letter . . . saw herself waving it like a captured flag.

Nan Livingston had used the letter in subtle ways to gain her objectives, just as she used Annie.

Why did she let her grandmother use her?

Because she so desperately wanted her approval.

Her footsteps resumed. In Annie, Nan Livingston had found a reluctant ally.

*   *   *

Cold seeped through Daniel's bone marrow. He burrowed deeper into his Chesterfield. Wind whipped the velvet collar, torn by brambles, against his chilled cheeks. He curled his body into a fetal position around the base of the teak tree and willed his mind to numbness, willed his mind to dream again.

The dream had been a pleasant one . . . of his parents, hugging each other, with Annie and him playfully trying to squeeze between them. Laughter, hot Christmas sunshine, cinnamon smell of plum pudding, hot spiced claret, evergreen decorations.

Like warm amber liquid pouring from a brandy bottle, the dream flowed from that Christmas holiday to another holiday, summer vacation. Home at last after his first year at Harrow. A sunny but cold July day and the letter. The letter from Harrow.

Daniel whimpered in his sleep.

He had been terrified at leaving home for boarding school. He had begged not to be sent away. His crying had irritated Nanny. She had had her way about Harrow, just as she had had her way about Oxford and her way in arranging every damned detail of his life. Even if it had meant using unorthodox means.

So, he had sailed away to England. More than nine hundred boys from twelve through eighteen lived and studied at the ivy-wreathed college. After

Sydney, with its wide-open spaces and sparkling waters and easy-going mateship, Harrow had seemed gray and crowded and oppressive.

As a colonial, he hadn't fitted in. Furthermore, he had been small and delicate and uncoordinated, which left him watching rugby and boxing from the sidelines.

Bespectacled Benjamin, a second-year student, had been the sunlight in that overcast first year. Slow but affable, Benjamin had offered consolation in return for guidance in ancient history, divinity, Greek, Latin, science, and mathematics.

"The first year is always the hardest for hazing, Daniel. Make it through that and you can make it through anything."

Desperate for friendship, Daniel couldn't deny the boy's request to help him cheat on those all-important exams. The exams that meant being sent back home a disgrace if one didn't pass.

It was Daniel who had been sent back home a disgrace. The letter from Harrow announcing his expulsion for cooperating in cheating had been a shame that he didn't think he could bear. Certainly unthinkable in the Livingston family. His grandmother had thought he had merely returned home for the summer holidays.

Of course, she was bound to learn the truth sooner or later. But to learn of his dishonor as she did—through the letter . . .

Dreading the coming confrontation with his

grandmother, Daniel had intercepted the letter from Harrow's administration brought by the mail packet. He had wanted to know its full contents and prepare her himself for the worse.

Mortified, he had been reading its castigation of his shameful deed when Annie had playfully yanked the letter from his hands.

Though she might have given it back immediately, the terror revealed in his face had prompted her to dash down the backstairs, waving the letter like a captured flag. But Nanny had captured Annie next—and the letter.

Heat from humiliation had burned red splotches on his cheeks. In his dream, he could even feel his cheeks burning.

Damn Annie. Treacherous Annie. Always spying on him, telling on him, siding with Nana. Annie wanted to be the cherished child. To the point of this latest betrayal that had resulted in his grandmother choosing his own wife. Damn Annie to bloody hell.

Something nudged him back to reality. The dream slipped away, and the burning in his cheeks was from the bitter cold morning.

And the nudging . . . he opened his eyes to find what it was that nudged him: the cold barrel of a Winchester jabbed at his genitals. "Bat an eyelash and you'll find your poke stuffed up your arse, lad," warned Frank Smythe.

2

1871

Gray, heaving water grudgingly permitted the curvetting bows of the NSW Traders' brig to enter the calmer ones of the Thames River. With her mouth thinned, Annie dismissed the Atlantic in favor of the measured booming of the glassy Pacific rollers off Australia's shoreline. She drew her pelisse closer around her shivering body. The month of September felt colder, damper, than any fall day in Sydney that she could remember.

The brig's once-swollen sails began to collapse with each nautical mile that drew the ship closer to Southhampton's grimy industrial port. She could tell that her grandmother was excited. Nana's high color surmounted the rouge painted on her wrinkled cheeks. According to the old woman, it had been over sixty years since last she had seen England and London.

She had been aboard a brig then, too. Sentenced to life in New South Wales, on the other side of the earth, she had not only survived but had triumphed over the horrors of the penal system and the cruel power of the military guards. She had forged a dynasty in that new world.

Ever the independent woman, Nan Livingston preferred to travel unaccompanied by servants. That left Annie to juggle the tedious details of the itinerary.

The voyage was to be another training period for her. Under her grandmother's tutelage, she had learned more than any man working himself up through the ranks of the shipping business.

If nothing else, Nana had taught her the art of shrewd investing. Against the advice of other ship owners, her grandmother had bought several freighters at an extremely low price during a depression. The venture had proven successful— and had proven to Annie that she could best learn from her grandmother.

Nevertheless, Annie had spent a year as an apprentice in NSW Traders's accounting department. She had dutifully learned the system of recording and summarizing the company's financial transactions. Her keen mathematical sense had spurred her into mastering the complexities of the shipping industry. She could analyze, verify, and report any results about which her grandmother inquired.

By the time this voyage was over—England, Spain, Brazil, and India—Annie would have learned all there was about ships, as well as the operations of the company's foreign offices in London, Paris, Calcutta, Shanghai, and a host of other cities with names that evoked exotic images.

"The factorage system has its beginnings in the West Indies, dealing with the home agents of England," her grandmother was saying. Nana's small, delicate frame was turned ever toward the ship's prow and the suburbs of London. "The factor acts at once as merchant and banker. It is important that we know our representatives abroad. Etienne Carondolet is the most accomplished of our factors. We will be his guests during the duration of our visit."

A pall the color of slate hung over the workhouses, factories, and warehouses that encroached on the river, which was itself a dingy gray. Oh, how Annie longed for the surging, ultramarine coastline of the Pacific.

Nan arranged for their trunks to be forwarded to Etienne's home address, and they kept only their portmanteaus. A stagecoach transported Annie and her grandmother on to London. The smoke-filtered sun cast a dismal light on the world's greatest city. More people lived in London than in any other city of the world, and the crowded slums indicated as such. At the littered Victoria Station, her grandmother shepherded her into an underground train.

As it steamed its way through a maze of tunnels, Annie sat petrified. The utter darkness, lit only by intermittent gaslights to assure her she had not descended into Hades, made each intake of breath an agony for her.

Sunlight. She needed sunlight and clear, azure blue skies and tall, green grass gently waving over the empty lands of Dream Time. How could she endure another moment away from Australia?

Had not the train at that moment reached their destination, she would have fled the coach. Like the heroine in the recent best-seller *Alice In Wonderland*, she would have rushed blindly in search of the hole leading back to the earth's surface.

Nan rose from their seat. "A marvel isn't it, Annie? Who would have thought we would be traveling by coach underground? Before long, it will be in the air, I vow."

The train disgorged its passengers, and Nan Livingston sniffed distastefully at the stench of humanity pressing upon her. All around, a strange blend of English assailed Annie's ears. The streets were narrow and dirty, and the sooty buildings blocked the sunlight.

Holding a scented lace handkerchief before her

nose, Nan said, "At my request, Etienne has reserved rooms near Covent Garden."

Annie noted her gaze had a faraway look and knew the old lady was recalling some long-forgotten memory.

"'Tis Brown's, I believe." Nan fished through her reticule and came up with a folded paper. "Aye, once we've refreshed ourselves, I'll send a runner to let him know we've arrived."

Brown's was in the West End, a district famous for its fashionable social life. London's merchants and bankers amassed their fortunes in the City but spent them in the West End.

Eager to feel the taste of open-air freedom, Annie would have dismissed the hack and wandered through Covent Garden's warren of bookstalls, al fresco cafés, map collections, and flower bins. Street musicians vied for her attention with the enticing shouts of the hawkers.

On the other hand, Nan appeared to have changed her mind about the desirability of the Covent Garden area. Before Annie's eyes, the old woman looked as if she were shriveling. Her personal power that at times was like an almost visible light seemed nonexistent now.

Once inside Brown's, Nan regained her formidable vitality. Like a field marshal, she sent the porters scurrying to accommodate her granddaughter and her.

Since 1837, Brown's had been one of the most

famous hostelries in the British Empire, a staunch guardian of properly maintained tradition. The hotel was a result of linking eleven townhouses. Pillared corridors, Venetian chandeliered lobby, and palm-court lounge for tea drew the Old Guard clientele. Particularly welcome were those whose names were registered in Burke's *Landed Gentry*.

The rooms were nothing short of sumptuous. Comfortable brass beds, spacious baths, salvers of fresh fruit, and copies of the *Times* welcomed them. Annie chose the luxury of a hot bath while her grandmother opted for rest.

Without disrobing Nan lay down on the bed, closed her eyes, folded her hands as if in death, and went into immediate sleep. Noting not for the first time that the old woman never wore jewelry, Annie quietly left the room. Did the process of aging make one androgynous? Or did Nan Livingston, in assuming the role of business leadership, most often masculine in gender, also take on male characteristics? Even the application of rouge and powder was more like armor than an adornment.

The thought was terrifying. Annie swore she would not let that happen to herself. That defeminization. Yet, to succeed in Australia, definitely a man's world, could she afford to be soft, gentle, yielding?

With a sigh, she began dressing. A gown of apple green washing silk was her selection. With a very elaborate fichu front, Watteau sac flowing down the back to the train, and elbow-length sleeves edged with lace ruffles, it was the latest in fashion. Her own statement of her femininity. Her raiment she could control; her wild red hair was another matter. She struggled to subdue it for a good half hour before restraining it in an expensive jade-beaded snood.

Too soon, Etienne's carriage arrived to convey them to the Carondolet home. The house stood in its own glorious parkland with a soft-flowing creek eddying below its grassy slope.

Observing the magnificent estate, Annie commented drily, "I thought you said Monsieur Carondolet was our factor."

"*Comte* Carondolet." Nan Livingston sat straighter in the carriage seat. She seemed to beam. "His family lost its land holdings with the French Revolution but have retained their title. Etienne is the best factor, or else I wouldn't have engaged him."

Two massive chimney stacks dominated the manor, built of rough lime-plastered stone. The French penchant for melding home and garden united fresh flowers, a conservatory, fireplaces, and sumptuous furnishings with a view of the rolling country.

Closer inspection revealed a need for paint and some repairs. The house was a little shabby but still retained its former grandeur. The exquisite Empire sideboard in the entry attested to the value of the mansion's contents.

Etienne greeted Annie and her grandmother himself. Portly, though only in his early thirties, his manner was aloof and formal. His attire was equally conservative, a single-breasted dress coat with stand collar, waistcoat, and peg-top trousers, all of dark worsted. He bowed, then surveyed his guests with expressive brown eyes. "You must be weary, *Mesdames.*"

"Oui, un peu, mais je m'attends avec plaisir à discuter des affaires de la société."

His eyebrows rose in his already high forehead, giving the illusion of a rapidly receding hairline. "As I, also, am looking forward to discussing company business. You speak French quite well."

A look of nostalgia softened the old woman's face. "I had the opportunity to learn it in my youth. A French friend." She brushed her black-gloved hands together. "My granddaughter, however, doesn't. Perhaps our visit will present the opportunity for her to learn the language."

That proved to be true as Etienne made himself available for Annie and her grandmother. French phrases were sprinkled in every exchange during a five-course dinner that evening and over the following four days when the two women accompanied him to his offices in the City, which were just east of the Tower Bridge near the Port of London Authority docks.

The use of French added confusion to Annie's study of the factoring aspect of the shipping business.

Etienne patiently and graciously expended extra time to explain the intricacies of his end of the business.

"I act as a commission merchant in the purchase of supplies and cargo and I discharge the functions of an agent in selling the products of my clients. *Est-ce que vous comprenez?*"

He was leaning near her, his hands braced on his massive, highly varnished desk, behind which she was sitting. Ledgers were spread before her, and she was busy deciphering the gist of the transactions. Every so often she would jot down a note or scribble a reminder for herself.

She sensed an intensity in his closeness. She glanced up over her shoulder. That close, she could see a speck of dandruff on his dark frockcoat. He was staring down at her. "Is something wrong?" she asked.

"*Non, non, mademoiselle.* I am only observing with amazement. I had thought your grandmother was one of a kind, an anomaly. I see her duplicate in you."

"Me?" She didn't know whether to take the remark as a compliment or not. In many ways, she admired her grandmother, stood in awe of her. And yet the way her grandmother used a person to achieve her ends, even if she thought it was in the person's best interest . . . Annie could not imagine ever being ruthless enough to manipulate people the way Nan did.

"Can you explain how you set up your contacts in the various cities abroad?" she asked with business-like efficiency. "What criteria do you use in gaug-ing the value of the commodities you represent? Do you correspond with—"

He held up his hands, and a smile squeezed wry lines on either side of his mouth. "You go too fast for me, mademoiselle. Most of my business trans-actions are simple and take place in coffeehouses."

Her smile echoed his self-deprecating one. "I have learned something, *Comte* Carondolet. Sim-plicity, even in business."

"Etienne, *s'il vous plaît.* Shall we join your grandmother?"

Nan had been inspecting a shipment of Ameri-can goods that had arrived in the warehouse below the office. She met them in the vestibule, patting the perspiration from her powdered face with her handkerchief. "An excellent system you have established, Etienne. No wonder you are so success-ful. Let the English take tea, I prefer wine."

"You are a lady after my own heart, madame. May I suggest that you and your granddaughter accompany me tonight to a reception being held at a hotel for a Belgian diplomat? The wine is only the best, and a jolly time is to be had there."

The reception was in progress by the time they arrived with Etienne. When dinner was served, Etienne escorted Annie and Nan into a private din-ing room. Its formal atmosphere was stifling.

Annie managed to sit sedately, her tie-back trained skirt arranged modestly. All the while she made polite conversation, when what she wanted to do most was flee the crowded room. Flee England. Return to the limitless plains of Australia.

Eventually, the guests, abetted by wine, relaxed. The formality between the French count and the Australian shipping magnate fell away noticeably. Annie picked up Etienne's lowered voice. "A woman of your stature, madame, should be presented at court."

Nan took a sip from her wineglass. "I would much prefer to attend a play at the Drury Theater." For an instant her gaze took on that faraway look again. "I once saw Goldsmith's *She Stoops to Conquer* performed there. The king was in attendance that night."

"Ah, but people have more respect for the throne these days. To be presented to Queen Victoria is an event one never forgets. She has the brain of a man with the heart of a woman."

For the first time, Annie spoke. "She has the brain and heart of a great human being."

Both Etienne and her grandmother stared at her. He nodded his head in acquiescence. "'The Queen will not be dictated to,'" he said, a quote oft attributed to the queen and one which he seemed to be making as an allusion to Annie. A reprimand or a tribute?

When the guests adjourned to the ballroom for a

continuation of the soiree, Etienne asked, "Would you care to dance, mademoiselle?"

Annie froze. She had had dancing lessons, naturally, but had never danced in public. As a child, she had been lanky and gauche. Haunting memories still made her movements stiff, awkward.

"Go ahead, child," Nan prompted.

"Come," Etienne said. "You will find the activity most enjoyable."

To demur would be less than courageous. She held up her hand and permitted him to lead her out onto the dance floor. Only three other couples occupied it. Etienne held her most properly, his kid-gloved hands never touching her bare skin. He moved well with the waltz's tempo, and after a few moments she relaxed.

Apparently, he did not. Perspiration sheened his high forehead. For a worldly businessman, a French count at that, he seemed very nervous.

A smile formed dimples at either side of her mouth. "You were right, *Comte* Carondolet. This is most pleasurable."

His intent expression lightened. "When we go to Paris, I will show you *l'Opera*, the racetrack, *le Comédie Française*. . . ."

She stiffened. "You will be accompanying us?"

He looked uncomfortable. "You grandmother and I discussed it. Since I have traveled extensively in the land of my forebears, it seemed quite natural that I should act as a friend and guide."

The suspicion that had been but a vague nagging now unfurled into hideous reality. She said nothing more. When they returned to the table, her grandmother peered at her in a searching manner. She knew now what her grandmother was looking for. She said nothing. Her rage was expanding, filling her entire body, consuming every thought so that the merest civilities were an elephantine effort.

When, at last, they returned to Etienne's manor and their own set of private rooms, her grandmother demanded, "What is it? You're a steam kettle ready to spew."

In tight motions Annie stripped her lace glove from her left hand. Her words spilled out like little spasms of the soul. "You tried to manipulate Daniel's life, Nana. He left. I shall, also, if it comes to that. You won't control me."

Her grandmother settled into the Sheraton chair and began arranging her black taffeta skirts. "Whatever are you talking about?"

She whirled on the old woman. "You know exactly what I'm talking about! Etienne. You are trying to arrange a marriage. I marry him and your dynasty inherits a title. He inherits a financial empire. That's it, isn't it?"

Her grandmother lifted an imperious eyebrow. "Is that such a bad exchange?"

"I—and only I—will decide whom I shall marry." She could barely control her rage. What scared her was the knowledge that her overwhelming anger was the result of her fear. That great fear that she would lose herself to that indomitable old woman.

Her grandmother removed a lace handkerchief from her sleeve, where she kept it tucked. "There is Dream Time to consider. I hardly think you could sustain the inheritance from your parents on the present woeful state of the sheep industry."

There. There it was. Her grandmother's metaphorical ace, removed as coolly from her sleeve as her handkerchief. Annie straightened. Her heart felt as if it were vibrating in her rib cage. She felt tears threatening. This weakness made her even more angry. "Dream Time is everything to me. But not the only thing. I am the only thing. My will. My independence. Me!"

The old woman's eyes flared. "Then we are at an impasse?"

Annie took off her gloves and tossed them on the oak commode. The careless gesture contrasted strongly with her emphatic words. "No. I shall do what you wish for the sake of NSW Traders. I shall devote my time to it most diligently. When I am finally allowed to take over the reins, I shall do my utmost to follow in your footsteps. Your business footsteps. Not your personal ones. My private life is my own!"

3

1874

Layers of wrinkles that were eyelids opened. Marble pupils stared up and through her. Clawlike hands reached for her, and she screamed and screamed and screamed.

Sweating, Annie sprang upright in the bed. Her heart thudded so loudly that surely it could be heard throughout the mansion. Except no one else slept in the house. The servants stayed in quarters abutting the carriage house.

She pushed back the swath of deep red hair that had tumbled across her forehead and breathed deeply and slowly until her pulse steadied. Then she swept back the damp sheets and swung her feet over the side of the bed and felt along the nightstand for a match. Light from the kerosene lamp soon spread a warm glow over her bedroom. The clock on the fireplace mantle showed half past four.

She thought about trying to go back to sleep, but she was afraid of dreaming again. That ghastly dream about the funeral two days before. How horridly waxy and unreal Nana had looked. Like one of her ships' figureheads.

Those frightfully boring ships. Mail packets and fishing smacks, cutters, barges, sloops, brigantines, coasters, frigates, even paddlewheelers. Only the clipper, that glorious clipper, the fastest kind of merchant ship, held any appeal for Annie.

For the last three years, Nana had made her meet every incoming ship with an NSW Traders' registry. "You must know the business inside and out, my girl."

Annie knew she would never have her grandmother's steel-trap business mind. Her grandmother knew it, too. Annie believed herself to be intelligent, blessed with a good education and a persevering spirit. Dutifully, she had learned the complexities of NSW Traders but had had no real interest in the company.

Dream Time had been both her life buoy and her albatross. To throw off the latter would be to surrender the former.

Try though she had to oppose Nana's will, she had waged a losing battle for her independence.

She had been too young, too inexperienced, during those years of constant conflict. Now she fully realized what Daniel had had to pay.

She had to be at the solicitor's office at seven. Whittens thought it best to read the terms of the will before his office staff arrived to disturb the privacy of the meeting.

Of course, only she would be there with Nan's solicitor. Daniel would be missing. Detectives hired by her grandmother had failed to locate him since his disappearance three years earlier.

Daniel, where the bloody hell are you?

And, Nana, where are you now?

All her life she had been second to Daniel. He had been Nana's choice. Dear God, but Annie had tried to get her attention. All those years. All those bloody years she had wasted herself, discounted herself. Well, damn it, now she counted!

She closed her eyes and felt the tears trapped behind her lids. *I do count, don't I, Nana? Someone? Please, I do count, don't I?*

Was she crying for herself, or for Nana, after all? The old woman had loved her, had been good to her. She would miss her grandmother. Substantial as a rock, Nan Livingston was, God bless her.

Wearily, she rose from the bed. The room was chilled, but she didn't bother to summon a maid to start a fire. She rummaged through her armoire for something suitable for the mourning period. A heavy black crepe dress with sable trim was her final selection. That and the crepe veil to her bonnet, black gloves, and a black-bordered handkerchief would be businesslike enough to lend her an authoritative presence.

Not that she really cared about the terms of the will with regard to Nana's shipping empire. NSW Traders could go to hell for all Annie cared. She had dutifully learned the intricacies of a business empire that included not only the shipping company, but also two sheep stations, four farms on the Hawkesbury River, a multitude of warehouses, the New South Wales Bank, and the Broken Hill Silver Mine—courtesy of a last-minute buy-out when the intended groom, Daniel, had disappeared.

Annie had also learned that with the cloak of NSW Traders on her shoulders she could understand Daniel's resistance to Nana's manipulations. Annie had come to respect Daniel for leaving.

She wanted only her half of her parents' legacy, the Dream Time station. When she reached the age of twenty-five, it would have been awarded to her anyway, and Daniel would have gotten the Never-Never station.

As it turned out, neither Dream Time nor Never-Never was available. Mr. Whittens explained that the two stations had been set up as subsidiaries of NSW Traders. Hands laced across the paunch of his stomach, the bespectacled old man broke the news to her in his solicitor's most matter-of-fact tone:

"While your grandmother awarded you and Daniel a total of fifty-one percent of the shares of NSW Traders, you must realize that, as a closed corporation, NSW Traders is controlled by the board of directors, who own among them thirty percent share of NSW Traders."

She folded her hands over the ivory knob of her propped umbrella. "Yes?"

He cleared his throat. "Donald MacInnes wants control of NSW Traders."

She stiffened. MacInnes was in a countinghouse partnership with James A. Balzaretti. It was his daughter, Caroline, whom Nana had hoped to induce Daniel to marry.

Had control of NSW Traders been MacInnes's intentions all along? "Are the other four board members behind MacInnes?"

Whitten's eyes widened. "Solidly." His tone held a timbre of respect that hadn't been there when she entered. "MacInnes is a wily, parsimonious Scot."

"I want a list of all the stockholders and how many shares they each hold."

A broad smile spread across his face. "I'll have it delivered to you at your office by the end of the day."

If only she knew where Daniel was. But then, for whose side would he cast his vote—MacInnes or her? The answer was obvious. Daniel cared not a fig for NSW Traders. Moreover, he hated her.

Maybe she deserved his hate. God knew, she had made enough mistakes to damn her in his eyes.

*   *   *

Like pubs, newsrooms were strictly masculine habitats. The aproned pressman behind the counter cast Annie a glance of scorn. She pushed down her rising sense of nervousness and closed her umbrella. June's heavy winter rains had soaked her.

She pushed open the counter's swinging half door. Copying Nana's regal mien, she passed by the newspapermen who worked in their shirtsleeves with their hats perched on the back of their heads. Disdainfully, she lifted her skirts out of the way of wadded paper, pencil shavings, and spittoons. The place smelled of printer's ink and stale cigar smoke.

A hand-lettered plaque on the door at the back of the newsroom declared the publisher of *The Sydney Dispatch* to be Ryan Sheridan. The newspaper was small and struggling against the publishing giant, *The Sydney Herald*, owned by the Randolph family.

Without waiting to be announced, she opened the door. Battling her grandmother's formidable will had taught Annie much about strategy. Selecting one's ground for doing battle and using the element of surprise were two effective tactics.

"Good morning, Mr. Sheridan." She felt fortunate to get the last syllable out. The man behind the battered desk stared back at her with piercing eyes.

All her poise began to waver. Groping for her nerve, she rapped his desk with the tip of her umbrella the same way she used her quirt in front of an insolent station hand who had insulted her gender. He had not questioned her orders again.

She didn't have to get Mr. Sheridan's attention if the steady focus of the disquieting, steel gray eyes was any indication. "I dislike being kept waiting, Mr. Sheridan, so I don't want to be announced."

In the silence, she heard the ticking of the cheap little Manchester clock on his desk. Slowly, he rose. He was tall, slender, and with an unnerving yogic self-control, if the stories circulating around Sydney were to be believed.

A widower who had come over in the second wave of Irish immigrants fleeing another potato famine, Ryan Sheridan had the look of a man who had faced everything and was afraid of nothing.

In his midthirties, his brows were still as black as his hair and as straight and stringent as his mouth, which was flanked by grooves reminiscent of a newspaperman's parentheses. The thought made her smile.

The parentheses responded likewise. "Had I known you were waiting, I would have—"

His easy charm alarmed her, and she took up her last strategy, the offense: Without waiting for him to come around the desk and pull out the spindle-back chair for her, she took a seat. She stabbed the umbrella tip between her feet. "Forewarned, you might have found reason to refuse seeing me."

He raised one level eyebrow. "Why would I do that?"

Drawing a breath, she went straight to the point. "Because you may have already cast your lot with Donald MacInnes."

He resumed his seat. "So, you've changed your mind about being a mere figurehead of NSW Traders?"

She repressed a start of surprise. Apparently not only was a takeover indeed in the works but this man sitting behind the desk knew more about her than she did about him. She kept a formal edge to her voice. "I don't recall ever making such a statement, Mr. Sheridan."

He smiled. A warm smile she wasn't gullible enough to trust. "Not publicly. To your grandmother. Often, from what I judge."

Inside her woolen gloves, her palms grew damp. "Were you a close friend of my grandmother's?"

"A business associate."

His terseness irritated her. "*The Sydney Dispatch* wasn't listed among the assets of my grandmother's estates."

He put his fingertips together. She noticed that his long, slender fingers were ink stained, though the nails were well groomed. He smiled over them at her. He was enjoying baiting her. "Mrs. Livingston owned no shares in my newspaper."

She frowned. "But you own six percent of NSW

Traders? That six percent would buy your newspaper five times over."

"Probably."

She leaned forward. Her jaw felt tight. "Mr. Sheridan, just what were the terms of your business association with my grandmother?"

"We can discuss that at another time. I think you had something else you wished to discuss?"

She didn't know how to proceed. A moment of hesitation separated her next words. "I couldn't care less about NSW Traders." She paused, then said, "You know, my grandmother was the only one who could manipulate me. I won't ever again willingly let anyone get away with that. I need controlling shares. My brother's twenty-five percent might have given me that, but he has not been located."

"Yes, I know. Your grandmother has searched the far reaches of the continent for your twin. With not a single clue."

"You were more than just a business associate, weren't you, Mr. Sheridan? More like a confidant, I would say."

He shrugged. His suit was a black, inexpensive one, and it tugged tightly across his broad shoulders. "What is it you want from me, Miss Livingston? My six percent? If so, you should know it is not for sale. That was part of the arrangement when your grandmother presented the shares to me."

"Presented?"

"Yes. With the provision that I never sell my six percent. Upon my death, they revert either to you or Daniel."

Her eyes narrowed. "Why would my grandmother give *you* six percent of the shares of NSW Traders?"

He turned up his palms. They were callused. "Why? Because I was the only person bold enough to take on *The Sydney Post* and Randolph—or foolish enough. The shares were more than just an act of support in my behalf. They were, primarily, another form of throwing down the gauntlet at Randolph."

She sighed. "Grandmother's implacable enemy. She thwarted his attempt to become governor of New South Wales. He's had one foot in the grave for half a dozen years now, and still she didn't give up."

"Will you? Give up on NSW Traders?"

Her gaze returned to those scrutinizing eyes. "My grandmother was ruthlessly ambitious. I'm not. But I am tenacious. I survived her machinations, loving though their intent might have been. I won't give up the battle with Mr. MacInnes, Mr. Sheridan."

"And you will assume the mantle of leadership of NSW Traders?"

"Yes—if you will pledge your six percent in my behalf at the upcoming stockholders' meeting."

"Why should I?"

She had anticipated that. "Because I am offering you the capital needed for the expansion you had planned for the *Dispatch*—a loan for which several banks have already turned you down."

It was his turn to look surprised. At last, he said, "There is still another thirteen percent of the shares outstanding."

"Belonging mostly to widows of board members."

"What's to keep MacInnes from persuading those widows to come over to his side?"

"If you knew of my indifference to NSW Traders's affairs, then I imagine Mr. MacInnes also knew. He won't be expecting me to force a showdown. Well, is it a deal, Mr. Sheridan?"

He tilted his chair back. "Obviously, it hasn't occurred to you that MacInnes might be more than willing to match your offer."

"It occurred to me. I'm taking my chances."

"I will agree to vote with you, Miss Livingston, on the condition that you also grant me a request should the time come when I need to make it."

"And that is?"

"I shall let you know at that time."

"It would be absurd to agree to do something when I don't know if I have the capacity to do whatever it is."

His smile unnerved her. "Oh, you do. I assure you, you do."

4

1875

Gingerly, Dan unfolded the newspaper clipping. Its edges tattered and frayed, it was from a three-year-old edition of *The Sydney Herald*. He knew its contents by heart. Still, the sight of those words always spurred him onward. New places. New faces.

"Five thousand pounds offered for the whereabouts of the missing person, Daniel Livingston. Please contact the solicitor's firm of Whitten & Assoc., Sydney, NSW."

The colony of Queensland in far northeastern Australia was a new place. A truly tropical paradise of color. Bright orange parrots and metallic silver crocodiles. Emerald green rain forests and purple orchids. The sea-foam green of the Pacific surf and the deep blue of the sky.

New faces, too. The color of the people was almost solely a golden brown. True, quite a few Chinese had immigrated to the gold fields of Queensland, but their yellow-hued skins were still a minority. The darker coffee brown of the aborigine was a rare sight now. The white man had seen to the aborigine extermination. Fortunately, the white man's numbers were few. So Dan felt safe among the warm brown of the placid Polynesians. His past was just that. In the past.

He had spent five years drifting with the Blue Mountain Bushrangers. Horse rustling and cattle duffering, robbing stagecoaches and gold escorts had been a wild rebellion against authority. Against all those years of submission to the autocratic authority of his grandmother.

Oh, the bushrangers enjoyed popular sympathy, though they kept the countryside in a state of terror with their raids. They represented pluck and daring. They were the underdogs, fighting the law, which was not highly respected in the pioneer communities of New South Wales.

Frank Smythe, self-styled leader of the Blue Mountain Bushrangers, would have admitted openly that he was no Robin Hood. The walleyed, shaggy-bearded man in the greasy, tattered greatcoat had wanted only the gold that flowed from the mines of the interior of New South Wales to Sydney, on the coast. He was an American who had come to Australia's gold fields in 1859 and found only the disillusionment of backbreaking labor. The lure of the strongboxes had been much more rewarding.

Daniel's interest had not been the strongboxes of gold dust and nuggets but the banknotes carried by the escort services shuttling between the gold fields and Sydney. A lot of the drafts he had noticed bore the stamp of NSW Traders. With each stagecoach waylaid, then, he had taken perverse satisfaction in abetting the bushrangers and Frank Smythe.

In return, forty-five-year-old Frank had become a father figure to him and had even introduced Dan to his first woman, the prostitute Flora Warwick. She had been, perhaps, the greatest gift in his twenty-five years. From her he had learned that he loved a woman's touch. After those awful years of Nana's domination and Annie's loyalty to her, he had been too insecure and afraid to be with women. How often he had wished the ground would open and swallow up Annie and Nana and NSW Traders!

He tucked the clipping back into his swag with his bedroll and meager possessions and swung it upon his back once more. The coming of the telegraph had brought an end to the bushrangers. With more and more of them swinging from the gallows, Frank had disbanded his merry men, and Dan was on his own once more.

Townsville was less than a decade old when he strolled down Finders, its main street, which bordered Ross Creek. Dominated by Castle Hill with its lookout perched on top, Townsville had been founded in 1864 by Robert Towns, a Sydney-based sea captain and financier. The place flourished, on the back of Kanaka labor—South Sea island natives imported to work on the sugar plantations.

Running out of money, Dan needed employment. This he found on a Monday afternoon on The Strand, a long drive fronting the Pacific Ocean and fringed with awesome banyan trees and coconut palms. Among the beachfront shanties was a clapboard warehouse perched on piers. The warehouse was designated Great Barrier Reef Sugar Ltd. Word was out that the company needed a bookkeeper.

On the building's veranda waited a line of more than a score of Polynesian men interspersed with a few women. They weren't chained, but they wore that haunted, hopeless look he had seen on the last boatload of convicts transported from England before the law was passed in 1868 ending transportation.

Felt hat in hand, his swag on his back, he approached the veranda steps. He shouldered his way past the Polynesian Kanakas. Their clothing was cast-offs, tattered and damp with the humidity that weighted the air. The smell of their fear smote him. Their dark brown eyes alighted on his fair skin and then shifted away. Apathy settled back in those dull gazes.

Inside, the office of Reef Sugar was little more than a reception room. Without glancing up from the ledger before him, a middle-aged man with thinning brown hair and eyeshades said, "I told you, mate, I'm not ready to inventory the blackbirds yet. I'm up to me arse in paperwork."

Dan cleared his throat.

The man looked up. "Yes?"

"I need work."

He nodded toward the screened door. "Those Kanakas can work cheaper than you."

"I wasn't interested in working in the cane fields."

"Oh, I suppose you want to just move in and take on the overseer's job."

Dan's eyes fell on the open ledgers overlapping each other on the already littered desk. "No. I'm more qualified for keeping books."

The man settled back in the chair and eyed him. "You are, are you? Just what qualifies you?"

An education at Harrow, which I doubt you have. He shrugged. "I've had some experience here and there."

The other's eyes narrowed, measuring Dan's bedraggled appearance: the riding boots, scuffed and worn down at the heels; the ill-fitting jacket and baggy, dirty trousers; an ill-kempt beard. "Like where?"

"Wallaby Mills, for one. Sydney." The fictitious company sprang to his lips with surprising ease. "Another one, a freighting company, went out of business."

"I trust it wasn't due to ineptness on your behalf."

At the man's dry tone, a half smile curled Dan's lips, almost obscured by his beard. His mouth's boyish softness had been chiseled away by those years of living a minute-measured desperado's life. "I'd like to prove my capabilities."

The older man tugged at one pendulous earlobe. Then, "What's your name?"

"Dan. Dan Warwick." Flora would be pleased. Her name was carried on.

"Well, Warwick, this office is just a depot for the Kanakas coming in and the cane going out. The main office is at the Reef plantation, some forty kilometers southwest of here. You talk to Master Brannaka. Tell him I sent you to apply. He'll make the decision."

Hope surged in Dan. He forgot his growling stomach. "Is there any kind of transportation going in that direction?"

"Only the blackbird barge goes that far upriver. Catch a ride with it. Ties up at the Dean Street Bridge and leaves at the eighth hour every Tuesday."

The forty-odd kilometers of river provided a panorama ranging from mangrove swamps and salt marsh to rugged ranges whose steeply rising peaks harbored tropical rain forests. Colorful birds were abundant: kingfishers, parrots, rosellas, kookaburras, lorikeets. A screaming cloud of black cockatoos exploded into flight. Their voices were a combination of fluting, raucous, deep melodic tones. Once, he spotted a red koala, disturbed from its sleep by the barge, clambering through a kari's boughs.

Occasional pockets of banana groves and rice and cotton fields marked the barge's arduous process upstream toward the Great Barrier Reef Sugar Plantation.

Queensland sugar had to compete with that grown by cheap black labor in Fiji, Java, and South Africa. In a colony where the demand for labor exceeded supply, it was impossible to employ whites in the cane fields except for wages that would have made the sugar unsalable.

So the sugar planters were importing labor from the Pacific islands to clear, plant, and cut the sugar. These laborers came to be called Kanaka, from the Hawaiian word for man. The Kanakas were seduced from their island homes or sold by their chiefs to white men, and then sold again on the wharves in Brisbane, Mackay, and Townsville.

Who was Dan to castigate—the white man for trading in blackbirding or the islanders themselves for selling off their own people? "A bloody mess," he murmured, then asked one of the Kanakas squatting nearby, "Are you hungry?" He had some cheese and still-warm bread he had purchased earlier that evening.

"Tonkil doesn't understand English."

The voice of a woman came softly out of the gloomy mist. He half swiveled to his right on his haunches. The gauzy veil of steamy vapor cast a mysterious beauty upon the very young woman, sitting with her back against the deckhouse. Her lustrous brown eyes steadily measured him.

He found his voice. "Who are you?"

"Kai. It is Polynesian for seawater." Her voice had a smooth, cultured quality that captivated him. So different from the strident doxies and gold-camp followers to which he had become accustomed over the past three years.

He turned to face her fully now. Her waist-length black hair entranced him. Free flowing, her tresses were in contrast to the bound hair of the so-called civilized woman of his culture. Her face was round as only a South Pacific moon could be. She wasn't really pretty by society's standards. "Where did you learn English?"

"From missionaries. The Baptist Missionary Society." That soothing softness momentarily deserted her voice.

"How old are you?"

"You ask a lot of questions. Questions whose answers are unimportant." She mimicked his clipped British tone: "'Are you hungry?' Does it matter? Feed Tonkil tonight and she will still go hungry for the rest of her days. Why bother?"

Her cynicism struck him like a slap. "You can't be more than fifteen."

Her smile was gentle. "Twenty-two. According to the missionaries' calendar."

He swung his swag off his back and reached inside to pull out the hunk of cheese, besmeared with the dirt of various hands handling it. He broke of a portion and passed it to her. She hesitated, then took it. "Thank you."

Her genuine gratitude affected him as no other woman had—his grandmother's interference, Flora's generous heart, Annie's little treacheries with her spying on him, telling on him, siding with Nana.

The young woman leaned forward to pass the girl her portion. Tonkil gobbled it like a starving rat. "Tonkil is my half sister," the young woman said. "We share the same father. A missionary. His other wives were glad to see us leave."

Dan could barely keep the scorn from his voice. "'Strewth, he believes in spreading the gospel of love!" He broke off another piece and handed it the young Polynesian woman.

"When we arrive at the plantation, the new workers will all be fed."

Dan glanced up to find who had spoken—Rob Fitzroy, the Reef's overseer. The lanky man had agreed to take Dan upriver to meet with the plantation's owner, Gunther Brannaka. "How long will that be?"

Fitzroy's spindly fingers tugged at his earlobe. The man had bristly gray sideburns and his fair skin had been burnt and wrinkled by the sun. "Oh, that could be around noon or late evening— depending, ye see, on the sandbars, the current, the traffic on the river, the number of hands who show up to man the barge."

"Tomorrow evening is a long time for these people to wait for food."

Fitzroy shrugged his bony shoulders. "That's Master Brannaka's system. But once the workers are on Reef soil, he sees to it that they are well cared for. Count on that."

The overseer shuffled off to check on the rest of the barge's human cargo. Dan turned back to Kai. "You will need the rest of this." He indicated the cheese in the greasy brown wrapping paper.

"You make a mistake."

She fascinated him. "How so?"

Her head tilted to one side. "I think you believe we can be friends."

He smiled. "We can't?"

She shook her head, and her weighty hair swished against her back. "No. Your spirit is chained."

He stiffened. His attention narrowed on her. "Why do you say that?"

She broke off a morsel of the cheese and slipped

it between her lips. The motion of her hands was incredibly graceful. "It is in your eyes."

Unconsciously, he leaned toward her. "And you're not? Chained? At least, physically? You are being forced to work in the cane fields, are you not?"

"My body, not my spirit." Her expression was adamant. "Your spirit is. Chained by anger and hate. Those are worse even than their fear." Her dainty hand swept out to indicate the nearby Polynesian men.

He felt uneasy with her perceptive statement. "That still doesn't explain why we can't be friends."

"Hate. It is a disease. It spreads. I do not wish it."

She was right. He had the disease. But his anger and hate and resentment had kept him alive.

He didn't know which was worse. Those feelings—or fear. Had he knuckled under to his grandmother, he would have surrendered himself and lived in fear of her benevolent tyranny the rest of his life.

He glanced over at the crouching, huddled Kanakas and knew he had made the choice that was right for him.

5

1876

    The leadership of NSW Traders was a lonely and isolated position. Annie's duties demanded all her time. England's flourishing new industries were producing a strong demand for raw materials, so, with the agricultural and mining potential of such a vast country, Australia's economic base was powerful.

Men like MacInnes, whom she had ousted in her triumphant showdown with the board of directors, would have taken pleasure in seeing her lose the business, so she worked just that much harder. She had to prove she could hold her own with any man.

Occasionally, she thought of Ryan Sheridan. It was like looking over your shoulder to see if you were being followed. The thought made her shiver like a kitten stroked the wrong way.

Ryan had made good his part of their bargain, throwing in his lot with hers. He had yet to take advantage of her promise that she would grant his request, whatever that might be. Sometimes, she wondered if it might be of a sexual nature, but that didn't fit with her assessment of the man's character: daring and demanding and maybe even ruthless but always above board.

As the owner of a gilt-edged shipping company and its growing number of subsidiaries, she was considered very attractive marriage material. She was courted not only by bachelors from the New South Wales colony but by men from as far away as the recently formed colony of Western Australia.

Trusting few, she turned down all proposals. At twenty-five, Annie found she was considered by some to be reaching that spinster stage. Tall and gangling, with large eyes that made her thin angular face seem vulnerable, she felt that all she could look forward to was being an old maid. Whoever wanted to marry her could only be suspect of wanting to marry her fortune.

Reluctantly then, she accepted the attention of the second earl of Dunraven, who was touring the colony. They met at the Queen's birthday ball and levee, held no longer at Government House because it was too small, but in the Exhibition Building.

Short and sparely built, Alfred was hardly the romantic image of an earl. But then, she was no blooming beauty. She no longer affected even the artifice of lightly rouged lips and cheeks. To do so seemed to her tantamount to a declaration that God didn't do a good enough job.

A reserved kiss on her gloved hand by the personable bachelor prompted her to agree to dance with him. He was slightly below her eye level. "I remember you passing through the greeting line," he said. "You are the famous Annie Tremayne."

"I would be difficult to forget, my lord. If not because of my height and coloring, then certainly because of my eccentric nature."

He grinned. "Gad, but you are a sporting creature. I expected to be bored tonight."

"Did you, now?" She paused as he whirled in place to the waltz, then said, "You wouldn't find boredom in the outback."

"Ahh, is it much more entertaining?"

"Entertaining, no. Challenging, yes. And I think you have never had to be challenged, have you?"

His eyes, the blue of Wedgwood pottery, took light. "Your outback. It is different?"

Her smile was dreamy. Her features softened. "There is nothing like it." She knew that nothing she could say would give an accurate description, so she chose the crude candor of the sheep herders.

"The magnificence of it would blow the fart end out of a kangaroo."

At that, he laughed so hard that the nearest couples paused in dancing to stare. The earl was hers. Recalling her grandmother's attempts to marry her off to that French count, she had to smile. The old woman was doubtlessly doing a jig at this moment, wherever she was.

After the birthday ball, she and the earl followed tradition and traveled by ferry to watch the fireworks at Manly Beach. A small resort, Manly Beach was named by New South Wales's first governor, Captain Phillip, after the physique of the local aborigines.

The newly constructed two- and three-story homes gave the beach the air of an antipodean Brighton, though English sunshine was feeble in contrast to Australia's brilliant light. Annie had seen the world's acclaimed seaside cities like Rio de Janeiro, Hong Kong, San Francisco, and none compared to Sydney and its beaches.

The palm-lined mall had numerous cafés and places to sit and view the Queen's birthday celebrations. With fireworks exploding in the black firmament, she and Alfred drank ale from frosted tankards and talked.

Or mostly he did. He was congenial and entertaining. "You must see the lawn tennis championships. I caught them last year at Wimbledon. Spectacular."

"You haven't seen anything spectacular until you have watched a kangaroo box. Oh, my, wasn't that breathtaking!"

Applause and sighs erupted around them in response to another flammable display of light and thunder overhead.

Nature, however, was competing with the man-made fireworks. Large droplets, heralding a sudden storm, stung the revelers' eyes. Table umbrellas fluttered wildly. Some of the spectators dashed for shelter in the tiny cafés.

"I think we'd best return to the ferry," she said. She wasn't ready to spend the night in one of Manly's few reputable hotels and have to deal with any amorous advances from the earl—or any man, for that manner.

Sometimes she wondered why she had no inclination toward a sexual encounter. Even the animals at Dream Time took more interest than she, she thought, and then had to smile at her own absurdity.

Occasionally, her lack of sexual interest caused her concern. Certainly, she felt empty and lonely. But she also felt resentful of her career since it made a relationship seem impossible. Mostly, she was confused about her role. She felt like a juggling act in a circus. So she just concentrated on not dropping the ball.

Lashed now by driving rains, the ferry pitched frenziedly in the water. Its passengers retreated to the cabin for shelter. Apprehension tightened their previously lighthearted smiles. Only a few benches girdled the cabin walls. Those were quickly taken. No one offered either the earl or Australia's most prominent female a seat. This was the egalitarian New World.

If Alfred was miffed, he comported himself with equanimity, considering he could move no more than a step in any direction, so crowded was the cabin. His nostrils quivered at the stifling odor of bodies, the rank odor of wet flesh and stale cheap cologne.

"Let's go outside," she suggested.

"Gad! You can't be serious. With all that tossing and torrent out there? I much prefer the safety—and stench—of the cabin."

Not her. Caring not a whit for what he might think, she deserted him and shouldered her way outside. The wind slammed into her, and she staggered against the bulkhead. Regaining her balance, she braced herself against the wind and inched her way across the rain-slick deck. Waves and troughs rocked the ferry like a toy boat. Lightning splintered the night and silvered the edges of boiling black clouds.

Her sopping-wet gloved hands clenched the railing for support. The expensive silk gown she was wearing was crushed and water stained, and her ostrich feather whipped back and forth across her face. Her shoes squished and her hose felt clammy.

She laughed exultingly.

"A banshee are you now?" a male voice shouted against the roar of the wind.

She whirled to find Ryan Sheridan standing beside her. This meeting was totally unexpected, since their paths rarely crossed except at NSW Traders's annual board meetings. At these times, he was always deferential, almost detached.

His black hair was plastered against his forehead and cheekbones, and his sodden frockcoat and trousers clung to his body like a second skin. Rain droplets glistened on his lips and spiked his long lashes. That same excitement she felt at this mighty demonstration of the elements glinted in his eyes as lightning bolts, one after another, lit up the night.

"Isn't it wonderful?" she shouted back. "The unrestraint of nature!"

"Its lack of restraint, Miss Tremayne," he asked at her ear, "or its danger?"

She shivered with that unidentifiable thrill that often accompanies the zephyr of fear. "Both."

He grinned, his teeth utterly white against his tanned skin. "That damnable feather is going to beat you to death. May I?"

Without waiting for her consent, he yanked the bow of her bonnet strings, which was tied beneath her chignon, and tossed her bonnet out into the night. For a horrified second, she watched it bob on the crest of a wave, and next it was swept from sight.

Laughing, she turned back to him. "It *was* a nuisance." Then she realized her hair had come loose from its coil to tumble riotously about her shoulders. At her age, unbound hair was tantamount to being seen naked. He stared down at her. An uneasiness compressed her lungs.

"A mistake," he said. "I have also loosed your greatest power."

"My greatest power?"

"Your femininity."

Her femininity. She had never considered herself especially feminine. If anything, to the contrary.

Off to her left, the lights from the Sydney shoreline came into view. Hastily, she tugged at her wind-tossed curls in an effort to subdue them into a genteel knot. Her fumbling attempts were not meeting with success.

"Here, let me," he said. He took her shoulder and turned her away from him. Pulling loose the bow of his white necktie, he lassoed her cavorting curls and secured them at her nape with the necktie.

By this time, the ferry had entered the protection of Sydney Cove, where the water was calmer. Some of the passengers were leaving the cabin to brave the rain, which had lessened. "Oh, there you are," came the earl of Dunraven's distinctly English voice. "When you didn't return, I was becoming worried that you may have been swept overboard."

"Thank you, Mr. Sheridan," she said, and calmly stepped away from him. "You're just in time to see the harbor lights at night, Alfred. Have you met Mr. Sheridan? He's the owner of *The Sydney Dispatch*. Ryan, may I present the earl of Dunraven."

With the introductions over and disembarkation imminent, she put the meeting with Ryan Sheridan behind her. In fact, in the days to come, Alfred took up most of her thoughts—and time.

She attended other functions with him: the Grand Bicycle Steeple Chase at the Albert Grounds, the horse races—where the crowd stood bareheaded in the grandstand for "God Save the Queen"—and various outings like rowing down the Hawkesbury, sailing, watching cricket, football, and even a prizefighting match.

But over the ensuing weeks, she came to realize that the earl was easygoing and indolent to the point of being a weakling. He had never had to work for his money. She soon wearied of him and felt relieved when at last he resumed his Grand Tour.

She returned to her office with a sense of near enthusiasm. But the long hours and demanding duties did not offer their customary distraction.

She was definitely restive. It was the city and all its congestion. That was it. Soon, as soon as her work permitted, she would get away. Take a holiday and return to Dream Time. Her respite from the pressures of her position—and her only plea-sure—came in her occasional escapes to her beloved Dream Time.

Only there would her soul find peace, her heart find contentment.

6

1879

    The event of Annie's twenty-eighth birthday gave her, at last, the impetus to forsake the desk of NSW Traders's chief executive officer and pack for a much-needed vacation, to be spent at the sheep station.

The railroad, which had been in construction for more than thirty years, had not even reached the border of New South Wales and Victoria. Along with other passengers bound for the interior, she boarded a stagecoach that would stop at the mining town of Broken Hill, the site of her mining company. She would use the pretext of inspecting its operations as an excuse to return to Dream Time.

Exhilaration sang in her veins. She longed to discard her heavy skirts and don bush trousers. For the tenth time she reached for the lace handkerchief tucked into her sleeve cuff and wiped at the dust that caked her face and the back of her neck. Canvas covers were dropped over the coach's window now to keep out the dust. The heat and the smell of the three unwashed passengers were even worse.

She, who owned a fleet of ships, should have owned her own stage line, her own private coach. But this was an opportunity to lose herself in the midst of ordinary people; people who neither knew, nor cared, who she was.

At every chance, a hat merchant from Brisbane complained of the miserable food of hard biscuits and dried beef, which they ate quickly at intermittent way stations, and the lice in the bed ticking at night.

Annie bore these discomforts with determined patience. What annoyed her was the unending proximity of the third passenger, Mick Harrison, the arrogant owner of a sheep station near Dream Time. His station had become famous for its prized breeding ram, Captain Cook.

The occasional contact between Mick Harrison's brawny shoulder and hers when the stage hit a rock, and his hand lingering at her elbow when she descended from the high step of the Concord coach, were opportunities of which he made the most.

When the coach reached the plateau of the western part of the colony and the canvas cover was rolled up once again, she kept her gaze on the tall grass that stretched across the eternal plains. She wondered how much more she could endure before she said something. Amicable relations were important in the isolation of the outback.

Worse, the reports sent back from Dream Time's foreman, Zab, indicated that her sheep station was foundering.

Broken Hill was composed of mostly dilapidated shacks that housed the miners, pubs, and brothels. At the stage station, she picked up her skirts and crossed from the boardwalk to the yellow building that was the assayer's office. An old man in a billed hat directed her to the Broken Hill Mines office. "Go up Iodide Street, it's at the end."

The end of the earth would have been better. She was glad she had worn sturdy shoes. The shack that served as the mine office was perched at the edge of the slope, and walking was precarious. Miners with picks and shovels entered the timber-supported mine. Pit ponies hauled the ore up the steep path.

She was perspiring freely by the time she climbed the wooden steps of the management building and entered the tin-roofed office. The relief from the sunshine didn't make her feel any cooler, as the office was an oven.

A bewhiskered man of maybe fifty sat behind a

desk. His spectacles didn't hide his tired, red-rimmed eyes. His pen scribbled on an open ledger. Perspiration dripped from his face on the grimy sheet. He glanced up and resumed writing.

She assumed her voice of authority. It never came naturally to her. "I'd like to discuss the silver mine with you."

"Yeah, so would Queen Victoria."

She smiled. "Not too pleased with the work are you?"

"Look, I don't have time for earbashing."

Without asking, she perched on a high stool near his desk. Her handkerchief was sopping wet yet still she used it to dab at her damp skin. "Do you need someone to help with your workload?"

He peered up at her, for the first time really seeing her. "Yeah, that would do for a start."

"What else?"

"Are ye fair dinkum?"

"I'm indeed quite genuine—and quite serious. I may be able to help you."

"Ye got an ear at NSW Traders?"

"You might say so."

He put down his pen. "Well, ye can tell the old lady we don't have up-to-date equipment. Carts drawn by horses don't get us nowhere."

"What else?"

"The cobbers who go down in the hole are dying from lung dust."

"What would you suggest to change that?"

He peered at her over the rims of his spectacles. "Better ventilation. An end to dry drilling." He shrugged. "I don't like to whine but someone's got to change or else the union is going to come in and then NSW Traders are going to have a no-hoper on its hands."

"I don't think the owner is aware of these conditions." She nibbled on her lower lip. "How long before the silver lode plays out here?"

"With the right equipment, you got until Armageddon." Those tired eyes lit up. "But it's not the silver that's the bonzer. It's iron ore. I like to fossick. Ye know, gems and semiprecious stones. But I've found more deposits of iron ore. Whole mountain ranges of solid iron!"

He hefted a heavy gray rock from his desk. "An ore sample." He passed it over to her. "Sweet as anything that ever went into a blast furnace. There's enough back there in them hills to supply the world for the next hundred years."

"What's your name?"

"Bleary. Timothy Bleary."

She handed him back the ore sample and brushed the dust from her gloves. "If Andrew Carnegie can do it in America, we can do it here. I'll tell NSW Traders about what you've said. If it works, Timothy, you've got yourself a royalty of three percent of Broken Hill Mines' production."

His expression was skeptical. "Not used to the heat, are ye? Well, tell the old lady up at NSW

Traders, ye need a fan when next ye speak to her."

He went back to his notes. Smiling to herself, she left the office. Outside her smile vaporized at the sight of Mick Harrison. He had been waiting for her.

"The veil and the dust—they don't conceal your identity. It's Miss Tremayne, isn't it?"

She continued walking. "It's Mr. Harrison, isn't it?"

Below a broken nose, his mouth compressed.

Good, she had irritated him.

He matched his pace with her crisp one. "I've been waiting until we were alone. I don't think there's much you can do to rescue your station. The drought's gonna do it in, if the rabbits don't."

"Oh? And you think your station will survive?"

He gave a smug smile. He had the ruddy complexion of a drinker. His bush hat rested in his hands, baring his thick, fair hair, which was slicked back from his high forehead. "I been tending it. You've neglected yours."

"Money can solve a lot of problems. Even those of neglect."

"I hear you're a wise businesswoman. Too wise to pour good money after bad." His brown eyes traveled from her leghorn hat past her dusty traveling suit to her serviceable button-up walking shoes. "Your sheep station doesn't appear to be the only thing neglected."

She expelled a long sigh. The man's insolence was incredible, but not worth losing her composure over. "I shall take your comment into consideration, Mr. Harrison."

She didn't speak to him during the remainder of the trip. At long last, the journey ended when the stagecoach reached the mining town of Mildura. Out in the far west, it was an oasis in the wilderness of an unwelcoming environment. Vineyards dotted the countryside because of the exceptional amount of sunshine.

Baluway and his nephew Zab were there to meet her in the station's old buckboard. Baluway was nearly blind, but his face, framed by gray hair and beard, perked up at the sound of her voice. His wife had passed away long ago.

The old aborigine had owned half of Dream Time, which her mother, Amaris, had given him for his years of loyalty, but taxes and legalities had proven more than he and his tribe wanted to cope with. Upon Amaris Tremayne's death, he had surrendered his half to Nan Livingston in exchange for the right of his tribe to remain on their old hunting grounds in perpetuity.

Annie kissed his woolly head. "I've missed you, Baluway. Both of you—you, too Zab."

"We're holding a ceremonial dance in your honor tomorrow night, Miss Annie," Zab said. In his twenties, he had been educated at the school Amaris had established on the station and acted more like a white man than an aborigine. His black features could never be mistaken, though, for anything other than those of his forebears: wide nose, kinky hair, thick lips, low forehead, and short arms and legs.

His septum had been pierced when he had come of age by aborigine reckoning, and either a bone, stick, or ring adorned his nose at all times.

Annie boarded the wagon. Her heart felt light for the first time in three years. She tugged off her gloves, removed her hat, plucked the pins from her hair, and shook its thick masses free. Oh, God, the delight of the breeze caressing her cheek and tossing her hair.

Her eyes caressed the countryside: the olive green of the oddly shaped dwarf eucalyptuses called mallee, the red-bronze dirt and the silver-blue rim of distant ridges. The land and sky and water were a part of her body and blood.

She stretched her arms wide, as if to encompass the sunwashed, wide open country within her heart. She felt no embarrassment before the two men. Their mystic, primitive side could understand her.

Zab and Baluway believed that rock, tree, and man were one. The earth had a spirit, a soul. They feared retribution if the rituals of life force were broken. If the countryside was not looked after, they believed nature itself would eventually die.

The station was built on one of the places called Dreaming sites, where a great spirit ancestor had completed its creative act and put itself into the landscape. According to the aborigines, the great spirit ancestors remained to this day and the sites still contained the power and energy of the aborigine's Dreamtime.

Normally, the savanna grasslands were colored with wildflowers: the flannel flower and desert pea, the kangaroo paw and Christmas bush. But this summer had been particularly hot, which must have accounted for their absence. The wagon passed several mustering camps with their yards, dips, and small horse paddocks. All empty.

Annie's ebullience ebbed as the wagon drew nearer and nearer Dream Time. Wooloomooloo Creek was only a dry bed. The wattles and eucalyptus were only brown branches. The ground was seared, as if a bush fire had blazed through.

The sight grew worse. Occasional glimpses of sheep corpses greeted the eye. The more recent victims of the drought were bloated, while other corpses were rotting. Flocks of buzzards took to the air when the wagon rolled by. She was viewing only the perimeter of the vast acreage of Dream Time.

What catastrophic figures awaited her full inventory? Why in God's name had she devoted her attention to the demands of NSW Traders when her real passion, Dream Time, lay dying?

At last, she could see the solid and comforting lines of the Big House. Only as the wagon clattered closer and the house's features became more distinct did she perceive how much the place had deteriorated.

The outbuildings needed painting. The shearing house's door swung crazily in the breeze on only one hinge. Fence rails were broken. Many of the drovers, shearers, bullockies, and other station hands did not even recognize her. Where once lavender blue bells of jacaranda had spilled over the veranda baluster, withered vines now clawed for support.

Her dismay must have shown on her face. "I wrote you about needed repairs, Miss Tremayne," Zab said. He spoke slowly, in a deep gruff voice.

She vaguely remembered the letter. She had put it in an abeyance file. Matters that had seemed more pressing had occupied her attention.

At the time a Sydney inventor had been besieging her with requests to view his ice machine. An insurance investigator had spent several days interviewing her about the loss of an NSW Traders frigate in a typhoon off the coast of India. There had been the christening of a new ship to inaugurate. Endless problems.

But now she was home!

She climbed down from the wagon before Zab could come around to assist her. "I'll see to it that Dream Time gets nursed back to health, Zab." She put out her hand for old Baluway, who had to feel around for his bearings. "The step is directly below you, Baluway."

Once inside the house, she gave way to her joy. She tossed her gloves and hat on the green-and-white-striped Hepplewhite settee and, skirts lifted in one hand, scampered up the wide staircase. Her other hand trailed along the highly polished maple bannister. Had she been going any slower, the gesture would have been a caress.

As if she were an art lover touring the Louvre, she wandered through room after room of the house. Her sense of smell delighted in all the old scents—the musty ones as well as the heady ones, like the beeswax polish on the old furniture.

Much of the furniture, as well as the drapes, needed to be restored or replaced, but the house itself had been soundly built and was little the worse for wear.

When she was satisfied, if only momentarily, she hurried back to her own bedroom, which ajoined the office Amaris had made out of a sitting room, and quickly changed into her old work clothes, which she found at the back of the armoire.

Bush hat in hand, she was soon descending the broad stairs two at a time. Her spurs clinked with each step. The men's riding pants gave her a freedom of stride she had sorely missed in Sydney.

At the bottom of the staircase, Zab had unloaded the last of her trunks and luggage and was taking orders from the housekeeper, his wife Vena. An aborigine also, her skin was as dark as his, and at more than three times his weight she towered over him. A mammoth of a woman, she cared for her Zab as much as she did the station, on which she had been born.

"Get the copper tub cleaned. The mistress will be wanting a bath when she returns from—"

"Afternoon, Vena," Annie said, smiling. "You've done a wonderful job keeping the house."

The woman bobbed her head. As Annie went out the door, she heard her murmur to Zab, "Reminds me of her mother, that one does."

The thought pleased Annie. Her mother had always seemed like one of the aborigine's Dream Time spirits. Superhuman. Indomitable. Nana had been like that, too, but also intractable.

When she entered the stables, Baluway was getting a saddle for her horse. Despite the old aborigine's near blindness, he was very much at home in the stables and could do almost anything a fully sighted person could.

"I thought you'd be down to ride, Mistress Annie." He stroked the muzzle of the gelding, quieting it. "The horse hasn't had a rider in a year now. He's mostly wild. Like you."

The last was said with a grin that showed his almost toothless mouth. Her responding grin was as wide, but with all her teeth—her best feature, she thought. Her unruly dark red hair definitely had to be the worst.

She mounted the pawing and snorting gelding, turned the horse from the yard, and cantered down the drive lined with majestic red gums. The drive opened onto the vast spaces she missed so much. The sun had taken the morning's mist off the paddocks and revealed the shriveled grass, dust, and saltbush.

Even the emu and those large red-gray kangaroos called the wooloomooloo had deserted the countryside for better fare. Her heart ached at what she saw. Would the drought never break?

Her horse picked up its ears. She stilled. Rapidly her gaze scanned the horizon. Then she spotted the source of her mount's agitation: a solitary figure silhouetted against the horizon. A man, if she judged correctly. He strode along the rutted wagon road. Apparently his destination was the Big House.

She waited and watched. A man afoot in the vast wilderness of the outback was to be regarded with caution. He appeared of average height and build but moved with the assurance of one who had mastered the powerful elements of land and nature.

When he was close enough for her to see his face she had to fight to control her expression. The lower portion of the right side of his face, the right side of his neck, and his right forearm, where the sleeve was rolled back, were badly scarred. The scars were a raw pink and slightly puckered.

"Easy," she said, gentling the horse's nervous prancing.

"G'day," the man said, stopping several meters' distance away. He touched the rim of his bush hat with fingers also scarred. His strange tawny eyes fringed by black lashes gazed up at her patiently. His laconic expression and relaxed stance belied the keen eyes.

She shifted in the saddle. Its creak was the only noise in that empty expanse. "Hello."

He altered his stance, tucked his thumbs in his dungaree's waistband. "I'm looking for work, Miss Tremayne."

"How do you know who I am?"

His crooked grin made him almost nice looking. Those eyes that were flecked with a fire the color of the tropical sun measured her from her hat to her boots. His attitude was amused and indolent. "No other woman, not even jilleroos, can wear a pair of pants like you do. Welcome back."

She felt stupid. He knew she wasn't a female station hand but the owner. "We've met before?"

"No. Not formally, anyway."

"You're stingy with conversation."

He chuckled. His expression changed as nimbly as a kaleidoscope. "You were twelve or so. My father and I had come to the Big House, seeking to buy a horse we'd heard Dream Time wanted to get rid of. You were long of leg and full of questions." He paused. "You still are."

Sadly, she didn't remember him. How old would he have been? With the disfiguring scars, it was difficult to tell his age. Maybe twenty-seven, twenty-eight, the same as she.

He answered her unspoken question. "I was only eight then. I never forgot the visit. The grandeur . . . of Dream Time. I decided then that . . . our station would be like that."

"Your station . . . it's nearby?"

"Was. That's why I'm afoot. Rivers Run—and all that was a part of it—is ashes now. Brushfire did it in. Burned it level half a year ago."

She certainly did need help. Someone who could help her get the station back in shape and then take over running it when she returned to Sydney. But how capable was this man? "I don't know anything about you. Your name, your experience, your educ—"

"My name's Reggie. Reggie Lewis. I'm a cattle man. What I know about sheep could be put in a thimble and then there'd be room for a pint of beer. But I'm a hard worker. I'm honest."

For all his humble statement, his expression was anything but that. Bold and proud were descriptions that came to her mind. "You forgot dependable."

He grinned again. "You forgot to button your top button."

She glanced down and blushed. The beginning of her cleavage was clearly visible. With her gloved hand she worked the button but couldn't get a good grip. "Very well," she said, still fumbling with the button and fuming at her discomposure. "I'll give you a trial period. The pay's the standard for an overseer. I won't always be here. You can write, I hope. I'll want a monthly report in my absences."

"Do you want help with your button?"

"Certainly not! You have any belongings— swag—that you need to collect."

"Nothing."

She wished he'd stop watching her with such patient amusement. She reached down a hand and took her foot out of the stirrup. "Well, it's a good three kilometers back to the Big House. We'll ride back double."

He swung up behind her, and her gelding shifted his stance to accommodate the additional weight. She wondered if she had been a fool to accept a stranger on his word. But over the last few years she had become good at judging character.

"How many sheep have you lost to the drought?"

His breath was warm against her neck, where her hair was tucked beneath her hat. His body was hot, pressed behind hers. "I don't know. Today is my first day back in a long time."

They discussed the effects of the drought, the price wool was bringing on the London market, and the need to build some kind of fence against the scourge of rabbits devouring the little vegetation left.

"You realize by hiring a cattleman, Miss Tremayne, you will be creating a scandal with the other sheep station owners."

"I'm no newcomer to scandal, Mr. Lewis. A female running any business is inured to scandal. Tell me, after owning your own cattle station, I wouldn't think you would be content to run some-one else's station."

"I'm not." His tone was terse. "I'll make a go of my own station again, but for now I need the job and you need me."

She almost laughed at his conceit, but upon their return to the Big House, he set to work on several projects, all in the interval of the remaining daylight hours. He talked extensively with Baluway and Zab about the ranch's history, saddled a horse and toured the immediate area for a cursory inspection, took a look at his own living quarters, and lastly asked to see the books.

This last astonished her. She took him to her office. Without her permission, he went around her desk, took a seat, and opened the first ledger. She watched him pore over its scrawled pages. "Not very detailed," he mumbled.

"Zab has been keeping the accounts in my absence. He hasn't had the training necessary." She knew she sounded defensive, but she hadn't origi-nally planned to be away from Dream Time so long. At first, it was for just a month or so. But the months had stretched into more than three years.

Then there was Never-Never to consider. Her father's station had been left to run wild over the years. Reggie Lewis's stewardship might just change that. Now was the time to diversify. When the price of wool and mutton were low, a run of cattle would make an excellent safety net.

Reggie was already pulling another ledger from the bookcase next to her desk. "We'll go over them another time," she said, dismissing him. She had no intention of working on her first day back.

After he left, she found Vena and told her she was ready for the hot bath. The steaming water, scented with lavender, relaxed her so much that she nearly drifted asleep in the copper tub. The hour had grown late. She washed the grit and dirt of four days from her hair. Dressing quickly in a chambray skirt and raw silk blouse, she bound her wet hair atop her head and hurried below.

Outside in the yard, the ceremonial dancing had already begun. The corroboree was a species of bal masqué of the aborigines. "Coo-ee!" cried the dancers in that peculiarly eerie, high-pitched, sharp tone.

The scene was powerful, something that might have been taken from the first page of the book of time: Around a fire danced the male aborigines, clad only in loincloths, their bodies painted with a blood red ocher. Outside the circle, the aborigine women stamped their broad feet in accompaniment to the primitive beat of a drum. The red lingering light of the last rays of the setting sun mingled with the turbulent red tongues of the fire.

She threaded her way through the workers and their families who had also turned out to watch the event. Respectfully, they made way for her. "Good to see you back, Miss Tremayne," a shearer said.

"Good evening, Miss Tremayne," said the wife of the station's baker.

Old Mick, a sheepherder with an Adam's apple as prominent as a shepherd's crook, bobbed his head in a happy greeting.

She nodded, calling those she met by name. She was gradually recalling forgotten faces. All of them were friendly. Suddenly, life seemed good again. She found a space beneath one of the ghostly peppercorn trees from which to watch the scene. Beneath her hands, clasped behind her back, she could feel the tree's rough bark. She could imagine the sap flowing, as if pumped by her heart.

Baluway would have said, "Tree, he is pumping our blood."

A warm wind burnished lights in the sky to flame. The corroboree was usually a reenactment of great deeds of the creator heroes of the Dream Time. Sometimes the corroboree enacted hunts or historical events like the removal of their tribes from their traditional lands.

As she watched, it occurred to her that here in the corroboree was her solution to the problem of providing for Baluway and his people long after she was gone. Once again, the answer was in

Never-Never. Reggie, if she could convince him, could teach Baluway's tribe to run cattle.

What if she could lease a portion of Never-Never, with all its rock art, as a national park for the benefit of all in return for the right of the aborigines to remain on the land in perpetuity?

The fire's light was warm on her face. The pounding of the drum found a partner in her pulse, beating at her wrist, her throat, in her ears so loudly she could not hear the chanting of the aborigines nor the laughing and quips of the station's families.

The aborigine believed in the union of sun and rain, in the satisfying circle of the rainbow. They believed in the strong energy of union of plow and sod, flint and tinder, mill wheel and water. A very sensuous, erotic, and romantic concept of life.

She closed her eyes, savoring the moment. She felt so full, her entire being . . . and yet, strung tight, tense. Her arms lifted of their own accord, as if they could embrace the entire world. All of life. Her head moved languorously, as if a heavy wildflower.

When she opened her eyes, she saw that across the dancing fire Reggie Lewis stared at her. Hunger glinted in his gaze as hot as the fire.

7

1881

"*I've fenced in* the last section. That should keep the rabbits from eating the Big House."

Reggie's derisive grin reminded her of her father. Like him, Reggie didn't give up. When other sheep station owners were declaring that fences would only slow down the rabbits, not keep them out, he doubled the fences, set out poison carts, stationed guards with guns.

Of course, Reggie couldn't play God and command the heavens to rain, but he had ordered a deeper pumping rod for the windmills and hired out-of-work drovers to dig irrigation ditches. The occasional light sprinkles that raised false hopes filled the bottoms of the troughs at least temporarily.

For more than two years now, whenever she was in residence at Dream Time, a mere five or six times, she and Reggie had treated each other with polite respect that bordered on camaraderie. The respect had a solid foundation.

She admired his knowledge of station management and his determination. The sheds and quarters benefited from yearly coats of paint. New double gates had been added, and the great stretches of boundary fences kept in repair.

In turn, Reggie was in awe of her business acumen, something of which the male-dominated society of Australia did not believe a woman capable.

One afternoon, she sighted Reggie from her office window. He was crossing the yard toward the sheering shed in that long, ambling gait of a stockman accustomed to sitting astride a horse.

The stockman was of a different caliber than the shepherd. The most obvious difference was that stockmen invariably used horses, while those working with sheep usually did not. Thus the stockman's success as a skilled worker of cattle depended on how well he could ride, and from this developed a rather romantic view of the stockman's life.

Reggie was highly skilled with the stockwhip. The better stockwhips, as his was, were made from kangaroo hide. With amazing proficiency, he could

ride at a canter, standing in the stirrups, and crack
his whip above a bellowing steer to draft it from
the others.

This drafting was something to watch. She had
witnessed him working a camp on Never-Never
and had never forgotten the sureness and fluidity
of his movements. The lanky, lumbering stockman
actually became graceful.

She put down her pen and rose from her desk.
That she checked her braided hair in the hallway
mirror before going outside was an indication that
her intention was not purely one of a business
nature, although this was not recognized by her
conscious mind.

Even those years spent in Sydney, away from
Dream Time, could not dull the vivid memory of
shearing season: greasy fleeces either stuffed in
bins or packed tightly in bales, hot and sweaty
workers, tar and oil that reeked, the teeth-grating
sound of men sharpening their shears, and, of
course, the holding pens.

For a moment, she didn't spot Reggie. Shearing was in full swing, and more than two dozen
itinerant shearers were wielding their blades over
124,000 bleating sheep. Then, he rose from a
kneeling position in the holding pen. Due to the
heat, he had stripped off his shirt and she saw
the splotch of scarred flesh that extended from
his cheek, down his neck, and around one chest
muscle.

Normally, if a woman were approaching, the first to see her would announce, "Duck on the water," as a signal to behave properly. Since she was wearing men's clothing, no one noticed her in time to issue the warning. So all stood frozen as she surveyed the half-naked overseer.

Rather than avert his eyes in abashed reaction or grab his shirt, Reggie stared her down. It was one of those indelible moments. Their gazes held for an inordinately long time, long enough for him to read what was in her mind. At least, she thought he must have because his eyes flared in what was unmistakable sexual response. She had witnessed it several times when dealing with businessmen who expected her to be neither bright nor attractive.

She broke the silence. "At noon, there will be buns, turnovers, and jam tarts to satisfy your hunger and tea to quench your thirst," she told the team of shearers.

She had planned to send Zab out to make the announcement, but she had to say something that would put the men at ease. "Mr. Lewis, I'd like a word with you when you get a chance to break free."

He nodded, then went back to inspecting a sheep that had apparently been injured by a careless shearer's blade.

She returned to her office only to pace. The memory of Reggie's chest, sun-browned and matted with light brown curling hair where the flesh wasn't seared, played havoc with her thoughts.

That and the fact that his eyes had recognized in hers raw desire.

About half an hour later, he came up to her office. He was now clad in a cambric shirt that was damp with sweat. He even held his hat in his hand, although his hair did not evidence a hat's sweatband ring, which told her he had come hat in hand to fortify the relationship of employer-employee. "You wanted me?"

She almost laughed. God, yes, she wanted him. Worse, he knew it, damn him. She resumed her seat at her desk for the simple reason that her legs felt wobbly when standing so near him. "I wanted your opinion."

A tiny smiled played at the corners of his mouth. "You're asking for *my* opinion?" Doubtlessly, her reputation for being obstinate and insisting on making her own decisions irrespective of advice from others had reached him.

"What do you think about Dream Time ordering some of those new shearing machines?"

He tucked his thumbs in his waistband as he was wont to do. "I think the shearers will have nothing to do with them unless convinced otherwise."

She folded her hands on her desk and smiled sweetly. "I'll purchase the machines. You convince the shearers."

His arrogant grin returned her unspoken challenge. "No worries, Miss Tremayne."

More than three weeks passed before six machines arrived from Melbourne. Those three weeks were tense for her. A tension had arisen between Reggie and her ever since that day she had seen him shirtless—and he had seen the desire in her eyes. They were both aware of this, and it made their once easygoing relationship strained.

Daily rain, however welcome it was, added to the tension, because it confined her to the house more than usual and halted a lot of routine activities that would have taken her mind off him.

When Zab and Baluway returned with the shearing machines in the back of the flatbed wagon, she and Reggie were both waiting on the veranda, neither speaking to the other, both hoping that this new project would ease the strain between them.

They stood shoulder to shoulder as two workers unloaded the machines that consisted of beltings, blades, and pulleys. Forty shearers stood on the far side of the wagon and stared stonily. They had moved on to the Dunlop station to shear but had returned to finish shearing another forty-three thousand remaining sheep owned by Dream Time.

"I don't think they're going to have anything to do with the machines," she told Reggie.

He looked down at her. "I guess it's my turn."

The shearers were picking up their gear. She and

Reggie watched them board barges and cross Wooloomooloo Creek to camp out on the other side.

"It looks as if it's going to be a showdown," she said.

He tucked his thumbs in the waistband of his dungarees. "Well, I think I'll go over and talk to them."

Lot of good talk was going to do, she thought grimly. She followed to watch him board a barge to be rowed to the other side, where three representatives of the striking shearers walked down to the bank to meet with him.

After handshakes were exchanged, he hunkered down on one knee. The other three did likewise and began talking in what looked like serious negotiations. A half hour or more passed, when the representatives rose abruptly and stalked away. Apparently, an accord hadn't been reached.

She expected Reggie to return, but he ambled over to where some of the shearers had taken up a game of horseshoes. To her surprise, he plopped down cross-legged alongside some of the shearers watching from the sidelines in the shade of a leafy gum.

The afternoon wore on like that. That afternoon and the next and the next and the next. Every day Reggie crossed the river to negotiate with the striking shearers. When they would listen no more, he joined them in whatever they were doing to pass the time. More than a week passed.

When she questioned Reggie about the proceedings, he would only say, "All in good time."

Then one afternoon, he was in her office discussing some bales of fleece that had gotten rain-soaked. She was trying to focus on what he was saying, but her mind was speculating about him, as usual. The man had an unbridled look about him. Did he find her attractive at all? Her gaze dropped to his sunbrowned, long-fingered hands, and her mouth curved with unconscious longings.

She reminded herself who he was, who she was. He, supremely male. She, fiercely independent. He could never bend to her in urban society. She would never bend to him in the outback. The fact that he worked for her only added to that conflict.

"Last night's high winds blew off a tarp," he was saying. "I figure we lost maybe forty-five—"

Zab appeared at the doorway. The bone in his nose fairly quivered with trepidation. "Miss Tremayne . . . Mr. Lewis, those shearers said to give you a message."

"Yes?" she asked.

"They said they wanted to challenge Mr. Lewis here to swim across the Wooloomooloo."

Reggie smiled. "The stalemate's been broken."

"God's blood," she said, "the creek's flooded!"

"That has nothing to do with it." He stared down at her with those sorrowful eyes more amber than gold. "If I don't succeed, they'll come up with something else. They want to find a compromise. They want to work."

"If you don't succeed," she said, "I'll need to find another foreman."

Thursday, two days away, was the time set for Reggie to answer the striking shearers' challenge by swimming Wooloomooloo Creek. "Give enough time for word to spread," Reggie had explained. "Either I succeed big or I fail big. I want as many people to be there as we can draw. This will make a statement—that Dream Time doesn't give up."

She loved his rare smile. Like a sunburst. This time it was wry but sincere.

He was certainly right about the challenged swim drawing a lot of spectators. Men, and a few women and children, had come from stations as far away as a hundred or more kilometers. They camped in tents and sleeping rolls on both sides of the creek.

The event was turning into a festival, and she soon found Dream Time providing food and drink for more than eighty visitors, not counting the itinerant shearers and her own employees.

Among the visitors was Mick Harrison. He occasionally called on her when she was in residence, ostensibly to discuss station problems. They ranged from the lack of a doctor when accidents occurred so easily to the exorbitant price of twice-yearly freighting in stores, usually transported by strings of camels.

Today, whenever the sun appeared from behind the dingy gray clouds, its rays glinted in Mick's reddish blond hair. She thought of Moses's burning bush. A warning?

He shouldered through the crowd of onlookers to where she stood on the wharf. She didn't bother to acknowledge his presence but kept her gaze centered on Reggie, who had stripped off his flannel shirt to the muslin undershirt beneath and then removed his boots.

"Worried about your overseer?"

The waters were brown and swirling and dangerous. "No."

"You made a big mistake hiring a stockman to run sheep."

"Four years at Dream Time and Never-Never have proved him quite capable."

"I still say one day you'll regret hiring him. Assuming he makes it across the creek."

She tilted her head so that she could see Mick's square face. Those curly lashes didn't hide the blatant lust in his eyes. "He will make it across, and I don't regret my decision."

Still, fear pounded its painful rhythm in her heart. Reggie waded in thigh deep, then lunged headlong into the rushing waters. His strokes were vigorous, but the mighty current was carrying him downstream, making the distance to the far bank ever greater.

Wildly, her only thought was that if he died, she would have missed loving him all because of foolish feminine pride.

Clapping and shouting, the spectators urged him on. Suddenly, in her peripheral vision, she saw an uprooted wattle tree bobbing in the current, hurtling toward him. She screamed out, "Reggie! Watch out!" But, of course, he could not hear.

Now the spectators knew of the impending disaster. All the waving of arms in warning accomplished nothing. The fury of the powerful current both blinded Reggie and drowned out all other noise.

In horror, she watched as the trunk slammed against his torso. For a fraction of a second, he seemed paralyzed by the blow. Then the waves took him from view. Her heart sank with him.

Oh, dear God, no!

"There he is!" a drover shouted.

Her gaze followed the direction the drover was pointing. "Yes!" she breathed. Maybe a quarter of a kilometer down river, Reggie was staggering ashore. A mighty cheer went up on both sides of the river. He raised a hand in acknowledgment, then collapsed.

"Zab!" she called. The young aborigine, never far from her elbow, stepped forward. "Get Mr. Lewis back to the Big House."

She pushed past a startled Mick Harrison and strode on back to the Big House to find Baluway

and Vena watching anxiously from the veranda.
"Vena, get some fresh tea started."

Annie hurried inside and ran up to her bedroom
to turn back the bed covers. In a matter of minutes
she collected towels, an extra blanket, and, from
her medicine chest, lineament, bandage strips, and
ointment.

By the time she had everything laid out, Zab
and an old shearer she recalled from other seasons
were supporting Reggie at either shoulder as they
climbed the staircase. "Put him in my bed," she
said, ignoring their surprised expressions.

After the two men deposited a limp and thor-
oughly wet Reggie on her bed, she began removing his undershirt. His lids fluttered open, and his
hand moved to the right side of his chest, where a
purple bruise mingled with raw scraped flesh. It
appeared no ribs were broken. She sighed in
relief.

"What happened?" he mumbled. His hand
groped at his injured side.

"You took a punch from an uprooted tree. Your
chest is beginning to discolor badly."

"Well, now, I guess that's kind of nice. Not every
bloke can say that the color of his cuts and scars
and burns and bruises match."

She felt an instant of anxiety. She had never
dared bring up the subject of his disfiguring burn.
Then, at the sight of his wry smile, she relaxed.
"Let's get you out of those wet clothes."

His brow raised. "My arms still work. I can manage to undress by myself."

Now her skin colored. She rose from the side of the bed. "I'll be outside. Call me when you're ready."

"One question. What am I doing in your bed?"

"Because that's where I want you."

"Why? My bed will serve just as well."

She paused, her hand on the door latch. By now she was experienced enough to know that the truth served best. "I've been wanting you there for some time now."

The silence and his searching eyes made her as nervous as a brumby. "You're a strong woman, Miss Tremayne. I might work for you, but I make my own decisions about the woman I make love to. Even under orders."

Her blush heated her skin. "It wasn't an order. Only a hope."

With a sigh, he closed his eyes. "What are we getting ourselves into, Miss Tremayne?"

"Go ahead and undress. I'll be back shortly."

For the next five minutes, she paced the station office. What a bloody fool she had made of herself. How could she ever go back and face him?

She paused in front of the window. The day was cloudy and made dreary by the rain pattering lightly against glass, installed only since her birth. Outside, the spectators had abandoned the field banking the Wooloomooloo, now empty except for several dingoes furtively paddling across.

Hardly a night passed in the lambing season that she didn't lose one to the wild dogs. They seldom ate their victims but just killed for sport, the blooming dingoes!

How could she not return to Reggie? A man went after what he wanted. By now she should have learned that if she was going to get what she wanted in the world, she would have to use the same tactics.

"Miss Tremayne?"

She turned. "Yes, Zab?"

He stood in the doorway, hat in hand. His teeth, and the bone piercing his septum, were white against the ebony of his face. "The shearers—they done agreed to return to the shed and those new machines."

She smiled. "Thank you."

When she opened her bedroom door, Reggie was sitting up in bed, his back against the doubled pillow. His chest was bare, and once again her breath caught in her throat. She tried to act insouciant. "Congratulations. You succeeded. The striking shearers have agreed to try the machines."

"You don't look pleased."

She tried to be honest. "I'm confused. My emotions are so tangled. I can't make sense of them. You see I want you. And I think you want me. If so, you're the first man who hasn't wanted me for either my wealth or position."

That wasn't quite true. Ryan Sheridan hadn't

wanted her wealth or position. The newspaper publisher had wanted something else—something he had told her he would make known should the time come when he would need it. So far, he had indicated nothing. In fact, the only times she ever saw him were at the NSW Traders's semiannual board meetings.

"You could be wrong about that, Miss Tremayne. About me not wanting either your wealth or position."

She stared down at him. The covers were pulled up to his armpits but didn't quite cover the crisp, curling brown hair just below his collarbone. Strangely, she no longer noticed the scarring of his scorched flesh. "I don't usually misjudge people. I think I'm right about you. Your face is honest."

His mouth twisted in a smile. "Honest but not handsome."

"My face is strong—but not pretty."

His eyes narrowed. "Who told you that?"

"My grandmother."

"She was wrong. Because of the strength in your face, you are strikingly attractive. That, Miss Tremayne, is better than mere prettiness."

She flushed and suddenly felt shy. Then she mustered her most businesslike voice. "Well, 'tis best we take care of those scrapes."

She picked up a washcloth and dipped it into the porcelain basin of warm water. After wringing the water from the cloth, she sat on the bed alongside of Reggie and bent close to dab at the dirt-flecked abrasion. Her hand braced on his bare shoulder. Touching him was like lightning shocking her. Quickly, efficiently, wordlessly, she finished her ministrations.

"I'll have someone look in on you later," she said, and retreated from the room.

But she herself came, drawn by an attraction to him she could not deny. Sleeping in the guest room, she could not help but think of him in her bed.

Over the next few days, she found it easier to talk with Reggie. He was entertaining. He loved the outback as she did and had experienced so many more adventures.

"When I was fifteen," he told her during one of her visits, "maybe thirty or more aborigines came to our camp and asked my father for powder for a musket they had. My father tried to appease them and gave them some tobacco, which they threw away. Then he gave them some flour.

"By this time, they seemed friendly enough, so my father asked to inspect their musket. In doing so, he opened the pan and drew his thumb across it to remove the priming. The aborigines did not notice. It saved our lives. Shortly afterwards, the black with the musket laid it on top of a fence post and fired at my father. He fired a shot of his own over the heads of the fleeing natives. They never bothered us again."

Early one morning when she looked in on Reggie she found that the window was open and he had kicked off the covers. His naked body was splendid. Treading softly, she crossed the room with the purpose of drawing the covers over him. But she couldn't resist touching that bronzed skin where hair whorled across his chest. At that same moment, his lids snapped opened.

"You must be freezing," she said.

He caught her wrist and drew her palm to his lips. "Then I guess 'tis time you warmed me, Miss Tremayne." His breath was warm against her flesh.

Her own breath sucked in. A tingling began deep inside her and began to spread outward like a summer-hot sun rising. "Please," she murmured, as his tongue stole out to stroke her palm. "Please, don't call me Miss Tremayne. Not now."

"One of us has too much clothing on, Annie."

The sound of her name on his lips did funny things to her. Made her breathing rapid and shallow. Made her pulse pound in her ears. Made her heart race.

"You mean—?"

"I mean I've been wanting you for a long time."

"Why didn't you let me know?"

"How do you tell your boss something like that?"

She swallowed. "You just did."

"You're going to have to help me undress you," he said. "I'm not in top form at the moment."

Undress before him? With daylight still flooding the room? "You'll have to close your eyes, Reggie. I'm not accustomed to taking off my clothes before anyone."

She could hear the humor in his voice. "You'll have to get used to it, Annie. Because once I start with you I don't intend to stop."

Disrobing in front of him was one of the most exciting things she had ever done, equalling, certainly, that showdown with MacInnes at that first board meeting.

And it was also one of the most disturbing things. Her self-confidence as a businesswoman dwindled when it came to being a female. Each article of clothing removed revealed more of her vulnerability. What if her almost boyish body failed to excite him?

Her boots were easy enough. And her men's trousers and shirt didn't tax her modesty too much. The feminine articles underneath, her chemise and drawers, took her forever to remove. At last, she stood naked, her arms crossed before her.

Passion darkened his face. He held out his arms. His voice was raspy, his smile wry. "Come here, Annie. Please come to me before I lose all good sense and get out of bed to take you on the hard, cold floor."

With that teasing initiation, she lost all restraint and crossed the remaining few feet to his arms.

His flesh was cold and she aligned herself along-side him, but soon her fire ignited him.

"Your breasts," he breathed. "I didn't know they were this large." He cupped one and brought it to his mouth.

She sighed. Against her stomach she could feel that male part of him grow hard. It pushed against her insistently. A part of her feared what would be demanded of her. Would she be woman enough to respond when all her life she had practiced masculine arts—both in her agrarian and mercantile roles of authority? Or was the act as basic and unemotional as the breeding of Dream Time's rams with its ewes?

When his tongue rolled her nipple between his lips, she gasped at the intense pleasure and forgot all else . . . until, without her knowing quite when or how, Reggie was atop her and his male organ nudging between her thighs.

"You've never had a man inside you, have you?" he asked at her ear.

She shook her head. "No."

He tunneled his fingers through her hair, loosening it from its plaits. "I don't know what you've been told or heard about—"

"Nothing."

His hands slipped down behind her to cup her buttocks. "There may be some pain, Annie. But, also, I hope, much pleasure."

He began nudging her gently even as his lips

made hot little forays across her cheek and down her neck. Excitement had built within her so that when he finally thrust fully inside her, her outcry was more of pleasure than pain, as he had hoped.

She wrapped her arms around his shoulders. Her voice was intimate and husky in the way of a woman fulfilled when she said, "Now that you've started with me, I don't intend to let you stop."

8

"Marry me."

Although Annie loved Reggie, those years of living under her grandmother's dominance had conditioned her to fear compromise and guard her independence. She knew she could never bring herself to marry. "No."

He did not express it, but he seemed to understand the reason behind her refusal. He said instead, "The child you carry is mine as much as it is yours."

Lying beside him in her darkened bedroom, she caressed his beard-stubbled jaw. "I know that. That's why I want our child born here. On Dream

Time. I want the babe to know its heritage—and its father."

He seemed to accept this. He gathered her against him and spread his hand gently over her mounded stomach. "As long as I have you in my arms, I can live without a wedding ring on your finger."

Annie leaned back in her chair. She was weary listening to the board members of New South Wales Traders, Inc. Halfway down the long, oaken table sat Ryan Sheridan. Beneath the black sweep of his mustache, the barest semblance of a smile tugged at the corner of his mouth. She knew the gesture was meant to comfort her.

Of all the members present, all men, naturally, he alone was not scandalized by her appearing at a business function in her state—most visibly with child and most notably unmarried. And past thirty, at that.

Ryan not only accepted her for the aggressive woman she was but openly admired her business acumen.

That acumen was required now. "I know that refrigeration aboard steamships has been a disastrous experiment," she said, "but I'd like to back this enterprise. If we can ship frozen meat from Sydney to London, we can provide mutton for worldwide consumption." And both NSW Traders

and Dream Time would reap more than fifty percent profit, by her calculations.

"Don't you think the losses sustained by James
Harrison indicate the disaster we're courting." This
was from an old codger, Smithby, who had argued
against every suggestion she had put forth over the
years.

"Harrison is bankrupt now," another board
member added. "That should convince us all."

"It only convinces me," Ryan said, his fingertips
pyramided together, "that the way is paved for
some progressive company to make a fortune. That
company can—and should—be NSW Traders."

Murmurs of agreement passed around the table.
When, a while later, a vote was taken and Annie's
motion passed, she felt the tension ease from her
spine.

With hostility toward cattlemen coming into
New South Wales's outback running high, she
wouldn't have chosen this particular time to attend
to business in Sydney. But, alas, she had been
groomed for these duties.

With the discovery of artesian water, New South
Wales had become the greatest artesian basin in
the world. Unfortunately, the discovery had made
it possible for cattle to become predominant. With
water, cattle could travel farther and were not limited by heat and dryness. Cattlemen were becoming the elite, while sheepmen were considered
almost a lesser breed.

Ryan met her at the boardroom door. The other men had already filed out of the room. His practiced eye ran over her ungainly frame. "You aren't thinking about starting back to your beloved station tonight, are you?"

She smiled wearily. "Running two businesses requires all my time."

"If you don't take good care of yourself, you won't be fit to run any business. You're draining yourself, Annie. Rather than blooming, as women do in your condition, you look wan and frail."

Her lips made a moue. "Only you would dare to speak of my condition."

He took her arm. "Come have dinner with me. I'll return you to your house on Elizabeth Bay tonight as untouched as you are now. You can get a good's night rest and leave tomorrow for Dream Time."

She chuckled. "Many would tell you I am blemished beyond recovery. My soul is damned. I am that scandalous Tremayne woman."

"You are one of the few real and fully feminine women I know."

She frowned. "Strange you should say that. I always thought of myself as rather on the masculine side."

He threw back his head and laughed. "Never, ever, think that, Annie. Now, I suggest we try the Remington boarding house. Widow Remington's cooking excels even that of China Johnny's."

She *was* tired. But, oh, she was so anxious to get back to Reggie. He was restocking his abandoned station site, Rivers Run, with the cattle he was gradually purchasing with his earnings.

She could almost summon his scent—the fresh way he smelled after bathing, his natural male musk upon awakening in the morning, and that strong sensual scent when aroused by her kisses all over his muscular body. His body with all its indolent grace excited her.

Only at that moment did she take note of Ryan's build. Tall, slender, wiry. He was an intense man, where Reggie was relaxed. She felt nothing for Ryan. Poor man. Was there a woman in his life who felt that pleasurable and painful yearning that she felt when out of Reggie's arms?

"Well?" Ryan prompted, a gleam in his eyes that completely eluded her.

She smiled. "Why not? And I buy. After all, I owe you something for supporting my views at the board meetings."

He took her arm and guided her out the door. "I told you I would have no hesitation collecting if the time ever comes that I should need to."

She halted before her secretary's desk. The bespectacled James was bent over a ledger, but she could tell he was listening to the conversation. She cared not, however. Her brow furrowed. "You've never told me what the nature of your request would be, Ryan."

It was his turn to smile. A raffish smile, she thought. "No, I never did, did I? Shall we eat now?"

She thought about his evasiveness on her return trip to Echuca, where Reggie was to meet her at the steamboat landing. Ryan might be her friend, but sometimes the newspaper publisher made her uneasy. There were too many layers to him. With Reggie, she knew exactly what was going on.

Anticipation at seeing him after three long months grew in her by the moment. By the time the hour arrived for the paddle wheeler to put in at Echuca, she was eager to rent a room in a hotel there and spend the night in lovemaking with him, regardless of how indelicate such a thing was considered for a woman in her advanced stage of childbearing.

She had purposely scheduled her work in Sydney so that she could take a vacation at the beginning of her seventh month. She had wanted their baby to be born at Dream Time, where she could enjoy a respite before returning to Sydney and NSW Traders.

When she disembarked from the steamboat, not Reggie but Zab was there to meet her. His ebony features wore a grave expression. She stopped at the base of the boarding plank. "What is it, Zab?"

He twisted his floppy bush hat in his hands. Sweat beaded his black skin. "It's Mr. Lewis, Miss Tremayne. He's . . . he's . . ."

Her heart went absolutely still. "He's what?"

"Dead. It was that Mick Harrison. He and some outraged sheepmen formed a vigilante committee. They done murdered Mr. Lewis. Hanged him, they did."

And now the world stood still.

The rifle was an old Sharp's carbine that Annie kept above Dream Time's mantle. As a child, she had been instructed in the use of guns.

Even then, occasional tribes of aborigines still intent on making war would pass through the station's lands. Their painted wraithlike figures could be spotted gliding silently through the thigh-high grass. They always passed on through, perhaps because of the influence of Baluway and his tribe, loyal to Amaris Tremayne. Nevertheless, Annie and Daniel had been taught always to be vigilant, always prepared.

Numb and vacant eyed, she took down the rifle now. Balancing it on her distended stomach, she dropped the breech, making certain it was clean.

Vena came into the room. Perplexity knit her dark features. With a worried gaze, she watched Annie drape a heavy bandolier belt with its supply of cartridges across her shoulder but said nothing.

"I'll be gone for quite a while, Vena," she said, picking up her bush hat and the canteen she had filled.

She headed out to the stables in a stride that almost matched fat Vena's waddle. In Annie's condition, trousers were out of the question, and she had had to settle for a loose-fitting riding jacket and a waist-slitted skirt of lightweight merino material.

Zab met her halfway across the yard. His eyes narrowed suspiciously, but his tone was, as always, measured with the utmost respect. "Where you goin', Miss Tremayne?"

"To hunt weasel-hearted rats, Zab. Would you see that Paddy is saddled?"

"Yes'm."

Watching him swing the saddle down from its peg, she could tell her foreman wasn't happy. His wide nostrils flared further, and the fierce-looking bone adorning them shifted.

"Should you be riding this late . . . with the baby coming and all?" he asked, pitching the saddle over the gray.

"I'll be fine, Zab. Your women manage to birth babies and resume their work in a matter of hours."

He grunted and fastened the leather cinch. She had not appeased him. He was a contradiction. He had a white man's technical education and an aborigine's extraordinarily complex set of religious and magical beliefs, superstitions, and taboos.

She could not preoccupy herself with his concern. She needed to focus on the task at hand. It would require all of her mental faculties. Her physical condition would be taxed to its limit. Her emotional and spiritual sides would have to be put on a back burner for the moment.

The carbine she sheathed in its scabbard before mounting. Even with Zab's assistance, she was clumsy and awkward. Once she was settled into the saddle's deep seat, though, her innate riding skills returned automatically.

The journey to Mick Harrison's station was a long one, almost five hours. She conserved her energy, stopping often and taking small restorative sips from the canteen.

Fortunately, the day was pleasant with clear skies, bright sunshine, and only an occasional gust of wind to stir the dust and grit, but the pleasantness of the trip began to diminish in proportion to each kilometer ridden.

Weary beyond comprehension, with her thighs chafed, her abdomen aching, her clothes sodden with perspiration, she nevertheless knew when she had crossed onto Mick Harrison's station. She had ridden boundary enough to know the exact extent of Dream Time property.

Since it was not mustering time, the sheep were shifting for themselves in paddocks. Her quarry would be somewhere around the Big House and its outbuildings.

As she rode closer to those outbuildings, two station hands paused in their work to look up and then went back to their tasks. Three boys and a girl scampered out of the path of her horse. She rode on past a row of cottages housing the hands and their families. A wife hanging laundry peeked out between two shirts.

Annie's presence went unchallenged. Apparently, Mick Harrison never expected a single woman, and one in her advanced condition, to take any retributive measures. Her mouth curled in contempt. A costly mistake on the man's part, dismissing a woman as inconsequential.

She found Mick Harrison in the breeding pen with Captain Cook and the ewes impregnated by the prizewinning ram. He had just removed his hat and was wiping the back of his arm across his forehead. A ring of sweat marked his fair hair where his hatband had been.

"Mick."

Startled, he looked up. At the sight of the carbine nestled in her arm, his eyes widened. "What the bloody hell is this?"

"It isn't a baby I'm cradling." Her voice sounded distant in her ears and as harsh and unrelenting as the hot summer wind.

"Are you crazy?" His brown eyes darted around the yard, looking for anyone to help.

"Aye. With grief. Know what that means? I'll do anything and not think about the consequences."

A muscle in his jaw twitched wildly. His hands opened and closed in spasmodic fury. "If you don't ride away now, I'll call for help. My hands won't make any allowances for a woman toting a gun, no matter what her condition."

She shrugged. "Like I said, Mick, I'm crazy with grief."

Sweat, appearing as if from nowhere, dripped off the end of his nose. "You'll never get away with this."

"Do I look like I care?"

He tried another tactic. "No. Right now you look like a slattern wench that has been bedded by a common stockman who didn't know his place."

He almost succeeded in riling her. Anger roiled her blood and hammered at her temples. She fought for composure. With a steady movement, she lifted the Sharps and looked down its barrel.

Mick Harrison's eyes scrunched closed. His entire body seemed to vibrate. "No," he gasped. "Please."

"Please what?"

"Please. Please, don't shoot me."

"Beg me."

He dropped to his knees among the sheep. Tears brightened his eyes. "As God is my witness, I didn't mean to kill Reggie. When he refused to leave, the boys and I were just going to scare him a little, but—"

"You're slobbering on yourself, Mick. Reggie wouldn't beg, and that angered you, didn't it? Look at yourself, Mick. You're a groveling worm, you are."

Slowly, her finger pulled back on the trigger.

"Oh God!" he gasped.

With the ringing shot, the carbine jerked in her arm. She peered over the barrel and its haze of white smoke. Captain Cook lay dead. Crimson splotched the prize ram's gray wool. The remaining sheep bleated in fright and ran to the pen's far corner.

Dumbfounded, Mick stared at the lifeless ram. A moment was needed for him to comprehend what had happened. Then, he screamed, "I'll kill you for this!" and charged toward her like a berserk water buffalo.

"Stop," a man's voice ordered.

Both she and Mick glanced around to see Zab standing at the corner of the nearest shed. The aborigine clutched a boomerang. Accurately thrown, it could shatter a human skull into a hundred fragments.

Mick came up short. He was panting. His gaze was wild. His hands were clenched.

Calmly, Annie removed another cartridge from the belt slung over her shoulder, dropped it into the carbine chamber, and fired again. One of the impregnated ewes staggered, then collapsed.

Behind Annie, a station hand sprinted up to the railing. "What's going—?"

"If your man tries to stop me, Mick, your brains will be splattered in the dust. Don't think I don't mean it."

His expression told her he believed her. She popped another cartridge into the carbine and fired again and again. When she had finished, the only living thing in the breeding pen was Mick Harrison.

Coolly, she sheathed the Sharps. "Set one foot on my property, lift one finger against me or mine, ever again, and you'll know what true agony means. I am told that the aborigines are marvelous at administering exquisite torture. Do you understand?"

He was quite audibly blubbering as he nodded.

"Jolly good, then."

She was suddenly extremely tired. So tired, she could hardly hold her head up. "Zab? Let's go home. To Dream Time."

BOOK TWO

*It spreads nor'west by No-Man's Land
Where clouds are seldom seen—
To where the cattle stations lie
Three hundred miles between.*

*Lest in the city I forget
True mateship, after all,
My water bags and billy yet
Are hanging on the wall.*
                              —Anonymous

9

1882

Sydney Harbor was gaily decorated with bunting. Schoolchildren, soldiers, squatters, and sheep herders joined Sydneysiders to celebrate the completion of Gladesville Bridge, the first span linking the north and south shores of Sydney Harbor.

Since the time Annie had forsaken the short skirts worn by little girls, she had witnessed the opening of the Suez Canal, which reduced by half the journeytime from Australia to Europe, a telegraph cable had been laid from Sydney to London, and all British garrison forces had been withdrawn from Australia. Not only was she witnessing history, she was partaking in its making. It was an exhilarating feeling.

Along with the premier of New South Wales and the mayor of the city, she was one of the dignitaries invited to speak at the completion of the bridge. She was the only woman of more than a dozen of Sydney's leading citizens seated on the temporary platform erected for the occasion. Fresh sawdust gilded the hem of her apple green skirt as she approached the podium. The sea breeze flicked the green ribbons of her saucy tam-o'-shanter.

"The iron link we have forged this day with opposite shores symbolizes the dawn of an era. An era that can bring peace and prosperity if we will but forge the link of cooperation and compassion with the people who were here first, with the people a continent away, with people the world over, and most importantly among ourselves."

Her speech was the shortest. The spectators didn't know what to think. What had she said? That she was for foreign labor? Was she on the side of the liberals from the bourgeois parties or the reformist from the labor side? Was she against the isolationists?

Only a smattering of applause followed her speech. "You confused them, Annie," Ryan said, as he accompanied her in her carriage back to the NSW Traders' offices. The French landau's leather top was down, exposing them to September's balmy sunshine.

She gave him a disgusted look. His wardrobe consisted of a much better quality of clothing these days, evidence of his flourishing newspaper. A top hat, gloves, and cane complemented his attire this afternoon. "Your candor is utterly comforting."

"I was bestowing praise, Annie. People are realistic. They expect duplicity. They don't want politicians and civic leaders to tell them anything good or promise hope or speak about the event at hand. They expect to be treated like children. You treated them as adults, as equals. You were truthful."

"Tell the truth and run." From beneath her parasol, she slid him a wry smile. "A Turkish proverb."

"Why are we stopping here?" he asked as her driver reined in the two grays.

She nodded up at the signboard. HOME FOR SINGLE WOMEN. "My mother founded it. Called it the Female Immigrants' Home. For the female convicts who were used mainly as whores and then abandoned."

"You never fail to surprise me, Annie."

She took his hand and descended from the carriage. "I trust I am not boring, at least."

He laughed. "Far from that."

An old nun in the black habit of the Sisters of Charity order met them and bade them enter the sparsely but comfortably furnished receiving room. "We're so glad to see you, mum."

"Thank you, Sister Veronica. It seems my visits are getting fewer and farther between. I stopped by to see if the shipment of medical supplies was delivered."

The nun's red cheeks broadened with her smile. "Aye, that it was. Just yesterday. Along with a bin of fresh vegetables, thank ye."

"The thanks go to the Bristol Restaurant. They volunteered their surplus." Though not without a bit of coercion. "If there is anything the home should need—linens, clothing—"

"We are low on kerosene. I've had to store the lamps in favor of candles."

"My secretary will take care of that." The need to leave as soon as possible became imperative as she felt her breast milk began to leak through her brassiere padding. "I'll try to make my visits less infrequent, Sister Veronica."

Once outside, Ryan asked, "Is this the same formidable woman who tackled Sydney's Goliaths, Balzaretti and MacInnes? Who took a Springfield to—"

"It was a Sharps." She climbed back into the carriage and instructed the driver to take them to her office. "The story has been blown out of proportion."

"But based on fact, you did take a carbine and dispatch Captain Cook, the five ewes impregnated by the ram, and its three offspring."

"Aye, but I did not dispatch Mick Harrison. Or render him . . . impotent."

Ryan threw back his head and laughed. "You're not afraid to take on any man are you?"

"And you're not afraid to champion the underdog." She referred to the shearers and factory workers, who had launched stringent attacks on the wealthy pastoralists and manufacturers.

"We've butted heads more than once over my editorials. If you weren't so headstrong and stubborn—"

"Me headstrong and stubborn? What did it gain you attacking Walter Phillips? The withdrawal of advertising support by manufacturers, that's what."

The American magnate Phillips had immigrated to Sydney to set up a subsidiary of the old New England firm of Phillips and Co. It was an express office that had branched out into construction.

"What does it gain you bearing and raising Brendan alone? Public indignation. At thirty-one, you have earned the reputation of an implacable, dispassionate spinster."

She flinched inwardly. "Of course, you can fight back by cutting the price of your paper, which should increase circulation—"

"We're not finished discussing you, Annie. Your black looks won't silence me."

She managed a shrug. "Come along then." They descended and entered the NSW Traders' offices.

When they passed by her balding watchdog-secretary, James, he peered up at her over his spectacles. "Are you ready for the Broken Hill report, Miss Tremayne?"

"No, send for Mrs. Heathcrest, please."

Ryan followed her into her office, where she stripped off her eyelet gloves and tossed them on the settee along with her tam-o'-shanter. He plopped down in one of the easy chairs opposite her leather-topped desk, one of the legacies of her grandmother.

"Mrs. Heathcrest?" he asked.

"My son's nanny." She seated herself in the other easy chair.

"So who is Sister Veronica? You're not a practicing Catholic."

"A convicted prostitute who came over on the last transportation ship in '68. Is this an interview, Ryan?"

The tips of his mustache curled upward. "We've known each other too long for that." He broke off at the discreet knock on her office door.

"Come in."

Mrs. Heathcrest entered. She was a short, middle-aged Welsh woman with a pouter-pigeon chest and a face as craggy as the Blue Mountains. Cradled in her arms was a squalling mite of humanity. Reggie's child. Annie had had a cubbyhole of an office converted to a sitting room-nursery for Brendan.

The nanny rolled her Delft blue eyes. "He's powerfully hungry, Miss Tremayne."

She held up her arms. "I'll take him, Mrs. Heathcrest."

When she cradled Brendan against her, his wailing stopped. He turned his head toward her covered breast and made little suckling noises. She had to chuckle.

Every time she stared down at those tiny flailing hands and soft fuzzy head, she experienced something that was as nigh to spiritual as she imagined she would ever get. Some called it a maternal feeling. A protective, overwhelming love for one's offspring. In a short month, the baby had altered her life forever.

"Your expression has softened, Annie," Ryan said. "Gone is that driven, relentless look of your businessmen."

"Businessmen don't nurse infants. Brendan's hungry."

A shy look crossed his face. He picked up his cane. "I'll leave, then."

"There's no need for that." She began unbuttoning her jacket and blouse. Little more would be revealed than what a low-cut ball gown exposed. "I'm sure you won't see anything that would offend you."

He settled back into the chair again. "I never found anything about females offensive. On the contrary, I felt they possessed a great mystery that we mere males would never divine."

She nudged Brendan's fat cheek in an attempt to guide his tiny mouth toward her nipple. "Why have you never remarried?"

His dark eyes watched her. She felt no embarrassment. "Why have you never married?"

"There was no need."

"My sentiments exactly. Tell me, Annie, do you never want . . . a man. Don't you miss what you and Reggie Lewis shared?"

"Of course I do. It can be a gnawing ache. If I let myself think about it."

But sometimes she did. How could you suppress the memory of ecstasy forever? Occasionally, memories of their loving would smite her at the most unexpected moments. Weakness would flood through her. If standing, she would clutch the nearest object, a chair—a doorjamb—Brendan's crib—for support.

Without even closing her eyes, she could recall with exquisite clarity Reggie's beautiful male body. Recall with haunting desire that part of him that had pleased her so wonderfully, its flesh pale pink against the rest of his sunburnt body. She remembered marveling how when holding it, it could be so hard and yet so soft to the touch, especially the underside of it. Like silk, almost. And its tip, a perfect mushroom cap that enticed her fingers to stroke it with mesmerized fascination.

"But you keep yourself too busy to give it much thought, don't you?"

She blushed and almost smiled. "I try to."

From beneath the concealment of her lashes, she studied him. Ryan Sheridan was undoubtedly a handsome man. He had to be nearing forty, or more. Glints of silver at his temples and lines of character formed by years of living, really living, were all that confirmed his approximate age. His vitality, his lively interests, his still-muscular body bespoke the years of a man much younger. "Do you miss your wife, Ryan?"

He looked down and spoke as if choosing his words carefully. "I miss what we had. More than I ever thought possible. Time hasn't diminished that. If anything, the years have intensified those things: the late-night shared secrets, the conspiratorial smile in a crowded room, the comforting hand on the shoulder, even the shouting matches. I miss that passion for life that can only come in sharing yourself with another."

"But there is a price to pay for what you describe," she mused. "'Tis called surrender. I don't know if I believe in totally abandoning myself to the mercy of another. Emotions can be very misleading. After all, our Maker did give us a mind for intelligent and discriminating thought."

His dark eyes appraised her. He opened his mouth to speak, closed it as if having second thoughts, then shrugged and said, "There is a balance to life, an equalization of the emotional and mental, that can only be enhanced, not diminished, by surrender, Annie. It's the great truism of all the world religions."

Brendan was asleep. With one hand, she began rebuttoning her blouse. "I don't follow world religions, Ryan. I follow my own inner voice. My instincts, my spirit guide, whatever you mystical Irish call it."

He rose now, straightening his jacket and collecting his cane. Yes, he was an extremely attractive man. "I commend you. You shouldn't ever know the loneliness of the soul, then. G'day, Annie."

10

1883

    As Dan unloaded the *Bertie Mae* of its cargo in Sydney Harbor, cedar from Lebanon and spices from Jakarta, he reflected on his childhood. What price had Sinclair and Amaris Tremayne to pay to be remolded by Nan Livingston and Australia? Was it worth it to them? He had felt less than human, only a symbol, a puppet. His boy's pain had been an outrage. Something he hadn't wanted to look at. So he hadn't, and it had been bearable.

    Losing Kai had been unbearable. Their unborn baby he would never know. But Kai he had come to love as he had never thought he could love another human being. With her he had fully become a man there at the Great Barrier Reef Sugar Plantation. At first, he had thought that she would merely make his life less lonely, that her presence would add a contentment. He had not been prepared for that wildly wonderful feeling that had stayed with him so that all he thought about was her.

He had been barely able to wait to return to his hut each afternoon. Even though her own work often hadn't been finished until after sundown, he had looked forward to entering the house and smelling her scent, a mixture of hyacinth, lavender, and her sweet skin odor, peculiar only to her.

He had looked forward to hearing the low lilt of her voice, her almost perfect English delivered in a delightful singsong manner and the way she peppered her speech with his Australian slang—dinkum for genuine and loo for toilet.

He had loved glimpsing the little things that had been hers: a sarong carelessly left at the foot of their rope-slung bed, wildflowers she had plaited for a crown for him, her tortoiseshell comb.

He had never given much thought to the consequences of their coupling—"rooting," as she had used the Australian slang. Except that in loving her he had become a man.

In those horrifyingly long hours of her labor he had come to understand that he had not been a man. He might have thought he was. In losing her, he had learned otherwise.

Would his brightly burning desire for her ever dim?

He did know he would never return to the rain forest where he had buried her. Perhaps that was why he had chosen to return to Sydney and the sea. The rain forest held memories of decay and rot, a swallowing up of the senses. The muffled heat of the tropical north was oppressive. While the sea with its wind and swells . . .

He put down a crate of peppercorns and stared at the rolling waves. Shades of aqua, turquoise, pale green, and blue. The goodness of sunlight, something one rarely saw in the rain forest. The fresh breeze wafting in from exotic lands unseen. The tangy salt air to pique the senses. Colorful longboats bobbing like ducks in the harbor.

More than a decade had passed since he had last been in Sydney. He could, of course, return to NSW Traders, but he supposed he was too proud and too bitter, which accounted perhaps for his interest in the fledgling labor union beginning in Sydney.

A series of strikes in the 1870s and an inter-colonial conference in 1879 had indicated the union's growing power. Maybe NSW Traders had met a worthy opponent in this union.

"Hey, mate," Richard called out to him farther

down the wharf. "There's a meeting at the grog shop after work. Gonna be there?"

Dan wiped the sweat from his forehead with the back of his hand. His entire body was highly muscled and deeply tanned. He had shaved off his beard but left the mustache to camouflage the grim set of his mouth. Few who had known the small, fragile Daniel as a child, before he went off to England for school, would recognize the man. "Bare-breasted jills couldn't keep me away, Ratbag."

Richard, or Ratbag, as Dan good-naturedly called the young man, was another of the union's subleaders. The short, dark, twenty-five-year-old had big ears, which had prompted the sobriquet. He had offered Dan a place to sleep when Dan had arrived on the docks, looking for work and broke.

Ratbag's place was a tenement in the worst part of Sydney, called The Rocks. The site of Sydney's first settlement, The Rocks was an area of warehouses, bond stores, brothels, and open sewers all perched on a rocky spur of land overlooking Sydney Cove.

Ratbag's flat was located in that squalid, overcrowded warren noted for its gangs of larrikins, from the word lair. More than once, Dan had had to fight these ruffians, who snatched purses, held up pedestrians, and generally created havoc.

Now he had his own place in The Rocks. Word must have gotten out, because he was no longer bothered by the larrikins. He dwelled in relative peace in his place on Suez Canal, an alley near Kendal Lane and its Chinese merchants.

That afternoon, Ratbag and Dan climbed The Rocks' steep cobblestone streets to the Hero of Waterloo Hotel, the oldest Sydney pub. Pubs were called hotels because of what he thought was a ridiculous law forbidding consumption of liquor except in residential premises.

A gas lamp supported by an iron bracket over the door guided travelers after dark. Concoctions like snowstorm, knickerbocker, sherry cobbler, claret spider, sangaree, and brandy smash beckoned the thirsty traveler to enter.

There in the dark and smoky bastion of its male patrons, the union members met to lift a tankard of ale and discuss the latest issues. Tonight, the issue was arbitration with the hardnosed American businessman Walter Phillips over improvements on wharf facilities.

"The meeting with Phillips is set for a week from tomorrow," said Crockett, a blazing-eyed, wiry young man. "He wants us to meet him on neutral ground. The highest ground, of course, for the likes of him. The Lord Nelson Hotel."

Dan chuckled. The hotel sat on Sydney's highest point, Observatory Hill. He puffed on his briar pipe, then said, "Phillips knows what he's about. It's called the art of intimidation."

"What do ye mean?" Ratbag asked.

"I mean the cobber wants to make us feel ill at

ease. The Lord Nelson Hotel serves pheasant under glass and offers a wine list as long as one of NSW Traders' ship manifest."

Ratbag narrowed his eyes. "How do you know that? I mean about the wine list. You eaten there before, mate?"

Dan swallowed his ale to buy time. His grandmother's preference for the place had caused him to endure hour-long courses and discourses. "I saw it posted on the board when I was looking for a job."

"Well, I'll skip its restaurant and its wine list," Crockett said. "Give me one of its rooms upstairs and Phillips's daughter."

Ratbag's large ears almost perked up. "What's the jill like?"

"A fair one. Blond. Blue-eyed. A saucy damsel. If I could . . ."

Whatever Crockett was saying, Dan never heard its conclusion. His gaze was fastened on one of the men at the bar. He was hunched over the bar. Nevertheless, his massive shoulders had that set that reminded him of a bull.

Without excusing himself, Dan rose from his chair and made his way among the tables of patrons toward the long mahogany bar. As dimly lit as the room was, the man's profile was unmistakable. Dan clapped a hand on the man's shoulder. "Frank! Frank Smythe! I can't believe it's you!"

The big man turned around, and for a moment

Dan thought he had been wrong after all, that the man was not Frank. Yet, one could not miss the man's walleye. Still, so many years had passed since Dan had ridden with the captain of the Blue Mountain Bushrangers. Maybe Dan was wrong about the man being Frank Smythe.

Looking into the haggard face with its gray, scraggly beard, looking deeper into the bloodshot eyes where utter despair was lodged, Dan knew it was the man who had been like a father to him.

"Yeah? What ish it?" Frank asked, his expression surly, his words slurred.

"It's me, Frank. Dan."

"So?"

"Why don't we go somewhere and talk?"

"Give it away, ocker."

Despite the command, Dan wasn't giving up. "You're going home with me, Frank."

He half expected his old friend, and Frank did look old, to swing one of those mighty fists at him. Instead, the man's shoulders slumped even more. "I'm tired. Give it away."

Dan braced an arm around Frank's waist to heft him from the stool and was dismayed by how much weight the once-burly man had lost. Mere flab remained on the ribs. At least Frank went with him docilely. He paused and over his shoulder called back to Ratbag, "Meet you at the Lord Nelson tomorrow night."

"But we haven't talked about the issues that—"

He grinned. "I'll handle Phillips, no worries, mate."

Somehow, he managed to support the staggering, half-drunk old bushranger through the dark, narrow streets. At George Street, Frank insisted on pausing to urinate in the cast-iron pissoir.

"Damme if I don't have a waterspout for a cock."

Dan didn't bother to tell the man that more urine splashed on the wall than in the pissoir.

Dan's place was little more than a monk's cell with the smells of cabbage, garlic, excrement, and sweat drifting in from the other flats. The furniture was of rough slab, the bed a hemp-slung straw mattress, and the crockery cracked and dirty. Old clippings from the *Illustrated London News* plastered the walls.

"A bowl of hot soup should do you fine, Frank."

"A pot of ale should do me better." He lay on the narrow bed and squinted up at Dan. "You don't look the same, me lad."

Dan grinned and set a pan on the dingy stove. "I could say the same of you."

He was barely able to get the soup down Frank, who dribbled more than he swallowed. After the man drifted off to sleep, Dan stayed up most of the night, going over the mass of papers the union had compiled on Phillips.

By the time he arrived at the meeting the next day, he felt prepared for the American industrialist.

What Dan wasn't prepared for was Phillips's daughter, Louisa, when the maître d' pointed her father and her out to him. She was small, prim, and golden haired. As the father and daughter stood outside the Lord Nelson Hotel, viewing the panorama of the Heads and the harbor's magnificent beaches, their backs were to Dan. December's hot sunlight reflected off the water and danced sparkles on her hair.

"Mr. Phillips?"

Walter Phillips turned around. He was of medium height but seemed taller with his ramrod bearing and iron gray eyes the same shade as his hair. He was dressed conservatively in gray vicuña trousers and frock coat, unbuttoned to reveal the gray pinstriped waistcoat. A four-in-hand necktie added that touch of a dapper appearance.

His daughter had the same aloof bearing, but her eyes were a different shade of gray, like the harbor waters at dawn. Dan estimated her to be in her early twenties. She wore a teal blue day dress with matching jacket and elbow-length sleeves edged with lace ruffles. In her hand, the flowerpot crown of her Rubens hat was trimmed with streamers.

Dan's clothing was definitely understated—trousers and a wharf jacket of East Indian nankeen—which was just as well. Let Phillips mistake him for an oaf. Dan figured that it gave him an edge.

"Yes?" Phillips asked.

"Dan Warwick." He stuck out his hand. "I'm the union liaison."

Phillips took it in a firm grip, although no cordial smile eased the lines of his face. "You're younger than I expected."

At thirty-two Dan didn't feel young. He cast a glance at the young woman. She was watching him with intent interest. "Will your daughter be included in our dinner party? If so, I need to make arrangements for another place setting."

"No. Louisa will be dining separately with her mother. Mrs. Phillips should be down shortly."

By the time Dan was seated in the fashionable hotel's restaurant, Louisa and her mother—an older, tired version of her daughter—were being ushered to their table.

About the same time, Ratbag and Crockett arrived. Dan made the introductions, and the four of them immediately launched into a discussion of the more controversial issues. "One of the points the union insists on, Mr. Phillips, is the use of products made in the Australian colonies for the wharf's construction."

Phillips dabbed his mouth with his linen napkin. "Impossible. Our pilings are built with iron gratings that only Virginia welders know how to fabricate exactly."

Dan shrugged. "Then our welders will have to master the process. But build the iron gratings they will."

Irritation, and mild respect, flickered in the gaze of the American. "I would have to have a sample of the craftsmanship before I could ever concede to such an agreement."

Dan shrugged. "That should be easily arranged. This will delay the construction process, naturally. Your company will have to be responsible for absorbing the cost of the delay."

Phillips laid down his fork. The lines around his mouth deepened. "You can't be serious, man."

"That I am, mate."

Dan's humor was not missed. Ratbag, or Richard, as Dan had introduced him, fought to repress a grin.

Crockett intervened and took up the haggling process. "Ye must understand, Mr. Phillips, that . . ."

Dan missed the point his union associate was making. Feeling he was being watched, he turned his head slightly to the left, where Louisa and her mother were dining. Louisa quickly averted her gaze, but not in time for Dan to miss the unmistakable interest that had been focused on him.

He had taken only a cursory and purely sexual interest in women since the death of Kai. Now Louisa's aloof beauty challenged him. What challenged him even more was the disapproving look leveled on him by Walter Phillips at that same moment. The American would definitely be in opposition to Dan's courting Louisa.

Both challenges were tempting, but not enough to take his mind from his purpose: to win the most concessions possible from Phillips in the contract negotiations.

Or, at least, he thought that was what he really wanted. Then Louisa and her mother stopped by the table when they had finished their dinner.

Mrs. Phillips conferred in a quiet, almost timorous manner with her husband over plans later than evening. Louisa chose that moment to smile and say, "The fish is excellent, isn't it, Mr. Warwick?"

From the corner of his eye, he caught the snide smile curving Phillips's narrow lips. "Mr. Warwick may not be familiar with barramunda's culinary qualities, Louisa."

Dan's smile came easily. "The fish is probably day-old and passed off as fresh by covering it with Chablis and blanched almonds."

Grudging respect glinted in Phillips's and Louisa's eyes.

Dan wasn't surprised when a messenger showed up at his tenement doorstep later than evening.

"It's a summons," Dan said, turning back to Frank, who was propped up in Dan's bed and eating meat pie that Dan had purchased from a street vendor. "From an American tycoon—Walter Phillips."

"I've heard of him," Frank mumbled, his mouth full. Color had returned to the face of the old bushranger. "He's in construction, isn't he?"

"He's involved in everything." He tossed the neatly penned message on the nightstand. "I'm to appear for a formal dinner next Friday."

"Where do they live?"

"Hunters Hill." The area was a suburb of Sydney that competed with Elizabeth Bay for elegance.

Frank chortled. "And I suppose you're going to show up dressed like a penguin, eh?"

"I don't own formal dinner attire, much less a black tie. I'm going to have to think about this."

Think he did over the following week. Was his desire to defy the arrogant and aristocratic Phillips an indirect urge to strike back at a resident of Elizabeth Bay, his affluent, estranged sister?

As more and more of his time was being taken up with union arbitration, Dan arranged to have Frank hired that week as his assistant. He dumped the miscellaneous arbitrations into Frank's loyal hands Friday afternoon. "Just look over the notes and brief me for Monday. I'm going out tonight."

Frank grinned cheerfully. "Going to the Mad Hatter's Ball, me lad?"

He rubbed his temple. "Though I'm far from the Mad Hatter." His irritation with himself and the Phillipses had prompted him to dress in the same clothes he wore to the Lord Nelson Hotel.

His defiance of tradition was duly noted by Phillips himself when he personally greeted Dan below the fanlight of the doorway. His gaze ran critically over Dan. "I'm glad you could make it, Mr. Warwick."

Dan scanned the room. Pots of palms and ferns graced the alcoves. Crystal chandeliers shimmered on glittering guests. Behind a Chinese silk screen placed strategically beneath a staircase, musicians played soft chamber music. Liveried waiters hovered discreetly, waiting for an empty glass to summon them. "You know, it's illegal to try to buy me."

Phillips laughed. "You said illegal. But you didn't say you couldn't be bought."

Dan returned his gaze to his host. "Is your daughter for sale?"

Phillips's face blanched. "I could ask you to leave for that."

"Daddy, there you are." Louisa came up and took her father's arm in a loving gesture. She was wearing a mauve silk organza dress that sloped off her creamy shoulders. "Mama's been looking all over for . . ."

She paused as if just realizing her father was engaged in conversation. Her gaze, silver in the gaslight, flitted over Dan. "It's Mr. Warwick, isn't it?"

"Last time I looked in a mirror I was."

She laughed gaily, and he reassessed his opinion of her. There was an element of spontaneity that mitigated her studied polish. He liked that. "Come with me," she said. "I'll introduce you to the other guests."

Her father's somber expression told Dan that he might be taking on an implacable enemy, but Dan had learned through union work that everything was negotiable.

"I want him, Father."

Louisa's father settled back in the wing chair and lit up a cigar. The smoke eddied from his lips before he spoke. "Is it the man who interests you—or the challenge?"

She moved languidly to the parlor window. Her fingers played with one of the leafy fronds that banked the high double panes. Her mind's eye recalled the young man's face, the color of ivory browned by age. "Queer, that's what he said to me, last night. That the kind of person I was challenged him."

"What else did he say?"

She didn't turn back to her father. From the kitchen, she heard her mother's high voice giving instructions to the cook. "That he hadn't made up his mind whether to tackle the challenge or not."

"In other words, whether you were worth it or not."

A smile curved her pink lips. "Oh, I'll make certain I'm worth it."

"Tell me, Louisa, what do you see in him?"

She recalled their brief discussion of Sydney's stupendous harbor, reminiscent to her of San

Francisco's. The conversation had drifted to her opinion of Sydney's people. "Not that much different from your American cousins," she had told him.

Dan Warwick's face, cold and thin, had become extraordinary sweet and gentle. People were important to him.

"The difference between Dan and other men I know, of course, intrigues me. His controlled, contained emotions. Yet I catch glimpses of a shy, melancholy side of him. His obviously educated background . . . it conflicts with his . . . uhh, well, his worker's hands, Father."

Her father read her mind. "That magnificent physique you so admire has been built by years of common labor. He is a common man. What do you think your life would be like with him?"

"I don't know." Her fingers stilled. Her child, barely stirring within her, would need a father. The man who had sired it was the profligate son of one of her father's business partners. Though her infatuation for the young man had ended quickly, the legacy of that foolish fling was just beginning.

"But I mean to find out, Father. If Dan will take me as his wife."

11

1884

The spring day was perfect for a picnic in Hyde Park with its delightful fountains—delightful, unless one realized that the old barracks facing Macquarie Street were once ex-convict quarters.

Ryan knelt on one knee alongside Annie, where she sat on a blanket with her legs tucked under her voluminous sprigged muslin skirts. She ceased humming the ditty, "Merrily Danced the Quaker's Wife," and took a sip of her lemonade. It was chilled by ice imported from Massachusetts. Cut from ponds, the ice was packed aboard NSW Traders' clippers in sawdust. She in turn sold the ice in blocks in Sydney at threepence a pound. A tidy profit for the company.

She looked up at Ryan. "Isn't Brendan beautiful?"

Ryan had removed his frock coat and slung it over one shoulder. The heat of the sun accentuated his male scent and the cologne he used, a subtle suggestion of Mexican orange, Indian sandalwood, and Thai amber. She ought to recognize the scent of his cologne. She had ordered it for his birthday from an Italian perfumery.

Both she and Ryan watched as her two-year-old son—and Reggie's—plowed his fat little hands into tufts of emerald green clover.

"Your son is beautiful because he is a replica of his mother."

She peeked up at him from beneath her leghorn hat. He was a brilliant listener and a keen observer. "Ryan, you know I'm grateful, don't you? So grateful for your friendship."

"Wouldn't anyone want to be friends with a living legend?"

The warm October afternoon wasn't responsible for the heat that suffused her face. "Pure luck, Ryan."

"You call it luck, your admirers say you bested Balzaretti because of your woman's sixth sense, and your detractors claim you knew all along and fleeced him in the bargaining."

She had to chuckle. Ryan was referring to her purchase of Rivers Run, Reggie's dilapidated cattle station. James A. Balzaretti had held the note on it. After Reggie's death, she had concentrated on putting his memory and that part of her life behind her. Until Balzaretti had offered the station for sale. When he learned she was interested, he had driven up the price. She hadn't cared. She had ended up paying an exorbitant sum for the station, far more than it was worth. But it was a part of Brendan's heritage.

Then, a surveyor she had hired to stake out the station's exact boundaries had found an alluvial diamond in a creek on the property. The Lewis Diamond Mine was expected to yield a million carats this year alone. Only about five percent of the Lewis diamonds were gem quality, but they included occasional rare pink diamonds that were selling for fifty times more than the usual white brilliants.

"I notice your editorials are still opposing Walter Phillips's business stance," she said, changing the subject. "And I don't notice him knuckling under to your mighty pen."

Ryan shrugged. "Then I'll champion an underdog Phillips can't fight—his own son-in-law."

"Dan Warwick?" She laughed. "An opportunist, using his wife's family as carte blanche."

"You don't know Warwick, then, Annie. He would—and has—walked into any drawing room without an invitation. He and his father-in-law are like cobra and mongoose. Each waiting for a weak moment in the other to strike."

He leaned forward. "Annie, listen to me. You

know me well enough to know that I would take you to print if I thought NSW Traders were stepping over boundary lines, don't you?"

His intensity confounded her. "Of course. I applaud your determined stand and powerful advocacy of the issues you believe in—although I don't always agree with you."

He had earned her unwilling admiration and support, but those she would never directly acknowledge—to him, at least. Nana had once told her, "Never put in writing what you can say. Never say what you can whisper. And if you have to whisper, then it shouldn't be acknowledged, at all."

"Then marry me, Annie."

Her eyes widened. "What?"

"You heard me."

"Brendan, come here." She glanced back at Ryan. "He's wandering too close to the pond."

"Annie, you're ignoring me."

Brendan came toddling back toward her, arms outstretched. She caught him against her and kissed his rosy, chubby cheek. "I don't need marriage, Ryan. I have my son to love."

"You need passion."

At the urgency in his low, melodious voice, something in her responded. She thrust the unidentifiable feeling from her and set her squirming son free. "I'm too set in my ways after all these years of ruling a virtual business empire."

"You're a woman, nevertheless. A passionate woman, though you would deny it."

She fastened him with a gaze that had quelled board members. "You don't know that." She rose and brushed off her skirts. "The afternoon is getting cool. I'd best get Brendan back to his nanny."

Ryan stood up as well, towering over her even at her height. "You're running, Annie. I had thought better of you than that." Then he smiled wryly. "I had expected at least a battle."

She had to laugh. "I'm flattered, Ryan. Truly. You're good for my feminine vanity. Please don't stop with the attention."

"I don't plan to. Shall we go? I have an interview with your opportunist, Dan Warwick."

"He's not *my* opportunist," she countered lightly, but a part of her was disappointed that Ryan could so easily dismiss her rejection of him.

You truly are vain, Annie Livingston, she told herself.

"All I am asking is for you to attend the reception for the tenor. It's not as if I am asking you to attend the opera, too."

Dan rolled away from her. She hated him when he faced the other way in their bed. She hated herself when her voice sounded shrill. She had always sworn she would never be weak and insipid as her mother had been.

"I told you before you ever responded to the reception that I had been elected to a state assembly of labor unionists. I can't help it that the times conflict."

"Politics! If it's not the union, then it's that new Labor Party. And if it's not the Labor Party to capture your interest, then it's . . . it's a woman."

"What?" He rolled back over to face her.

In the dark, she couldn't see his face, but she knew every beautiful line of it. In the six months they had been married, she had come to know every muscle in his body, every nuance in his words, but not the thoughts that went on behind those turbulent brown eyes.

"A woman? Are you out of your mind? Even if I wanted another woman, when would I have time?"

"I don't know," she whispered. She pushed back the mussed hair that had fallen across her cheek. In the span of time it took her to perform the gesture, her confusion vanished. "It's a woman you knew before me. Someone from the past. Your experience . . ." She could feel herself blushing. "You haven't been celibate all these years. Who was she?"

She felt the bed shift. In the darkness of the night, she could barely perceive his silhouette as he paced before their four-poster. Her four-poster. After their marriage he had agreed to move into the Phillips family home, at her father's urging. Dan seemed to adapt so easily to the trappings of the affluent.

"You're right, of course, Louisa. There was someone else."

Her breath caught.

"Her name was Kai."

"I don't want to know anything about her."

"She was Polynesian."

She put her hands over her ears. "I love you. I want you to love me."

"We both worked on a sugar plantation in Queensland. She had been sold into slavery. By her father. A Baptist missionary. He sold off both her and her sister. A bully of an assistant overseer raped her sister. Tonkil could have been no more than twelve or thirteen. And she conceived."

She couldn't take any more of his dispassionate voice saying such horrible things. She sprang from the bed and wrapped her arms around his waist. His flesh was icy steel. "Stop it! Stop it, Dan!"

"I suppose that was when I knew I didn't want to leave Kai there at the mercy of those beasts. When I found out she was carrying our child, I made up my mind to leave and take her with me. That was tantamount to stealing property, of course. The plantation owner wasn't about to let me get away with stealing a human he owned. He set his bullies and his starved mastiffs on us. She died there in the rain forest. I buried her—and our child."

Her tears seeped between her cheek and his back, where her face was pressed. "I am giving you another child, Dan. Just stop loving her. She's dead. I'm alive. I'm here. Feel me." She grabbed his hand and cupped it under her small breast. "My flesh is alive and warm and wanting."

She moved his hand down to her full belly. "Feel the child I am bearing you! Oh, Dan, kiss me, darling."

He whirled around and scooped her up against his chest. She could feel the anger and frustration and resentment emanating from him as he carried her to their bed, but she didn't care. At least he was warm with life again. And those feelings weren't directed against her. If only she could make him feel love for her.

12

1885

From her office window, Annie watched the procession of three hundred unemployed men and women along the quay to the Wool Exchange. They were led by the Cardinal Raleigh. Clad in cassock and miter, he carried not his pastoral staff but a huge cross on which was nailed the effigy of a downtrodden man clad in tattered rags, his side besmeared by red paint, and on his back the words, "Murdered by the rich."

In general, the clergy responded to the depression in the cities with sermons mocking the destitute by attributing their misfortunes to improvidence, drinking, and gambling. But not Cardinal Raleigh. He was throwing in his lot with the union workers, stirred by radicals like this newcomer, Dan Warwick.

A financial crash in Argentina, which had been a center of world speculation, was having its impact on Australia. So far, thirteen banks had closed their doors in the Australian colonies of Victoria, Queensland, and New South Wales.

As one of the wealthiest and most prominent of Australia's entrepreneurs, Annie was being singled out. It did not matter that she had fought to keep the Bank of New South Wales open and had made certain that the tellers funded each and every person who sought to withdraw their money.

When the banks that had managed to stay open did not cut their interest rates, the squatters and farmers suffered badly. So she had cut her rates and even loaned out additional sums.

Hard hit by the depreciation of land values, the ranchers began to employ nonunion labor. In retaliation, the wharf laborers in Sydney and Melbourne refused to handle wool shorn by nonunion labor.

Then silver, lead, and zinc miners at Broken Hill began striking. Annie had acceded to their blind demands. Did they not realize that by overthrowing the capitalist society they condemned they were killing the golden goose?

She picked up the folded copy of *The Sydney Dispatch* and read again Ryan's latest editorial. ". . . looking forward to the day when there will be

Join the
Timeless Romance Reader Service
and get four of today's
most exciting historical
romances free,
without obligation!

Imagine getting today's very best historical romances sent directly to your home – at a total savings of at least $2.00 a month. Now you can be among the first to be swept away by the latest from Candace Camp, Constance O'Banyon, Patricia Hagan, Parris Afton Bonds or Susan Wiggs. You get all that – and that's just the beginning.

Preview at home without obligation and save.

Each month, you'll receive four new romances to preview without obligation for 10 days. You'll pay the low subscriber price of just $4.00 per title – a total savings of at least $2.00 a month!

Postage and handling is absolutely free and there is no minimum number of books you must buy. You may cancel your subscription at any time with no obligation.

GET YOUR FOUR
FREE BOOKS TODAY
($20.49 VALUE)

FILL IN THE ORDER FORM BELOW NOW!

YES! *I want to join the Timeless Romance Reader Service. Please send me my 4 FREE HarperMonogram historical romances. Then each month send me 4 new historical romances to preview without obligation for 10 days. I'll pay the low subscription price of $4.00 for every book I choose to keep – a total savings of at least $2.00 each month – and home delivery is free! I understand that I may return any title within 10 days without obligation and I may cancel this subscription at any time without obligation. There is no minimum number of books to purchase.*

NAME_____

ADDRESS _____

CITY_____STATE_____ZIP_____

TELEPHONE_____

SIGNATURE _____

(If under 18 parent or guardian must sign. Program, price, terms, and conditions subject to cancellation and change. Orders subject to acceptance by HarperMonogram.)

GET
4
FREE
BOOKS
(A $20.49
VALUE)

friendlier feelings between employee and employer, when shipowners abandon ruinous competition among themselves . . ."

Only a slap on the hand. Still, she was incensed. Was he or was he not her friend?

She decided to pay a call on him that evening. Ryan lived in Wooloomooloo. The 'loo was one of Sydney's older areas, with many narrow streets and some fine old homes built in the Regency style. She told her carriage driver to wait and was about to descend from the landau, when she sighted Ryan exiting from his doorway. He wore a Talma evening dress coat and carried top hat and cane.

She almost hailed him, when a woman stepped forward from the vestibule. In the gathering dusk, Annie could not tell much about her except that her raiment was of fine quality. The brim of her toque shielded her face. She looped her arm over his and, looking up at him, gave a little laugh to something he said.

Puzzled, Annie watched them set off down the street. Where could they be going afoot this time of evening, pleasant though it was? "Follow the couple," she told her driver.

She felt a prick of what she could only term indignation. Why had she not heard about Ryan's love interest?

Of course, a man like him would not be practicing abstinence. Still, they were friends. She hid nothing from him. He had known about Reggie and her, hadn't he? Pique stiffened her spine.

Soon, Ryan and the nameless woman reached Queens Square at the northern end of Hyde Park and turned into a doorway. Astonished, Annie could only stare. St. James Church. They were attending mass!

Why, she had never considered Ryan to be spiritually oriented. She had often thought churchgoers hypocritical and weak. Those descriptions certainly were not applicable to Ryan. Obstinate, opinionated, stuffy even, but not hypocritical or weak.

Who was the woman?

At times like this Annie missed having a woman friend in whom to confide. The nature of her business dictated that most of her acquaintances were of the male sex. After her long working hours were finished, she had so little time to seek out anyone else.

Her discreet inquiries over the following days elicited no information of value about the woman Ryan was seeing. Apparently she did not move in the same social circles as either Ryan or Annie. Frustrated, she at last determined that she would ask him about the woman point blank.

Brazen, aren't you, Annie? she told the mirror as she tucked a stray russet curl into place before sallying out to the offices of *The Sydney Dispatch*.

Ryan was back in the pressroom with rolled-up shirtsleeves and a pressman's apron. Ink matted the hair on his left forearm. "Annie, what prompts you to tread on the hallowed ground of the male domain?"

Her smile was as tart as his question. "I feel more as though I'm treading on spring ice. Do you have time to take me to lunch?"

"I'm working on a late scoop. Two union leaders have been arrested for armed skirmishes with the police."

"Any chance one of them was that Warwick hooligan?"

"Not him, but two of his mates. You underestimate Dan Warwick. He doesn't let his passions overrule his good judgment."

Passions. She was reminded of why she was calling upon Ryan. "Perhaps later, then."

He grabbed up an ink-smeared rag and wiped his hands. "If it's important, Annie, I think I could snatch some time for dinner tonight."

She almost demured, but instead, she said, "I'd like that. I'll be back for you at eight."

As the hour approached, she grew agitated. She paced the floor and thought of half a dozen excuses to beg off. She should have kept it as merely a business call. Now, having dinner with Ryan—inquiring about his personal life, would lay her open, make her vulnerable. She was getting far more involved than she should.

Still, she dressed and summoned her carriage. It was a dulcet autumn evening, the first of March, and the landau's top was down. When she arrived at Ryan's office, he was just coming out and struggling into his frock coat. His bowler was slanted across his eyes.

"Working till the last minute, I see," she said, trying to keep her tone light as he climbed in beside her.

With an apologetic grimace he stretched out his long fingers. "Didn't get all the ink washed out." He put his arm on the back of the seat. "Now, what's this all about? Something's troubling you, Annie, isn't it?" He knew her so well.

"How does one of the open air cafés down on the harbor sound?"

"Grand. After a day in the print shop, the ink fumes tend to give me a headache. Then the eyes start to blur." He flashed her a wry smile. "I know I'm getting older when my body protests daily in a dozen different ways."

He also knew enough not to press her. The café she chose was near the site of the proposed tram depot, overlooking the cove. Just enough light of day was left for them to view the myriad boats and tangle of sails and spars. Nearer, wattles ablaze with orange flowers shaded the small café and offered a nest to the tame kookaburras.

They selected an umbrella-topped table nearest the water. After ordering a bottle of red wine, they studied the menu and talked of inconsequential things like politics and weather.

He was patiently waiting for her to say what was on her mind. She sat across from him and surreptitiously appraised his chiseled profile. Was she in love with him? No. He was a good friend, that was all.

At last, she asked in a soft voice, "Who is the woman you are seeing?"

One dark brow raked upward. Beneath his ebony mustache, his lips twitched. "That's what this is all about?"

She never moved, not even to touch her wineglass. "Yes."

"I see. You're serious, then." He took a sip of his wine. "Mary McGregor. She's a widow. Her husband was the dean of Sydney University. Is that all you wanted to know?"

Mary McGregor? Annie searched her memory and came up with the face to match the name. A lovely woman with flaxen hair and deep brown eyes, maybe thirty-five or so. "Are you in love with her?"

He settled back farther into his chair and observed her over the rim of his glass. "Is that important to you?"

"Yes."

"Why?"

She took a fortifying swallow of her wine. "Because should you two marry, she might object to our friendship. And our friendship is important to me. I don't want to lose it."

For a moment he said nothing. There was only the swish of the water against the embankment, the quiet tones of the other diners, the clink of glass and dinnerware. "Should I marry, Annie," he said quietly, "I would hope my wife would not possess the unpleasant quality of jealousy. She would understand about my friendships with others, whether they be men or women."

From a nearby wattle came the mocking laughter of a kookaburra.

She had been too long without the love of a man. She knew that now. The disastrous evening with Ryan had made that clear. Her feelings for him were becoming demanding and selfish. Jealousy was an abhorrent word. She was grateful that he had been honest with her before she had overstepped her bounds.

The problem was that she met many men in the course of her business engagements, but neither she nor they knew where the person at the helm of New South Wales Traders ended and the woman named Annie began. Annie intended to find out for herself.

An opportunity presented itself shortly thereafter. She had been invited by the Melbourne Shipowners Association to inaugurate the launching of an entertainment ferry, replete with dancing and gambling. The inauguration was timed to coincide with the opening of Moomba.

Moomba was an aboriginal word for a big party and was comparable to the French Mardi Gras. It was held in March when the grapes were ripening.

In "Marvellous Melbourne," as the city fathers designated it, she would find anonymity, at least for one evening.

In 1883, the connection between the railways of New South Wales and Victoria had been completed, the iron link having been driven at Albury, a border town on the Murray River. Taking the train, she slipped into Melbourne without any fanfare. Her hotel was near the City Square at Paris End where graceful trees shaded the street.

Her civic duty, inaugurating the ferry, wasn't until tomorrow, so the afternoon and evening were hers.

A few costumed revelers were already cavorting down Swanston Street where it crossed the Yarra River, sometimes called the River that Runs Upside Down because of its muddy brown color. It was really an attractive area of the city. Here more merrymakers were already in pursuit of pleasure, drinking, laughing, carousing. A fat man dressed in a harlequin costume stood drunkenly in a canoe to shout at passersby and almost tipped his fellow passengers into the river.

The weather had a sublime quality that made Annie's spirits light. A hawker at the Flinders Street Station was selling dominoes, and she purchased a scarlet one with black-sequin-lined eyes. Now she was truly incognito.

In the Royal Botanic Gardens she bought scones and cream from a refreshment kiosk. She carried her fare along a stone-paved path through a lush garden to a picnic bench overlooking the Yarra. Exotic flowers scented the air. Cockatoos, possums, and rabbits were her immediate companions.

For a while, she found contentment in her surroundings. But amorous couples strolling along its leaf-canopied paths or rowing with the river's gentle current impressed upon her just how isolated she was. The solitude of the sensual gardens was not where she would find companionship.

Or so she thought.

"You're missing the best part of the park," a man said off to her left.

She turned to peer through the gathering dusk. He wore a pirate's bandanna and earring. "And what is that?"

"The fairy-tale carved tree." He ambled toward her on bowed legs that definitely proclaimed him a horseman. Which was it a—a polo player or a common stockman? Did it matter?

"How do you know I haven't already seen the tree?"

"I followed you. From the time you left our hotel."

She supposed that alarms should have gone off. She was alone in a secluded park. "You're staying there also?"

"I'm in town to meet with my son. He's doing time at Melbourne University."

She had to smile, and the man smiled back. He was a big man, stocky almost, but his smile appealed to her. It suggested a nuance of the forlorn. "Where are you from?"

"Echuca. Got me a cattle crossing up near the confluence of the Murray and Campaspe rivers."

She had been right. Her romantic intruder was a stockman. Although one could hardly designate Timothy Abernathy as a common stockman.

They had never met, but she had certainly heard of him. His crossing had become a vital transshipment point for inland commerce, aspiring to be the Chicago of Australia. His wharves could unload seven riverboats at once. He was in his midforties and he had seen two wives buried.

Yes, she knew of Timothy Abernathy, and he knew of her, most certainly. But did he know she was this lonely woman on the park bench?

"And you?" he asked, propping a black riding boot on the bench and resting his arm on his knee.

"I'm here as a tourist, for the opening of the entertainment ferry tomorrow."

"And tonight?"

"Tonight is for magic."

"Then let's make it, shall we?" He offered his arm.

Foolish she knew she was, but she took it. She wanted magic and romance and to believe, if only briefly, that a man could be attracted to her for appearances sake only.

"First the fairy-tale carved tree, milady. Then Chinatown."

She looked up at him. He was definitely a big man. "Chinatown?"

"Best part of Melbourne to go for Moomba."

He made light talk as they sauntered toward the fairy tree. "I've often thought about renting a canoe while in the city, but then wondered, why bother? That's for courtship, and romance isn't exactly a prospect at my age."

"Oh, I should hope it isn't reserved just for the young."

Neither she nor he had exchanged names. Beneath the spreading branches of the fairy tree, he carved his initials in the fading light. "And yours?" he asked.

"A. T." She watched as he penned her initials just below his and enclosed them within a heart.

From there, they wandered back into the town central, where the streets were blocked off for Moomba. The crowds were denser here, and more rowdy. Imaginative costumes ranged from Cleopatras to kangaroos.

From a vociferous vendor he bought a bottle of locally produced wine and offered it to her. She hesitated, then tipped the bottle to her lips. "Tart, strong, and tasty," she said, fighting back a wheeze with a smile.

The Chinese quarter on Little Bourke Street was a narrow lane thronged with shops, joss houses, laundries, and tiny restaurants. Decorative paper lanterns and garish tiled archways over the lane enticed the curious pedestrian to enter the strange and mystical-looking district. Sandalwood incense commingled with the sharp odor of fish and the piquant scent of green tea.

A bright vermillion placard with spidery black lettering welcomed customers in two languages to the House of Fong. Timothy chose a minuscule table for them to watch the parade of merrymakers and ordered tea.

"I think the wine is sufficient," she said. "I feel tipsy as it is."

"Ahh, but tonight is the time to throw caution to the winds. It's a time for magic and pleasure, isn't it?"

"Why did you follow me?"

"What man in his right mind wouldn't? Your red hair is a siren's lure."

Her eyes narrowed. "You know who I am, don't you?"

At that moment, little explosions rippled through the street. Bright red snakes of firecrackers heralded writhing fifty-meter papier-mâché lions and dragons. He had to wait for the infernal din to pass before speaking. "Everyone knows who you are."

"Yet we've never been properly introduced."

"No." He had the grace to flush. "I watched you sign the hotel register."

She felt the tug of heartache that came with her guarded nature. It was an ever-present suspicion that invariably prevented her from accepting male admiration at face value.

Did Timothy Abernathy already suspect that the railroad's eventual thrust into the outback would ruin his riverboat trade?

She looked into his tired eyes and saw what she had chosen to avoid earlier: desperation. With that, she knew her own desperation. That she was condemned to her life of solitude.

You've won, after all, Nana.

13

1886

Dan swallowed back the lump in his throat. As he watched Louisa breast-feeding their daughter, he had to admit that in the depths of his soul he had not believed he could ever come to love another human being as he had Kai.

Yet ten-month-old Chevonne had stormed his heart with her gurgling communication and open smiles.

"She has your delicate beauty, Louisa." Indeed, there was no hint of his own heritage in his daughter.

His wife's gaze flew to his. Surprise, then pleasure, were reflected in her normally cool expression. "It's difficult to tell, what with her eyes changing color constantly."

"And her hair, too." He rumpled the honey-colored silk curls with his fingertips. His and Louisa's joy in Chevonne had bridged their initial disharmony. "The labor union is hosting a fund-raising dinner two weeks from Friday. Would you like to attend?"

Her voice, with its Yankee clip, softened. "I'd love to."

He and Louisa rarely went out together, mostly because he refused to have anything to do with Sydney's ton. Or was it that he wasn't prepared to encounter his sister? From what he heard, she still ranked high on any invitation list, despite her decidedly eccentric behavior.

With her free hand, Louisa spread her maroon day dress and gave him a cautious smile. "Trite to say, but I really haven't anything to wear. What with growing large with Chevonne and then nursing her, I've put on weight that my clothes don't accommodate."

"Then it's time we called upon the best modiste in Sydney. You're too comely to forgo the dinner for lack of proper clothing, Cinderella."

He sincerely regretted his indifference to Louisa over the past year and a half of their marriage. Had they been married in some bush church, their marriage might have gotten off to a better start. For a newly married couple, the outback was the best start one could get. Nowhere to run to, and you had to learn to talk to each other.

But then, the outback and its widely interspersed stations had never interested him. Not the outback nor Dream Time nor Never-Never.

Often he vowed to cement better relations between himself and Louisa. More often, though, his union work had come first. But now, their daughter Chevonne was making him take a look at what was really important in his life.

On this occasion, he kept his pledge and even accompanied Louisa on the round of milliners and modistes. He had expected to be bored, but Louisa's joy in the outing was contagious. With each fitting, with each chapeau, she turned and postured and swirled before him. Her elan had returned.

With his hat on his lap, he watched and made honest observations. "The last dress, Louisa—that was most flattering."

His practiced eye noted how much weight she had gained. Apparently, it bothered her. The few times they had made love since their daughter's birth, Louisa had seemed distant, as if she couldn't lose herself in their lovemaking. The death of her mother, due to a liver disease, had added strain to Louisa's disposition.

In that first year of their marriage, her ability to do just that, to lose herself to the force of their passion, had astonished him, because she usually appeared so contained and controlled.

He wondered if she would ever regain her desire, or if that was gone forever.

And his own desire? What had happened to it? It wasn't that he had lost interest in Louisa so much as that his sexual drive had dwindled.

"Dan?" Louisa halted before him, the lavender taffeta skirts of the modiste's creation held wide. A puzzled frown drew down her brows. "For a man who comes from the streets, you have an uncanny predilection for selecting quality clothing."

He rose. "There is no mediocrity in my kind of background. One either aspires to the heights or surrenders to the muck."

Louisa left it at that, but Dan wasn't sure that his explanation satisfied even himself. His duplicity should relegate him to the world of muck. He had rationalized that withholding his background from Louisa and her father wasn't hurting them. Frank, who occasionally visited the household, never indicated that he knew otherwise.

Despite Louisa's father's condescending attitude, Dan detected an element of respect that the rigid American grudgingly ceded him. Because of that, because of Louisa, because of Chevonne, he had encouraged his less than cordial father-in-law to invest in a rail program that would lay track across the outback.

Dan believed in the enterprise, but his interest and finances were captured by something stronger: the fledgling Labor Party, which was expressing strong opposition to the practice of importing Kanakas.

In addition, an expansionist mood was reflected in the party's increasing radical nationalism and strongly egalitarian outlook. The Labor Party supported the growing hostility to the Old World with its hereditary privileges, landlordism, and class distinctions—all of which NSW Traders represented to him.

"The track would connect Sydney with Perth," he had told Walter. They had sat in Walter's mahogany-paneled library in the Elizabeth Bay house. Dan had wondered if Walter knew the mahogany had been transported on NSW Traders' ships.

Walter snorted. "You might as well decide to turn the tide and order the wind to stop. Have you ever seen the outback?"

His smile was thin. "Upon occasion."

"Then you have some idea about it. You'd have to cross the Nullarbor Plain. It is one of the most desolate regions in the world. The plan would never work."

"Think about it," Dan said, tamping on his pipe. "A trans-Australian railway. Should the enterprise succeed, your investment would reap a very healthy profit."

And would drive a coffin nail into his cool, self-reliant twin's monopoly on Australia's continental trade.

14

1890

When the expansionist boom took over Australia in the early 1880s, Annie had begun making plans for the inevitable bust that must follow. One of those plans consisted of wisely reinvesting her profits in the corporation. The second plan combined business and personal concerns.

For several years now, she had been systematically buying wool from all over the world—Scotland, the United States, Argentina. After explaining her strategy to Ryan, she paused, sat back in her chair, and said, "I'm giving you a scoop, Ryan. The scoop of the year."

He lit up his cigar, then asked, "And what's that?"

"That I am flooding the wool market."

She had to give him credit. His expression didn't betray any astonishment. He let out a helix of smoke. "Why would you do that, when you own one of the largest sheep stations in Australia, among other smaller ones?"

"I have been secretly undercutting a certain man's sheep prices no matter how low he goes, so he cannot unload his sheep or his wool."

"My question is still why?"

"I want to bankrupt this morally corrupt man."

Through the haze of smoke, Ryan's eyes narrowed. "Mick Harrison?"

"Yes."

"And after him, then who, Annie? Who's next on your list?"

She looked up sharply from the latest copy of the *Dispatch* he had tossed on her desk. His nationalist-isolationist newspaper was now championing Dan Warwick, who was campaigning for election to the new independent Labor Party.

"I sound hard, do I? Well, Ryan, if I surrendered every time some man tried to put me in my place, then NSW Traders wouldn't exist." She pointed to the article about Dan Warwick. "If this man is elected, then before long his kind will control the parliament and dictate the policies of wealthy pastoralists and mining and shipping companies. In answer to your question, Ryan, Dan Warwick will be next on my list."

"And if I take editorial opposition to you politically, then am I next? Personally?"

She couldn't meet those black eyes.

The equally black mustache, despite his forty-odd years, twitched. "Is that why," he said more quietly, "you won't let me love you—as a woman should be loved? Because then you would be vulnerable to me, wouldn't you? And that's a woman's greatest sin, according to Nan Livingston, wasn't it?"

She rose from her chair. Her head was held majestically, her auburn hair a flame red in the sunlight streaming through the office window. His affair with Mary McGregor, if it had been that, had gone its way, while the friendship between him and herself had remained constant. This conversation concerning love between them took her aback.

"And if I let you make love to me, would that guarantee me immunity from one of your editorial attacks?"

A regretful smile curled the ends of his mustache downward. "No."

She chuckled, then at his start of surprise, grinned. On a male, the grin would have been described as rakish. "After all these years, Ryan, I do believe I am ready for you to make love to me."

* * *

Cool, autocratic Annie Tremayne, who was always in control, was nervous. An attack of nerves before a business dinner or a board meeting was an occasional occupational hazard. She always could handle it as she did any business decision— analyze what exactly it was that made her nervous, gather all the information she could, and determine the worst that could happen. This linear process gave her a sense of calm, of control.

She approached the tryst with Ryan Sheridan in the same analytical fashion. Yes, she was nervous, she reasoned. Why shouldn't she be? It had been years since she'd been in bed with a man. My God, almost eleven years. She was no longer youthful. All these years of hard work, with little time for herself, showed in the mirror. She was too thin and gaunt. All hollow eyes and cheeks.

Tentatively her hand touched the silk fabric gathered over her breast. A man wants a woman. A soft woman with generous curves. She was hard and vigilant rather than generous. She'd had to be.

Tears glistened in her eyes. What had happened to Dream Time? All she'd wanted was to live out her life at the station. Sometimes, she thought Dan was the lucky one. Gone from all this, or possibly even dead.

Nevertheless, from the vantage point of an upper window of the Regency-style Orient Hotel, she couldn't help but feel pleased by what she saw. The prestigious old hotel overlooked Circular Quay, the original landing point for the First Fleet almost a hundred years earlier, and the Tank Stream, a creek that had provided early Sydney's water supply.

Now spacious Bridge Street crossed the stream, and the quay was a veritable forest of sailing and steamship masts, a good portion of them belonging to NSW Traders.

A rap on the door instantly shifted her thoughts from NSW Traders to herself, although she wasn't certain where the essence of one began and the other ended. "Yes?"

"Your dinner, Miss Tremayne."

She crossed to the door, pausing only long enough before the sitting room's oval mirror to tidy her hair. A few auburn tendrils lay upon her nape, and the remainder of her tresses were swept up in an imperial coil at her crown. Below the auburn slashes of her brows, hazel eyes stared steadily back.

Good. She was in control again.

A waiter in red livery wheeled in a cart and stood with hands folded while she lifted the various covers to inspect the evening's fare: succulent roast pheasant, snow peas, creamed corn, and bread pudding drenched with brandy. The wine was properly chilled.

She nodded her approval. "Put the cart over

there, please," she said, pointing to the chintz-covered settee and matching overstuffed chair.

When the waiter turned back to her, she saw that he held an envelope in his hand. "A gentleman asked that this be given to you, Miss Tremayne."

With a serenity that belied her thudding heart, she accepted the ivory envelope. "Thank you, that will be all."

Once the door was closed, she opened the envelope's flap, unfolded the parchment sheet, and read:

> My dearest Annie,
>   A gentleman, I know, never stands up a lady. However, I lack the inclination to perform on command. You're not ready, neither am I. Our passion will keep. When the timing is right . . .
>   Your obedient servant,

She stared at Ryan's scrawled signature. Fury swept through her as hot and fast as an outback bushfire. She picked up the sterling silver dome covering the pheasant and hurled it against the wall. The reverberation loosened the baroque-framed mirror. It hit the floor, then shattered into a hundred silver slivers.

With dismay, she observed the result of her unbridled anger. Never, not in all her years beneath Nan's tutelage, nor after she had taken the helm of NSW Traders, had she ever lost control of her emotions. That was a luxury only permitted to people without responsibilities.

Slowly, her fists unclenched. Gradually, a smile took possession of her strongly delineated lips. Then laughter erupted. Laughter that vibrated throughout her tall frame. To have one's body vibrate with feeling . . . God, it felt wonderful!

"You've got to ride with the best of them, son," Annie called out to Brendan. My, but he was handsome. He'd inherited his father's extraordinary height and dark Celtic good looks.

Anxiously, she watched Brendan mount the brumby again. The wild horse was determined it wasn't going to be mastered. Her nine-year-old son was determined he would be the master.

English and aborigine stockmen girded the corral and rowdily cheered Brendan on. Dust flew. The white brumby bucked. It twisted and reared. It neighed, kicked, and tried to bite its rider. Brendan was barely managing to hold his seat.

The presence of Zab, skilled in horsebreaking, reassured her. He would step in if he thought the heir to Dream Time and NSW Traders was in real danger.

She glanced over at him. His white smile reassured her. The bone through his septum never did.

As a girl, with her father Syn watching, she had had to prove her own competence in just such fashion: learning to ride like a stockman, to yard sheep, to shear wool, to keep the station's books. Her grandmother, though, had abducted her from Dream Time and forced her to learn the intricacies of the shipping industry.

She thought of all those years when she had been slighted as the insignificant twin. For an instant she let herself feel the anger she harbored against Nana.

Nana, I paid the price as your chosen successor, but Brendan won't be required to.

She was determined to give Brendan a taste of both worlds—NSW Traders and Dream Time. Brendan would have the opportunity to make a choice, or choose both, if he so desired.

"It is time you let him become a man, Miss Annie," Zab said at her side. "Time for another corroboree."

Could she relinquish her son for this rite of manhood? For too long he had been under her woman's influence. He needed the guidance of a man wise in the ways of the spirit and nature.

Because the aborigines were an integral part of nature and the land, they were the land. Baluway had once told her, "White man got no Dreaming. Him go 'nother way."

The other way was a road contrary to nature, according to the aborigines. The road led to eventual destruction. "I will send Brendan to you next year, Zab."

She turned her face, bare of powder and rouge, to the high noon sun and closed her eyes, feeling the calm steal over her. Returning to Dream Time always did that for her.

It was her escape. This time her escape from Ryan's rejection.

No, he hadn't rejected her. He just hadn't submitted to her, and she was accustomed to being in command. Yet, as always, he had earned her unwilling admiration and support by adhering to both his professional values in the face of financial ruin and his personal values in the face of losing her and all that she represented—power, prestige, wealth.

She knew he loved her. His letter, lying on her nightstand upstairs, admitted as much. But it also demanded her submission, though not in those exact words: "This platonic relationship can continue forever. Or it can be much, much more. Richer. But we both have to bend. Yield. Can you do that, Annie? Could you surrender to the compromise of marriage?"

She knew she loved him. But marriage?

Damn it, Ryan Sheridan, I can't bend that far for you!

Ryan Sheridan sat behind his desk in a position that would have been familiar to Annie had she been there, watching his visitor over the pyramid of his

fingertips as if they were a gunsight that focused
and sharpened his perception of the person.

Today, the object of his attention was not Annie
but her twin, Dan Warwick.

Gradually life had revealed to Dan who he was.
He had learned to be independent, to think for
himself, and finally to lead others. All that Nan
Livingston could have hoped for, had she had him
with her the last of those very formative years
before he reached full manhood.

Dan took the initiative. "Want to tell me why
you have agreed to work as mediator between the
union and the shipping industry?"

Sheridan tilted back in his chair. "We have
known each other for some time now, Dan. I
believe you to be honest and well intentioned. I
think you care about people—and your country.
Do you really think a dockworker's strike is going
to serve Australia's best interest?"

"Her best interest is her people."

Sheridan nodded. "You believe that. I believe
that. Miss Tremayne believes that. Let's keep that
in mind as we try to arbitrate the threatened
strike."

"Annie Tremayne is representing the shipping
industry at this meeting?" He would have
thought she would have been too busy and would
have delegated someone in NSW Traders' upper
management.

"This issue is as vital to her as it is to you. You

and the union are against importing cheap labor. That's the bottom line in this issue, isn't it?"

Memories of the cruel treatment of the Kanakas, as well as a fleeting vision of Kai's sweet, sultry face, assaulted him. "Yes." The single word came out clipped, void of emotion.

"Miss Tremayne and the interests she stands for see this strike not only as an act against private enterprise but as another act of racist legislation, another bid for that nationalistic feeling—'Australia for Australians . . . Preserve the purity of white Australia . . . A white Australia!' The sort of thing that headlines other newspapers."

"Compromise is not likely, but—"

Dan broke off as Annie swept into the room without being announced. Head held high, she took the other chair opposite Ryan and spread her skirts as old Queen Victoria must have done each time she met with her cabinet and prime minister. "I presume you are Mr. Dan Warwick?"

"I go by that name."

Watching the dawning recognition in her expression, the blanch that drained her complexion, he couldn't repress the satisfaction that tugged at his mouth.

"Daniel." Her single word was barely a whisper.

Sheridan shot him a questioning glance.

"Sister meets estranged brother," Dan said with a cryptic half smile.

Whatever imperial mannerisms Annie Tremayne

may have used vanished as tears welled over her eyes and her lips trembled. "All these years, all the heartbreak. You don't know how I have searched and searched for you, hiring investigators to ferret through every bush village in Australia. And now you're here. What happened to—"

"I can't imagine you being heartbroken. Not when you command an empire, Annie. You have become no better than Nan. Striving for the ends while turning a blind eye to the means, forgetting that human hearts are involved."

She flinched, as if he had actually struck her.

As far as he was concerned, everything was against their reconciliation. Not just their childhood differences, but their views on immigration as well as labor and management. He continued relentlessly. "All along you wanted NSW Traders, Annie, and now you have it—if you can keep it and the stations."

With that, he shoved back his chair and strode from the room, slamming the door in his wake.

15

1893

Not quite twelve, Brendan had grown into an awkward, almost homely boy. He was tall and straight like the magnificent stringybark tree used for shelter in wet season places. His energy had shed his boy's chubby physique, and his facial bone structure had narrowed, giving him at that age a hatchet jaw and big ears. In growing taller, his body had lost its childish grace.

Today, he was anxious. He stood on the veranda of the Big House and looked out at the violet smudge of ridges in the distance. And nothing in between. Nothing but rust red sand and the comical baobab trees, short and squat as a dwarf or tall and grotesque. The outback was a weird land of monstrosities.

His mother had left Dream Time the day before, leaving him behind for the summer. Leaving him behind to learn about the ways of the aborigine.

Bugger the aborigines. Oh, Zab was all right, but what was so bloody important about learning how to track a man in the bush when he lived in the city?

Except that Zab and Vena and Baluway knew some kind of secret that had power. And he was supposed to learn it. At least, that was what his mother had said. And it was the learning that frightened him.

What if he failed? What if he wasn't man enough? His mother never failed. And she wasn't even a man.

"You ready, boy?"

He spun around. Zab stood at the gate. He wore white man's clothing, but the stick through his nose proclaimed his adherence to his own civilization. Brendan remembered his mother telling him that Zab could pick up sheep tracks by seeing no more than a broken twig. From it, he would know that not only had sheep passed that way, but had done so within the last day or so.

Brendan bobbed his head. "Yes." His voice sounded like a croak.

"We go to Never-Never and the sacred sites."

"I'll get my clothes."

"You won't need any."

He nodded again and swallowed.

He and Zab set out afoot. Baluway was too old. Baluway, Brendan's mother had said, was changing lives. Why couldn't she call it dying, like normal people did?

Traveling with Zab seemed like following a spider web. Zab strode just ahead of Brendan, who kept his gaze fixed on the back of the wavy hair. The black man had changed into a skin cloak, and he carried with him a spear, and a boomerang tucked into the band of his breechcloth.

For miles they walked across a treeless plain, and then the country gave way to dry limestone and saltbush. Once through open ironbark country, they wound their way through a eucalyptus woodland. Several times, they circumvented termite mounds twice as tall as they.

Brendan did not notice the gradual change of the landscape. It seemed that all at once he and Zab were climbing a steep escarpment and passing through ocher-colored fissures and fractured rock passes.

Eventually they came to a deep canyon through which snaked a gurgling stream. Lingering sunlight cascaded through weeping paperbark trees lining the creek. Brendan was exhausted and sank down beneath a paperbark to watch Zab deftly spear a perch for dinner.

The tranquillity of the evening hushed Brendan's

worried mind. The fresh air, the mouth-watering smell of perch sizzling over a fire, Zab's reassuring presence. A grand camping trip this would be. He fell asleep with a full belly and anticipation for the morrow.

The next day the journey resumed with what seemed like more crisscrossings of the rocky and fissured terrain. Brendan's feet were blistered. Despite his bush hat, his neck was sunburnt. He was so weary. Each step, putting one foot in front of the other, was a monumental effort.

At last, they came upon a small canyon blanketed with lush ferns and trees. Brendan could hear a creek falling down in a dim gorge. Saliva welled in his mouth at the thought of cool, fresh water. Even the air was cooler.

Zab tracked a path that wound deeper into the forest, negotiated downward over slippery boulders, and ended at a sandy stream, shaded by the rustling foliage of tall tea trees. The banks of the stream were steep and made of loose sand. A pure, haunting, oboelike birdsong echoed off the rocks and broke the silence of the glade.

"That is the spirit of woman calling out for her lover," Zab told him. "We eat, rest, then we begin your training for initiation."

Brendan started to question Zab about what kind of training he would be receiving, then thought better of it. Soon enough he would learn.

Too soon, he did.

The first few weeks were filled with rigorous instructions in surviving off the earth. Naked but for a breechcloth of animal skin, he learned how to find and cook crayfish and emu eggs. They used the grease of the emu as protection against the sun and the wind. The eucalyptus wood they used for cooking had the scent of piss but did impart a wondrous flavor to the food.

He discovered how to glean the blackberries from their thick tangle of bushes and to gather honey by scaling a tree, using his bare feet as nimbly as his hands. Snails were scooped up with the toes.

Zab taught him how the tribesmen twisted fishing lines from pounded bark fiber, and how bamboo and cord made an excellent net for trapping schools of fish. Brendan was shown how to watch the wedgetail eagle for signs of nearby habitation, how to use the boomerang to bring down a wild turkey and the spear to stop a fleeing emu. He learned how to imitate the faint bleat of the kangaroo. He watched Zab perch motionless high on a tree and grab a bird as it came to roost.

But this was all nothing compared with moth hunting. Zab took him to where the fields of snow daisies bloomed and the smell of heath filled the air. With a kangaroo skin and a fine net of bark fiber he had fashioned himself, Brendan collected moths by the hundreds and roasted them in hot ash. They had a sweet, nutlike flavor.

"Moths, they make the eater fat," Zab said, rubbing his distended black belly and laughing. The longer Zab was away from civilization, the more his language reverted to an English that had an almost poetic explicitness.

He demonstrated perfect concentration and great endurance by sitting poised for hours with his fishing spears beside a water hole. Brendan despaired of ever learning but within three days, he had speared his first fish. He was elated. Then Zab reprimanded him for laying his wooden spear on the ground, lest it should warp or be trodden upon.

When a certain plant flowered, Zab said, the aborigine knew that in the faraway ocean the stingrays would be fat and ready for harvesting.

Brendan's hands were bloodied and aching from cleaving a knife from a quartzite block by hammering with a stone. But the knife became a prized possession.

Exhausted by nightfall, he would lie on the ground and look at the heavens. Since man had begun to read the stars, he had known that the Southern Cross pointed northward. Brendan felt drawn up into that glittering cosmos. For him, there was something consoling about finding the Southern Cross leaning on its axis. It was for him a sort of personal signpost on the infinite.

At last, after more than a month, Zab took him to the base of a six-hundred-foot cliff, where a thin stream wound. Staring at him at eye level were hundreds of figures: people, spirits, kangaroos, cranes, goannas, echidnas, and everywhere fish. The art gallery, painted in red and yellow ocher and white clay, was alive with all the creatures, real and imagined, from the outback.

"This sacred site is Rainbow Dreaming," Zab said with quiet reverence.

That evening, Zab built a fire. Sitting opposite Brendan, the aborigine began his story of the Dream Time, which explained the cohesion and interdependence of all living things. It referred to the beginnings of life and its continuation into the future.

In the firelight, the aborigine's face glowed. His voice rang out against the canyon walls like a messenger from another world. "Long, long ago, before the Dream Time, before there was time-count, the earth had no shape. It was mushy and shaky. Then came mighty Rainbow Serpent, Almudj. This was the start of Dreamtime."

He pointed out on the rock face an ocher painting of a snake. "After assisting other Sky Heroes with creation, Almudj split the rock and forced her way through. There." His gnarled finger indicated a vertical fissure in the precipice. "Rainbow Serpent created hills, stone archways, and deep pools. Every year she brings the wet season and a renewal of life. She can then be seen standing on her tail as the rainbow."

It appeared to Brendan that all this was leading up to something, but he was lost as to what that

might be. As Zab talked, Brendan was startled to
see a ghostly figure silhouetted against the fire's
light. The guest turned out to be an old aborigine
with a skirt of grass around his waist. He said
nothing but silently took a seat at the campfire.

Into the night, Zab talked. He told about the
Mimis, those elusive spirits that lived inside the
rocks. "The Mimis are so thin that the slightest
wind will break their long necks."

At this point, another visitor arrived. An aborigine of middle age with shells suspended from his
waist and ankles and neck. He, too, joined them at
the campfire.

Unperturbed, Zab continued with his story of
the Mimis. "Only when it is calm do they come out
to hunt and paint. If anyone comes or a breeze
springs up, they blow on the rocks. The rocks, they
then part to let them enter and close behind them
again. People must be careful, because sometimes
the Mimis will lure them into the rocks and then
lock then up."

Other aboriginal men had drifted into the camp,
but by this time Brendan had learned to ignore the
stealthy arrivals of the wraithlike visitors, maybe a
dozen in all. Besides, he was enthralled with the
story. "When do the Mimis come out?"

"Every evening, but we can't see them. They
leave messages. Like this leaf, or a painting."

Brendan felt a tickling and tightening of his
scalp.

"The white people teach aborigine school," Zab continued. "The aborigine, he forget the importance of Dreamtime. If no one remembers the old ways, the life force is broken."

Zab paused and fixed him with a piercing look. "You are ready for the secret rite? To earn your secret name?"

Even in his immaturity, Brendan knew this was a momentous decision. One of responsibility. He swallowed. "Yes."

"Good! We are ready then for the initiation ceremony."

The rite seemed simple enough. Zab scooped up white clay from the banks of the stream. "First, you leave the signature of your hand on the wall."

Brendan watched in amazement as Zab mixed the white clay with water from the stream, then took a mouthful of the pigment. Holding Brendan's hand against the rock face, near a painting of Hawk Dreaming, Zab spewed the white liquid around Brendan's hand to create a stencil.

The vigilant aboriginal visitors made grunts of approval. Zab said, "Your hand print is a symbol. Responsibility to your heritage. Your secret name will be Woorunmarra, Keeper of Dreams."

Brendan thought the ceremony was over. He was tired and ready to sleep. Zab had other plans. "We dance."

"What?"

"It is the final part of your initiation rite."

Zab and the other aborigines fell to painting their naked bodies with ocher and white stripes. "The ocher is the same as blood, and blood he give life to animals in the paintings."

The old man with the grass skirt had taken up a five-foot-long hollow bamboo trumpet, a didgeridoo, and began blowing on it—a piercing, droning note as eerie and funereal as any bagpipe. The shell man began dancing, and the shells made a clacking sound that kept rhythm with the bull-roarer. This was a piece of wood whirled at the end of a long string. It emitted a fluttering, fateful noise, something between a groan and a shriek.

The rest of the visitors joined in the dance. Their fierce features possessed a male arrogance that stirred Brendan. Zab indicated that he was to dance, also. He attempted to follow the men's steps and shrill chants and shrieks. The dancing by the glow of the campfire continued for hours.

When there was a pause, Brendan thought he would drop where he stood. Then another tribal dance with a different pattern of intricate steps resumed. So did Brendan. At some point, he became caught up in the energy and freedom of the ceremony. The aboriginal dancing had induced an atmosphere of high excitement. A frenzy entered his body. He leaped and writhed and shouted. He felt a deep kinship with these aboriginal males.

Dawn was drawing near when Zab and the others

ceased dancing. In a trance of utter weariness, a
dazed Brendan watched Zab approach him.
Numbed by the greatness of the occasion, he
docilely submitted as Zab took him by the shoulders
and positioned him on the ground, spread-eagle.
Another man gagged him. Still, another held his
arms pinned. Someone else anchored his ankles.

Above him, Zab held in his hand the same knife
of stone that Brendan had made earlier that month.
Brendan was stripped of his breechcloth. One aborigine pointed at his penis, saying, "*Con-do-in.*"

Sudden fright seized Brendan.

There was much blood. Excruciating pain. His
screams coming from afar. The circumcision was
barbaric. At one point, he thought he was going to
faint. He left his body and floated above to watch
the final jagged incision into his foreskin.

Through a haze, he heard Zab pronounce, "Now
you are a man, Dream Keeper."

At almost eight, Chevonne Warwick was teas-
ingly called a cornstalk by her father, because
stalks quickly grew tall when planted in New South
Wales. With small features, she was tall, slender,
and fair complected. And she was restless and
reckless.

Especially today. For three weeks, she had been
practicing her role for the amateur theatrical per-
formance being staged for Anniversary Day, the

holiday that commemorated January 26, 1788, the day the Union Jack was first raised at Sydney Cove. The play was centered around the members of the famous First Fleet, that first shipload of convicts, soldiers, and their families. She played one of the twenty-five children, half of whom were illegitimate offspring of female convicts, and the other half the children of the marines' wives.

By 1868, only twenty years before, transportation had finally been abolished, after more than 162,000 convicts had been sent out to Australia. Almost everyone in Australia had parents or grandparents who were ex-convicts. But no one in Chevonne's family history had been a convict. Her mother was from America, and her father's family, as far as she knew, were immigrants who were no longer alive.

Chevonne couldn't imagine being a prisoner. She couldn't imagine submission of spirit in order to survive. She would rather die than be docile and yielding.

So, when her mother was rehearsing her part in the play, Chevonne stole outside. The Sydney Theater Company had created a home out of an empty warehouse on the wharf. Its ships beckoned. Their sails whispered in the sea breeze of faraway lands.

One, in particular, called out to her. A small merchant sailing ship, the *Elissa*. Hat in hand, Chevonne stood watching as the sweaty dock workers unloaded hogsheads from the three-masted iron bark.

"Built in Aberdeen, she was," a man's voice said, coming from slightly behind her.

She turned and stared at him. A big man with a dark, wiry beard, he reminded her of her father's friend and employee, Frank Smythe, except that this was a young salt. His eyes looked out in the same direction as her.

"Where is she coming from?" Chevonne asked him.

"Just arrived from India with a cargo of ivory and jute. We sail at dawn to pick up a load of bananas from Townsville." He looked her over. Was he trying to decide whether she was worthy of high adventure? Whether she was seaworthy? "Would you like to see her?"

"Yes."

"Come along, then." He touched her shoulder, guiding her up the gangplank amidst the coming and going of the dock hands. "I'm Captain Watson, and whatever you want to know about ships, I got the answer. Sailed from Greece to Galveston to Gallipoli, I have."

The *Elissa* was a comparatively small freighter. However, having been raised in a seaport city, Chevonne was savvy about ships. She recognized the beautiful sheet line of the *Elissa*'s rails and desk, that slim look from her bow to stern.

A thrusting figurehead of a female goddess

scanned the seas from her vantage point under the bow. "Looks like the Queen, she does," the captain said.

The relief of Queen Victoria on coins Chevonne had seen didn't look like the figurehead, but she said nothing. "Can I go up to the wheelbox?"

"Of course. From there you can get a fine salt spray. Just like you're under sail."

Looking out from the wheelbox was a taste of freedom. From that position, she could see a coterie of porpoises cavorting. They called her to come to sea.

"We've just overhauled the captain's quarters aft. Ever seen a sextant? It measures the angle between two points, such as the sun and the horizon."

She shook her head.

"Sailors used it to steer by the stars," he added.

That sounded exciting, steering by the stars. Excitement and adventure. Boys had it. Girls didn't.

"Come along, I'll show you."

She followed him down the dark companionway to the officers' accommodations. The captain's quarters were elegantly paneled. A small porthole let in the only light. The room had a moldy, damp smell.

"The sextant's there, on the table," Watson said.

She crossed to a table, where there were unrolled dogeared sheets of maps with strange markings. No sooner had she bent over one than the door closed behind her. She looked up. She was alone. Then she heard the key turn in the door lock.

Instantly, she knew something was wrong. She tried not to be scared. She went to the door and tried to open it, but it was securely locked. Dropping her hat, she spun around and ran to the porthole. In attempting to jar it open, she scraped her hands and broke a nail below the quick.

The room was hot. She looked around, wildly wondering how she was going to get out. The slant of sunlight through the porthole told her it was midafternoon. By evening the man would surely be returning.

Up above, she could hear the tramp of feet. She screamed. And screamed again and again until her throat felt raw. Nothing. Either the dockworkers did not hear her or they didn't care.

Detesting touching anything, she disdained both the chair and the bunk and slumped down against the maple-paneled wall. All of her life, she had been cherished and adored, safe and secure. Now she knew that something really horrible was about to happen to her.

Her mother would miss her but would not know where to find her. Even if someone had noticed her board the *Elissa*, they wouldn't think enough of it to say anything. Not in time, anyway. Not by dawn.

Lingering sunlight stenciled the top of the far wall. Soon, too soon, the man would be returning.

She felt sick to her stomach. And scared. And hot.

The room grew dim. Tears welled in her eyes. She wanted to be home. She wanted her mother and father. She didn't want adventure. Never again.

At the sound of footsteps thudding down the companionway, she began to tremble. Her heart pounded loudly. Her chest ached. When the door opened, she jumped to her feet. The freighter captain said nothing, just looked at her. He closed the door behind him and locked it again. She backed up as far as she could, until the table halted her retreat.

"Let me go."

He licked his lips, as if he were nervous. "I won't hurt you. If you do what I tell you to."

"My father will miss me. He's a member of Parliament. He could have you arrested."

"Not on the high seas, he couldn't." He moistened his lips again. Then attempted a smile. "I just want to touch you."

"Then you'll let me go?"

"Yes."

He put his hand on her chest. "No breasts yet. I miss having children aboard."

She shuddered.

He hunkered on one knee and reached under her short skirt to tug at her long, lacy drawers. "So fine and pretty."

She gasped. On the table behind her, her clutching

fingers found the frame of the sextant. She brought it down hard on the man's head. Not hard enough to knock him unconscious, but it didn't matter. The bright blood gushing from his eye socket told her the point of the sextant's arc must have blinded her.

Yelling in pain, he staggered to both knees. Quickly, her hand found his pocket and retrieved the door key. She let herself out and ran up the darkened companionway, across the poop deck, down along the main deck. No one was aboard to stop her flight.

Her breath wouldn't come. Her chest felt as if it would burst. At last, she gained the gangplank. Her feet flew down it and out along the wooden wharf. She ran. She was crying now that the danger was past.

At last, she reached the Village Green and Holy Trinity Church. It was empty. At the parish hall, she found the rector. The gray-haired old man recognized her at once. "Child, child, your parents have been worried about you."

She was hiccoughing. "I . . . I got locked in . . . one of those old warehouses. I screamed. No one could hear me."

He poured her some water. "Sit down and rest. You're all right now. How did you get out?"

She drank a calming sip of the water and thought rapidly. "An old tar. He had drunk too much and fallen asleep just outside the door. He let me out."

"Well, let's notify your parents you are safe and get you home. You must have taken the chill. You're shivering, child."

She couldn't stop shivering. Not even after her father fetched her home. Her mother and Minnie and Alicia, employees who had been in the Phillips' service for years, clucked after her.

"'Tis a fever the girl has taken," the rotund Minnie said. She was so fat her upper arms swayed when she moved them to bathe Chevonne's face with a cold, wet cloth.

"Chicken broth," said skinny Alicia, the cook. "That's what she needs.

"A paddling," Louisa said, quite sternly. "That's what my daughter needs. Where is your hat? This should teach you not to wander off alone. Maybe this will get the wanderlust out of your soul, Chevonne Warwick."

For all her lecturing, Chevonne's mother smoothed back her daughter's damp hair with tender hands. Chevonne was only vaguely aware of their soothing touch. Her body burned. Her mind drifted.

She dreamed. Strange dreams. Not of ships and sea but of fire and flames. Of aborigines and their Rainbow Serpent, Almudj, who brought the renewal of life.

16

The *Sydney Dispatch* called the event on the waterfront that September the Great Maritime Strike.

For Dan it was worse than any nightmare.

He and Frank had agreed to leave early for the strikers' demonstration along the docks. At the last moment, Chevonne begged to go with him. "Please, oh, please, Papa."

He stared down at his nine-year-old daughter's face. He used to think that he was prejudiced about her beauty, but the many people who stopped to comment convinced him otherwise. Chevonne had Louisa's golden blond hair, and a wealth of it. His daughter's merry, bright blue eyes were solely her own. They laughed, they dared.

No wonder he took her out with him so often, much to Louisa's displeasure. Especially that morning. "You're busy, you get distracted. For God's sake, Dan, this isn't some holiday parade. Something could happen to her."

He glanced over his shoulder at Frank. The big bear of a man was playing with Chevonne's braid, which she was unplaiting. She grinned back at the big man.

"That's no little piggy, Chevonne," Frank said in a mock gruff voice. "That's a big one."

Dan turned back from her childish laughter. His daughter adored Frank. "She'll be all right. We're both here to look after her." He didn't remind his wife about his daughter's escapade two years earlier, when she had strayed from the Anniversary Day play rehearsal.

Louisa's stony expression irritated him. Whatever he wanted to do, it seemed to him she was hell-bent on opposing it. Obstinate, inflexible, unwilling to see the other side.

After some more fruitless arguing, he yanked his hat from the hall tree and stormed from the house. Frank and Chevonne hurried to catch up.

The scene at the docks was in some ways like a parade on the sunniest of days. Banners and placards were waved on high. Sea gulls and terns took flight with the passing of each cluster of impoverished strikers, half of whom were shearers and most of the other half miners. Only a few dozen were actually dockworkers.

Their discontent could be detected in the muttering of their voices as each group shuffled by, sounding like the intermittent whistle of a teakettle and then gathering full steam into belligerent shouts.

Some of the strikers moved like fire dancers on their holy mission. As if entranced, or in a seizure, the sea of protestors yelled, gesticulated, rolled their eyes.

Although Dan was no longer head of the labor union, he had campaigned and been elected to the newly formed Labor Party on the platform opposing the importation of cheap labor, chiefly the blackbirding of the Kanakas. Foreign labor was a major sore spot for the labor union.

Nevertheless, he would have advised against this demonstration taking place on the heels of the arrest of one of the union party members. The man, Henry Benton, had been drunk and had aggravated a government official in front of the Royal Theater. Police had been summoned and had had to beat Benton into submission.

Today, the name of Henry Benton had become a war chant. As the meagerly clad workers moved apart and came together like flotsam on a tossing ocean, one worker stood on a wagon, exhorting the people to revolt.

Dan recognized him. Crockett, one of his old union cohorts. Ratbag was probably somewhere nearby, and Dan scanned the crowd until he located him passing out leaflets to the people gathered around the wagon.

"We have nothing to lose but our chains!" Crockett was yelling, his fist clenched above his head.

Dan thought they had a lot to lose, beginning with their lives. Working toward a goal required the use of both emotion and intelligence. The man had gone past reasonable thinking. But then, Ratbag, not Crockett, had always been the smarter of the two union leaders.

Chevonne tugged at his hand. "Papa, why do they look so angry?"

He glanced down at his daughter. Intelligence glinted back at him from her eyes, made bluer by the reflection of the harbor water. "They are angry because they are the have-nots."

"The have-nots?"

"People who have no hope," Frank put in.

Dan recalled those years of bushranging, when Frank had become an actual Robin Hood, giving away more money to the goldfields' destitute than he kept.

In a way, those bushranging days had been the best times for Dan. Excitement, adventure, even when all they lived on was tea, mutton, and damper—bush loaf made from flour and water;

even when they rode fifty miles or more a day from their home base.

"No hope of better jobs," Frank was explaining. "No hope of when they might eat again. No hope of knowing if they will have a place to sleep that is warm and dry."

"We are the haves, Papa?"

Should he be reassuring? He chose honesty. "For now, yes. We are the—"

Screams interrupted him. Then gunfire. He spun in their direction and saw mounted soldiers charging down the street. Those afoot scattered. One woman, watching from the sidelines, went down, blood crimsoning her flowered dress. The sea breeze took her hat and spun it crazily along the street as a child would a hoop.

Around Dan, people were stampeding, crazed by fear, knocking down anyone who stood in their path of escape. He felt an unaccustomed surge of panic. He whirled back to a wide-eyed Chevonne, but just beyond her Frank clutched at his shoulder. Slowly, the big man sagged, then buckled to the ground.

"Frank!" Dan shouted. He released his daughter and ran to kneel beside Frank.

A small hole in his jacket marked where he had been shot. Dan tore the garment away. Frank moaned. His face had that same pasty look as the day Dan found him in the bar, far gone on alcohol.

"Hold on," Dan said. A crimson-edged hole in

Frank's shirt duplicated the jacket's. Even as Dan struggled to get Frank erect, the spot grew in size. "Oh, God, Frank, just hold on. We'll get help."

He half dragged, half carried, his old friend over to a dilapidated farm cart nearby that had been abandoned in the melee. "There," Dan said, tucking one of Frank's dangling legs onto the wagon bed. "We'll be out of here in no time, mate."

In the next second, the awful, paralyzing truth electrified him. Chevonne! She was gone!

His heart squeezed shut. He was stunned. His mouth would not work. He could not call out. His blood congealed in his veins. The one thing he cared about most in the world, he had neglected.

"Who are you?"

Brendan stared down at the girl. The tiny saucer hat atop her curly blond locks was awry. Dirt smeared one cheek. The ruffle at one shoulder of her yellow dress was torn. It had been his doing, but she would have been hurt by that run-away horse. "Brendan. Brendan Tremayne. Are you all right?"

She nodded. She was actually laughing. At least, her eyes were. So big, so pure blue. She hadn't screamed or cried silly tears when the horse hooves had almost struck her. She had spunk.

"Can you talk?"

She nodded again. "My name is Chevonne Warwick. You have a cut on your cheek."

His hand went to his cheek and came away with blood. Probably a deep enough cut to leave a scar. He didn't know how or when he had gotten hurt. Cuts and scrapes and bruises were nothing to him. Not after that summer two years ago.

Another shot zinged by, and he pulled her into a grog shop entryway. "Where are your parents?"

For the first time, her intense focus shifted from him back to the street. People were still dashing for cover from the mounted soldiers or running away from the area when a group of patrolling soldiers had trotted past. "I came with my father. He got lost."

Brendan smiled. "You mean, you got lost."

She smiled back. "No, he did. I didn't move. Until you pulled me out of the way of that horse."

"How old are you?"

"Ten. Almost. And you?"

"Twelve. Well, soon I'll be." He felt infinitely older. After all, he had been initiated into manhood, hadn't he?

"Brendan!"

He spun around. His mother, with her skirt hem lifted to expose her high-button shoes, was running across the street toward him. Behind her was Ryan. "My mom," he explained to the girl. "She'll help us find your father."

His mother wrapped her arms around him. The flowery scent of her perfume wafted around him. The smell triggered pleasant, though unnameable feelings.

"Oh, God, Brendan. I was so frightened. I thought . . . when I turned around and you were gone . . . I thought . . . I don't know. I'm just so relieved."

He was surprised to see the tears on his mother's cheeks. His mother never cried. After all, she was Annie Tremayne. She could break a horse, navigate a ship, shear a sheep, and run a business. She could do anything.

"Mom, Mom, I'm all right. This is Chevonne. She got lost from her father. Can you help her get home?"

Beneath his hand, he felt his mother's shoulder stiffen. Chevonne stood there, quietly observing them. He liked that. She didn't get all emotional and talk a lot or cry or anything. "Chevonne? Chevonne Warwick?"

Chevonne's gaze darted to Brendan and back to his mother. "Do I know you?"

"No," his mother said slowly, "but I know you. And your father, Daniel."

"Dan," the girl said. "No one calls my father Daniel."

"They used to."

Brendan stared at his mother. She had that far-away look, as if she had sailed off on one of NSW

Traders' vessels to China. "How do you know her father, Mom?"

"It's a long story," Ryan said, coming up behind his mother to grasp her elbow. "Let's get young Chevonne back to her family."

His mother glanced up and down the cobbled street. Except for a few soldiers riding by and motley groups of frightened men and women huddled in alleyways and building recesses, the area around the harbor appeared empty. "It should be safe enough now to leave. My office isn't far, Chevonne. We'll send a messenger to your house to let your father know where to find you."

The four of them went unchallenged through the carnage of the riot-stricken harbor. Bodies littered the street like trash. Brendan gaped at the sight, unable to conceive that these people who had been so alive and vociferous only moments before were silent.

The New South Wales Traders building rose a full three stories above Argyle Street. Once a one-story warehouse, it had been renovated over the years into a stately establishment fitted with elegant furnishings. The actual shipping and receiving warehouses had been built along Dawes Point.

Office employees had deserted their desks to watch the riot from behind the safety of the windows and the partially opened door. Annie Tremayne reassured them that the situation was under control and shooed them back to work.

Brendan followed his mother and the girl into the main office, where his mother presided like some queen. At least, in his imagination.

A sideways glance showed him that Chevonne carried herself in the same stately manner. She took a seat in the big leather chair with an aplomb he had not noticed in other girls. She pulled her short skirts over her hose-capped knees, then primly folded her hands, waiting.

"My friend, Mr. Sheridan, will see that your parents are notified," his mother said, removing her gloves. Strange, she seemed nervous to him. Most likely all the shooting and bodies.

"I imagine we'll be hearing from them shortly," his mother continued in that brisk voice he heard her use when she was discussing business. "In the meantime, would you like some tea and scones, Chevonne?"

"Yes, ma'am." The girl's gaze was taking in all the objects in the office—a gold pen and inkwell, a painting of a storm-tossed ship, a sailing vessel done in brass that his mother's fingers often stroked when she was thinking.

Then his mother did something out of character. Instead of requesting James, her secretary, to serve, she left the office to get the tea and scones herself. With Ryan busy getting out the message to the girl's parents, Brendan was left alone with the girl. He plopped into his mother's office chair, which almost fit him, so fast was he growing.

Chevonne's roaming gaze settled, at last, on him. "Your father works here?"

"I don't have a father. My mother owns New South Wales Traders. You know, Annie Tremayne."

"No, I don't know her. Should I?"

He gaped. "Everyone knows my mother."

"Not me. Not my parents. Leastways, they don't ever discuss her. You were very brave today. My father will do something nice for you."

"You have laughing eyes." The curious way she looked at him made him sorry he had blurted out the last.

His mother returned, wheeling in a tea trolley herself. Set with a fine lace cloth and a silver teapot and milk jug, the tea service was reserved for important guests. A mound of scones sat on a doiley.

As though Chevonne were one of NSW Traders' important clients, his mother poured tea into exquisite china cups and plied the girl with polite questions. They seemed polite to Brendan, anyway, because they were boring ones.

Instead of asking if she had ever been to China or boxed with a kangaroo, his mother asked about her father—what he looked like, what he was doing, the things he liked doing best.

"So, he smokes a pipe now," mused his mother. She sat on the settee, with the tea service on the table between her and Chevonne.

Chevonne's expression became alert. "You must have been good friends with my father."

"At . . . one time." His mother leaned over to refill his cup.

All that bloody excitement, the running and panting, had made Brendan beastly thirsty. Why did girls take such dainty little sips? Maybe they didn't ever get real thirsty.

At the knock on the door, his mother straightened. "Yes?"

Ryan entered. Behind him was a man, a little shorter but with that same . . . Brendan didn't know how to describe it, except he was a sort of "I am here" person. A person you didn't forget.

"Papa!" Chevonne set down her cup and saucer and flew into her father's outstretched arms.

He picked her up and hugged her against him, then began raining kisses all over her face. "Chevonne, I was so bloody scared!"

She wriggled from his embrace and took his hand to pull him into the center of the office. "This is Miss Tremayne. And this is her son, Brendan. He saved my life, Papa. A horse almost trampled me, and he shoved me out of the way. Isn't he brave?"

Her father merely glanced at him before his flinty gaze traveled to Annie. All pleasure faded from her countenance.

"Your son will be sent a check as a token of my gratitude," he said

His voice seemed very stiff to Brendan, especially for someone who obviously knew his mother. As stiff as the man's body.

"Daniel." Hand outstretched, his mother half rose from the settee.

"G'day," the man said. "Come along, Chevonne. Your mother is very worried."

Brendan jumped to his feet, but Dan Warwick took the startled girl's hand before he could say anything and left the office with her in tow.

"Well," Ryan said, "it would seem our newly elected member to the Labor Party remains adamant in his scorn for you and all you stand for?"

Brendan's mother glanced at him. He was surprised to see how pale she looked. The riot that afternoon must have shaken her more than he realized. "Why did he seem angry at us, mother?"

"An old feud that goes back as far as Dreamtime, Brendan."

Dreamtime. Every Australian worth his name knew about Dreamtime. It was more than just the aborigines' explanation of how that vast featureless land was formed by giant spirit creatures making epic journeys across it to create its rivers, rocks, animals, and plants.

Dreamtime was also the aborigines' highly specialized form of trance, as unique as the other growths of that strange land. Brendan thought his mother looked as if she were possessed by Dreamtime.

17

1895

"*I've waited patiently,* Annie. Now it's time that I remarry."

She laid her fork across the edge of the gilt-rimmed plate. The Adams Hotel dining room was virtually empty at that time of night. She took her time before replying. Picking up her linen napkin, she calmly patted her lips and refolded it in her lap. "This is a departure from the subject of our conversation."

Ryan settled back in his chair and summoned the waiter to refill the wineglasses. "Overexpansion and the decline of the price of wool are boring subjects." He pulled out his watch fob and checked the time. "Almost nine-thirty." Beneath his well-trimmed mustache, the corners of his mouth rose in a wry smile. "Five years and four hours and thirty minutes since I last asked you to marry me."

"You have been patient." *About marriage, anyway,* she thought.

About sexual relations, she could not expect him to have the celibacy of a priest, and even that was questionable. She was rather certain that he had had several affairs. Mary McGregor had come closest to disrupting her relationship with him.

Tonight, in the table's candlelight, she saw that he was very serious. "Is there someone you want to marry?" she asked, startled by her sudden shortness of breath.

"At the moment, for the last one million moments, only you. But I grow lonely, Annie. Dining with you or attending a play or a business function together once or twice a month isn't enough. I'm too old for this. I plan to turn my attentions elsewhere. Don't ask me where, because honest to God I don't know. I don't want anyone else but you."

She picked up the heavy silver fork and turned it between her fingers. "I've waited too long, too." She glanced up at him. There was no coyness or subterfuge in her gaze. "I want you, Ryan, and I love you."

"We were discussing marriage, not love."

"You were. Oh, Ryan, I've been so contented

with you all these years, but I am too set in my ways after all this time. I'm nearing forty, you know."

"I know."

She ignored his wry smile. "Will you take me to bed? Will you make love to me, at last?"

He sighed, studied his wineglass, then looked at her. "It's a start, Annie. But on my terms. Here. Tonight. In one of the rooms above."

Her breath evaporated. After all this waiting, repressing the wanting of him, she wasn't ready. "I can't. Not on command. I . . . I don't feel . . . that way."

He chuckled. "You will."

She half resented his statement, that he was so certain of himself. Or, maybe, so certain of her. And yet a minuscule point of anticipation took light deep inside her, in her center, and began to spread gradually.

Their conversation resumed, touching on the most prosaic of subjects. She almost lost her patience when Ryan launched into a diatribe on the country's "artificial prosperity" created by overseas investment, and went from there to the danger of overoptimism. But the glint in his eye told her he knew exactly what he was doing.

By the time he pulled the chair out for her to rise, she was giddy with excitement. She drew on her gloves, looked up at him, and laughed softly. He took her hand and touched the underside of her wrist, at the glove's oval slit, to his lips. She shivered. Waiting for him to arrange for the room only heightened her nervousness.

In his early fifties, he was still very handsome, very male, and tonight very debonair in his formal black evening jacket, tie, and trousers. His deep voice with its Irish lilt had that faint suggestion and self-assurance of a man who knew himself, his foibles, and his strengths.

When he came for her at the foot of the curved staircase, she placed a trembling hand in his and said, "Tomorrow there will be talk all over Sydney."

"Tonight will only enhance your image," he said, tucking her hand inside his elbow as they mounted the stairs. "Every woman will envy your courage to be yourself, and propriety be damned. Every man will wish he had a woman like you."

"And tonight you have me."

He paused at a door halfway down the gaslit hall. His eyes were dark and passionate. "Only tonight?"

"I don't know," she answered honestly, her heart beating at her throat. "It depends on what happens tonight."

With a chuckle, he opened the door and drew her inside. He took her chin between his thumb and forefinger and tilted it upward. "You like making it difficult for a man, don't you, Annie Tremayne?"

Hearing the humor in his voice, she returned it. "I am completely shameless." Unnerved by her rampant feelings, she drew away. Her critical eye appraised the suite, obviously the best in the house.

"Why?"

"Why what?" she asked, unbuttoning one glove as she moved into the next room. A four-poster bed draped in white netting. The bridal suite, of course.

"Why do you like making it difficult for a man, Annie?"

Slowly she turned. Thumbs tucked into his vest pockets, he stood in the doorway, watching her. She knew that, in surveying the room's appointments, she had been stalling. And he knew that, too. His blunt question rattled her. "What makes you ask that?"

He crossed to her and began unbuttoning her other glove for her, then peeled it off. His touch on her bare skin sent a little spasm through her. "You won't let any man past that wall where you keep your feelings locked."

He was so close she could feel his breath on her face. "It has been the only way I could survive in a man's world."

His hands cupped her shoulders, bared by the cut of the red gown. "Let yourself surrender, Annie. Only in surrender do you really win."

At these words she felt a curious weakness. "I

don't know how to do that. Surrender."

"Tonight I am going to show you. To begin with, I want you to take down your hair. While I watch."

Slowly, she nodded and began removing the pins that anchored her coil of hair. She let each pin drop onto the carpet. The excitement that flared in his eyes aroused her as well. When the last pin was removed, the mass of her fiery red hair tumbled about her shoulders, almost down to her waist.

He reached around and deftly unhooked her gown. She stood immobile. His gaze never left her face. Her lips parted as he assisted her gown in its slipping, slithering course down her body, revealing her breasts, which were pushed high by her corset. He quickly unlaced it and then removed her chemise.

His dark eyes ran over the length of her body, her long legs and the spot where they apexed in tight red-gold curls. "Touch me, please," she whispered.

Still holding her transfixed by his consuming gaze, he reached out a hand to caress her nipples. A little gasp escaped her. Her knees went weak, and she grabbed his shoulders. "Oh, God, Ryan, take me to bed now. I've waited too long."

"I know." A wistful smile creased brackets at either side of his mustache. "All the years we've wasted, love."

He surprised her then, sweeping her up in his arms and cradling her against his chest. She had always thought she was too big for a man to do such a thing. She put her arms around his shoulders and buried her face in the hollow of his neck, fragrant with the scent of his now familiar cologne.

"Thank God, the bed's only a few feet away," he said with feigned shortness of breath as he dropped her onto the big bed.

When he leaned over her, hands planted at either side of her hips, she shoved at his chest playfully. "Sir, you are not at all gallant."

He pushed himself back and unknotted his cravat. "Ah, Annie, how can I be gallant, when there is a raging fire inside me?" He stripped off his jacket and shrugged out of his vest. "I want you. I want only you. I've wanted you since the day you boldly came to my office as an eighteen-year-old and tried to bargain with me."

"Tried? I did. By the time I finished, you yielded your vote to me."

He took off his trousers. God, but he was bloody beautiful. "I had already made up my mind to cast my vote with you the moment you entered my office." With infinite tenderness, he stretched out beside her on the bed and pulled her to him. "Which reminds me. I am claiming that request you promised to grant me should the time come when I would want it."

She didn't know which disconcerted her more— that after all this time there was something he wanted from her, or the feel of that hard cylindrical part of him pressed against her belly. "Yes?" she whispered. "What is it you want?"

His hand slipped between her thighs and spread her legs. She moaned when his fingers found that most intimate part of her. She felt as if moisture must have gushed from her, so excited was she. Still exploring her with an expert touch that made her wriggle, he buried his face in her mass of hair and whispered against her ear, "I won't ask you to marry me again, Annie. You'll have to come to me of your own accord. All I am asking for is your love."

He removed his fingers and shifted his weight atop her. "Oh, Annie, I need you to love me."

She felt him prod into her, then gain entrance. She heard herself sigh. "Me loving you . . . what does that mean to you?"

Gently, he kissed her lips. "It means just having faith in me, Annie. In us."

18

1897

    Louisa stood before the mirror and pinned the yellow flower to her white merino jacket. The bottom half of her dress was frilly and flouncy, while the top half was relatively plain.

This was the New Woman fashion, championed by those who now marched for rights and at the same time had an unwillingness to relinquish the advantages of clinging femininity. She herself was experiencing conflicting inner desires.

She affixed a yellow ribbon to the crown of her pleated-brim hat, tilted at an angle. She had only an hour left before the meeting at little Macquarie

Place. Should she tell Dan the truth about where she was going?

She thought not. It would only add fuel to the flame. There was nothing she could do about what she had become. Snippish and headstrong and totally unsuitable as a politician's wife. But one didn't throw away almost fifteen years of marriage, especially when one loves someone the way she loved Dan.

She straightened the brim of her hat so that it shadowed her eyes and their discontent. On her way out the door, she paused at her father's study. He had an upset stomach and had stayed home from the office. She opened the door and peeked in. He was busy writing. "Father? Feeling better?"

He put down his pen and smiled. "Yes. Sometimes a man needs a day away from the office."

He was completely gray, and it seemed to her his face had become wrinkled overnight. He was no longer the powerful autocratic figure in her life. Dan had replaced him. "I am going shopping. Will you be needing the phaeton?"

"No, I'm not planning on stirring from here." His eyes, which she used to think were as cold blue as Norwegian fjords, actually took on a warm glow. "I hear Chevonne practicing Mozart. She's getting good."

"When the piano tutor leaves, will you remind her to return to her studies?"

"You really should send her to a finishing school

back in New England, Louisa. You received an excellent edu—"

"Father, Dan and I are making certain Chevonne receives the best education available."

"Bah!" He thumped down his pen. "Dan is so bullheadedly patriotic, he is sure that everything Australian is the best way."

"We are the Americans, not Chevonne and Dan. You've doubled your financial holdings since moving here." She blew him a kiss from her gloved fingertips. "The day is positively too bright for us to argue. I'll be back by dusk."

After giving the old coachman, Witherspoon, her destination, she settled back in the carriage. In a way, she agreed with her father. She had never been able to make sense of the wild, strange country she had immigrated to. The seasons were upside down, the animals weird, and the water circled the wrong way down the sink.

She tried to relax as the phaeton's horse clip-clopped down the steeply sloping streets of Paddington and through the narrow lanes of the inner city. Today, however, guilt battled her determination to go to the meeting. Neither her father nor Dan would have approved.

At the corner of Loftus and Bridge streets, the site of the first bridge in Australia across Tank Stream, she instructed Witherspoon to wait for her. With a small nervous twitch in her stomach, she descended from the phaeton and glanced around Macquarie Place. Three pubs, a tobacco shop, *The Sydney Dispatch*, and several other small businesses faced the square.

Women of all ages were gathered beneath the shady Moreton Bay figs, clustered around the stone drinking fountain, trussing the gaslamp posts. All the women were dressed in white and adorned with some kind of yellow article.

Like Louisa, they had come to attend the first organized meeting of the New Woman's movement. Their yellow ribbons, flowers, sashes, hats, represented their causes, foremost the right to vote.

As one stout woman mounted a hastily constructed platform and began speaking, Louisa realized she had not been prepared for the subject matter. With cropped hair and dressed scandalously in sandals, the woman preached about anarchism and free love.

After her, another woman, this one in flowing white robes, mounted the platform and began to talk about the necessity of birth control. Louisa reflected that if she had known more about birth control fifteen years earlier, she wouldn't have had Chevonne. And she might never had found the courage to prompt Dan to marry her.

She found herself blushing crimson as the woman discussed the intimate details of preventing conception. But she felt that what the woman had to say was justified.

"Shocking, isn't it?"

Louisa turned. It was that Tremayne woman. She was gowned in the white of purity. Her parasol was yellow, as were her gloves. With the deep red hair untouched by gray and eyes as bright as a child's, she could have passed for twenty-five.

"I'm Annie Tremayne."

"Yes. I know you."

She shrugged. Her smile was wry. "Doesn't everyone in Australia? A curse at times, I am afraid."

"You're one of my husband's arch rivals in political philosophy."

"Well, that, too."

Louisa gathered her pluck. "Look, Miss Tremayne, my loyalties—and my love—are for my husband. And will always be. But I feel I owe you an apology."

The other woman's eyes narrowed. The wary look of the persecuted came into that direct, sea green gaze. "Yes, Mrs. Warwick?"

Louisa glanced down at her daffodil-colored handkerchief, a twisted square of linen in her nervous hand. "I know you two don't see eye to eye on a lot of things, including business and social differences, but he had no right to do what he did at the reception for the new commissioners."

The whole affair had been disastrous. Louisa and Dan had been talking to a commissioner appointed to the Court of Requests, who had washed down his pork and kangaroo with too much wine and porter. His wig had even slipped to one side. On the other hand, Dan had drunk very little, so there was no excuse for what had happened next.

Annie Tremayne and her son had entered the reception hall. Dan could be bloody curt sometimes, but he had always been willing to meet people halfway. Therefore, he had shocked Louisa and everyone in the reception room with his most audible comment, "'Tis that Tremayne woman and her bastard."

Later that evening, after Louisa and Dan had returned home, she had berated him. "That was totally uncalled for. And not like you at all. We all make mistakes, Dan." She certainly had. "Who's to say that marrying the boy's father might not have been the greater mistake?" But Dan had remained obdurate, and she had given up the subject.

"Would you care to have a sherry with me?" Annie Tremayne asked now. As if embarrassed by her impulsive suggestion, she looked away, nodding toward a nearby doorway. "The subject of voting rights won't come up for a while."

She glanced over her shoulder. The place was O'Brien's Pub. "A pub?"

Annie's grin was close to roguish. "Women shouldn't be allowed a sherry?"

"But in a pub?"

"Where better?"

She laughed. "I think I'd like a sherry, thank you. Miss Tremayne."

"Annie, please."

The tall woman ushered her into the dim, smoky interior of O'Brien's Pub. It possessed a warm ambience, with its Tudor-timbered ceiling and polished mahogany bar. A constant, low talk said that this was definitely male domain.

The aproned waiter didn't look surprised to see women enter the establishment. With a nod of his head, he said, "G'day, Miss Tremayne," and led Annie and Louisa past the men drinking pints of porter and bitter, to a more secluded table in a private room.

"Irish coffee t'day, Miss Tremayne?" he asked.

"No, we'll have sherry, Timothy." She winked boldly. "The best, naturally, drawn from one your ancient casks of Amontillado."

Louisa sat, hands folded primly, while her eye took in the masculine surroundings. How much women missed, sequestered in the home and only permitted to go out for limited excursions like picnics, parties, and theater.

"Well, what do you think?" Annie asked with a sly sparkle in her green eyes. "Does this look like some Arabian den of iniquity where an innocent woman might be kidnaped and sold into some sheik's harem?"

A slight smile came to Louisa's lips. "A really quite placid place." She reminded herself that she must use caution. Perhaps the Tremayne woman had an ulterior motive in seeking her out. Louisa certainly didn't want to divulge anything that could in any way hurt Dan.

She sipped at the sherry and occasionally made her own contributions to a conversation that ranged from free speech to new art to the "insane treatment of the insane," as she succinctly opined to Annie.

The Tremayne woman signaled for another sherry, then said, "Alas, I sometimes think I'd rather be insane than a female. For that matter, many people think I am insane. Men especially."

Louisa chuckled. Annie had a vivacity that she admired. She was relieved that the subject of Dan was never raised, and the afternoon passed quickly. Louisa enjoyed herself more than she could remember.

Her intellect was stimulated. Furthermore, this cautious friendship with another woman based on respect fulfilled a need she hadn't realized was there. It had to be like a person who didn't know that she had poor vision until she donned a pair of glasses.

Reluctantly, she said her good-bye with a promise to get together at the next rally for women's rights. She returned home in high spirits—and with the intention of educating Chevonne more on these issues. Her daughter needed to realize that there, in a continent that was bigger than

Europe and where the men outnumbered the women six to one, women were ignored in all matters but one.

No, Chevonne would be raised differently!

The rally wasn't responsible only for Louisa's exuberance. The eye-opening experience had inspired her to tell her daughter the truth about her parentage. She called Chevonne into the drawing room. "Sit down," she said, patting the space beside her on the settee. "There is something you need to know, darling. A secret I have been carrying far too long."

Chevonne's blue eyes widened but she said nothing as she sat down.

All of a sudden, Louisa's relief turned to nervousness. She smoothed the dimity flounces of her skirt. "When I was only a little older than you, I made a mistake. I didn't known anything about . . . about contraception."

The word sounded so stilted. She couldn't look at Chevonne. "I was infatuated with a young man who was worthless when it came to character. When I realized I was . . . with child . . . carrying you . . . I was desolate. Then I met Dan. I knew I loved him at once. I was surer of this than my own name. Fortunately, Dan wanted to marry me, although I never told him the truth about you. I think it would break his heart."

Did Chevonne understand what she was asking? That the silence in this matter was for Dan's sake, not her own?

"In any case," Louisa finished, "I don't want what happened to me to happen to you. Would you like to accompany me to the next rally?"

Chevonne laid her hand over hers. "Yes, Mama. To both questions—the unspoken and the spoken one."

Louisa looked quickly into her daughter's eyes and saw a maturity there she had not suspected. Choked with gratitude and love, all she could say was, "Why don't you tell your grandfather we'll be eating soon."

After her daughter left the room, Louisa remained where she was. She was weak, even giddy, with relief. But that relief vanished in the next moment when she heard Chevonne's outcry, an eerie wail that reminded Louisa of the legendary banshees. A shiver crept up her spine. Following the wailing sound to her father's office, she arrived at the same time as the startled servants, Minnie and Alicia.

Chevonne's blond hair spilled across the chest of her grandfather, who lay prone on the Aubusson carpet. With a sob, Louisa dropped down beside her daughter. "Oh, God, what has happened?"

Chevonne looked up, her eyes glazed with shock. Her breath was coming in gulps. "I came in to tell Papaw I had finished my work. He smiled and was telling me he was . . . proud of me when . . . he grabbed his shoulder and fell over. Mama, he won't talk. I think he's dead!"

Louisa tried to maintain control. "Minnie, send Witherspoon for Dr. Hallerum. Alicia, summon Mr. Warwick."

Gently, she took Chevonne by the shoulders and told her to run upstairs and get her smelling salts. Of course, Louisa knew smelling salts were useless. It was too late. Still, she had to give Chevonne something to do until the girl regained composure.

After everyone had left the room, Louisa placed her ear against her father's chest. Nothing. One arm was outstretched, the hand curled like a claw. A bit of blood mottled his mouth and cheek. Strange she should think of Dan now and the razor nick of blood on his jaw that morning.

An absurdly futile hope prompted her to try to rouse her father. No response. No movement. "Oh, Papa!"

Now it was safe to cry, and tears coursed a trail through the fine powder dusted on her cheeks.

Her father had been the one remaining link with her past. With America and childhood memories and all that was safe and secure and familiar. Her father had adored her. She was a perfect daughter to him just as she was. Now there was no one who fully loved her.

For Dan, she could never be fully what he wanted. And Chevonne, well, Louisa knew her daughter loved her but also knew that it was her father she worshiped, even though she now knew he was not her natural father.

Quickly, she dried her tears. How childish of her and how selfish. She was a grown woman. Yet another tear spilled over.

"Mama, here are the salts. Is Papaw . . . dead?"

Managing a calm countenance, she said, "Yes. He's with God now. You must help me. I want you to find his best suit, that pinstripe one, and lay it out on his bed. I need to stay with him until the doctor and your father come."

The two men arrived simultaneously. At once the portly old doctor began examining her father. At that point, Louisa fell apart. Trembling, she covered her face with her hands and wept copiously.

Dan took her in his arms and led her from the office. "You've done all you can, Louisa. You'll need to save your strength for Chevonne and me. Let Dr. Hallerum take charge of the details."

Startled, she peered up at him. "Save my strength for you?"

"Yes, me." In the darkened hallway, she couldn't make out his expression. "Your father and I didn't always see eye to eye, but I admired him. He was like a rock. Always there. Always certain of where he was going, what he expected from life."

Then Dan really surprised her. He bent his head and kissed her temple. "You are a vital part of your father. Strong like him, whether you know it or not. His death reminds me how precarious life is. I don't want to lose you. Come along upstairs. I want you to rest while there is still some measure of quiet in the house. I'll have the doctor prescribe a measure of laudanum for you."

"You won't leave me?" she asked as he led her into their bedroom.

He pulled back the quilted coverlet and eased her onto the bed. "No. I'll be right here. All night, Louisa. I promise."

As he removed first one of her high-buttoned boots, then the other, she watched him in astonishment. This gentleness, this compassion, were an unexpected side of him. Then he drew the coverlet up over her and pulled a chair alongside their bed.

Seating himself, he took her hand in his. "You know, I can still remember the first time I saw you, Louisa. I was determined to have you, if only because I sensed you thought you were too good for me."

A faint smile erased a bit of the grief from her mouth. "I was intrigued by the difference between you and other men I knew. You were so controlled, your emotions contained. Your obviously educated background conflicted with your magnificent physique that had to have come from years of common labor. You were a walking dichotomy. You still are."

A shadow of a frown crossed his face. "There are things you don't know about—"

A knock at the door cut him short. The interloper was Alicia, with a small blue glass bottle. "Your laudanum, Mrs. Warwick. Dr. Hallerum said to take a dose twice a day for the next several days."

"Thank you, Alicia," Dan said, taking the bottle from the bony old woman.

After she departed, he poured out the medicine. Gratefully, Louisa swallowed the acrid-tasting liquid. At the moment, she wanted only to retreat. She realized Dan was talking to her, telling her about his morning session at the capitol and the bill that had been defeated.

"Ever since George Reid was elected premier of New South Wales, he has pushed for a federation of Australia's colonies. I think he's right. There's no limit to what Australia could . . ."

The only thing she could focus on was the small razor nick on his jaw. Like her father's small splotch of blood. The thin red line expanded like a blazing, bloody red sun, warming her and frightening her at once. Then merciful sleep overtook her hallucination.

"Mama, you are sure that Miss Tremayne invited us to lunch with her after the march?" Chevonne asked. "The newspapers say that she and Papa have been feuding for years over everything from politics to business."

Louisa considered her next words carefully. She

felt a loyalty to Annie, who had introduced her to a whole new world of business and politics that was open to women, and she was grateful for the friendship the woman offered her. On the other hand, Dan was everything to Louisa. The death of her father had hit her hard. Dan had been slightly skeptical about the issue of women's suffrage, but when the bill was passed, Louisa knew she had won his full admiration.

By initiating her own interests, she had liberated herself. She was no longer afraid to take charge, and yet be submissive at times. All inhibitions gone, she and Dan had reached a new plateau in their marriage—and in their passion.

She felt a blush steal over her cheeks at the memory of the night before. Her growing sexual boldness amazed her as well as her husband. And it pleased him. Especially last night, when she had taken the initiative to touch his genitals and gently massage them. His groan had turned to a gasp as she had bent her head and enclosed him with her lips. She knew he had been startled by her sultry chuckle, so atypical of her, and her whisper, "I've been passive long enough, my husband."

She refocused her thoughts on her daughter now and gave her hand an encouraging squeeze. "Whatever ill feelings may exist between Annie and your father are just that, Chevonne. Between them."

At almost fourteen, Chevonne was acquiring the

features of a young lady. Her baby fat had melted away, leaving a beautifully sculpted face. Her dazzlingly clear blue eyes were fringed by dark brown lashes, and her dark brows starkly contrasted her summer-child's blond hair. Today she wore it loose with the sides pulled up and secured at her crown by a small bouquet of fresh posies.

Until a few years ago, her skirts had been worn short, protest though she might. This afternoon, she wore a becoming blue gingham dress gathered into tiers of lace in the rear. The vision of youthful innocence took Louisa's breath away. Hadn't she been only a little older, sixteen, when she fell in love with Dan?

The march was being held down at the Circular Quay where the Great Maritime Strike had led to a riot that marked the gaining strength of the labor union and her husband's Labor Party.

This time, she hoped, the outcome would be much more peaceful, and the march would accomplish the desired goal of giving women the legal right of contraception.

Annie was waiting beside her hansom cab. Louisa had come to realize that Annie was actually very shy. And very private, although to others she seemed stiff, reserved. Annie and Ryan Sheridan now lived together openly, flagrantly ignoring public opinion.

For Louisa, Annie's smile came easily and warmly. "I was afraid the spectators jamming the streets would delay you. Hello, Chevonne. How lovely you look, doesn't she, Brendan?"

For the first time, Louisa noticed Annie's son. It had been at least a year since last she had seen him. He looked more like a young man, though he could be only . . . what? Sixteen? His gangly body and lantern-jaw look had matured into hard, fuller lines that were declarations of purpose and strength. A thin, pale scar along his cheek added rather than detracted from the purity of his features.

She recalled that he had been instrumental in finding her lost daughter the day of the riot, although Dan had never fully explained the events of that day.

Brendan executed a formal little bow and smiled. "A pleasure to meet you, Mrs. Warwick." He turned his hazel-eyed gaze on Chevonne. "Remember me?"

"Yes. My white knight without a horse."

Louisa had been expecting a girlish giggle. Her daughter's aplomb dismayed her. Something in Brendan's smile struck a chord in her heart. Something that both pleased her yet caused her disquiet.

Only the discovery of gold in Western Australian back in 1893 had been keeping the sagging economy afloat. NSW Traders, almost a law unto itself, was successful so far in plugging the leaks in its ponderous ship of business. So, too, had Dan managed to steer Phillips Enterprises through the rough waters.

The Australians themselves were suffering. There was little work to be had. The price of wool had declined, and banks and businesses had collapsed. These events in turn caused the unions to lose ground in their struggle.

It seemed that everywhere in Sydney Dan went men were waiting in lines for work. Women and children begged on the streets. Swagmen, those with their gear on their back, became a familiar sight once more, as hundreds of men took to the "wallaby track" in search of work in the country.

Dan stayed at work late many nights, trying to find solutions for the homeless and hungry. One of his projects was the Trans-Australian Railroad, in which he had urged his father-in-law to invest. Walter had halfheartedly given the project his attention. As a result the railroad ran only half the distance of the continent, stalled at Port Augusta, the doorstep to one of the most desolate regions of the world, the Nullarbor Plain.

The course of the track lay across a thousand miles of scorched, treeless limestone, through miles of red sandhills covered with saltbush and bluebush and desiccated acacia trees. December's summer sun often exceeded one hundred degrees. Names like Lake Disappointment were evocative of that eternally barren land of harsh stone deserts and dry lakes.

Here, Dan thought, was an opportunity to put jobless men to work. If camps were set up, railroad gangs could inch the line across the Nullarbor Plain. Camels could be used to transport the necessities of life.

"An ill-conceived plan," wrote the *Sydney Post*, but Ryan Sheridan championed the idea in *The Sydney Dispatch*. So did Louisa, who in addition entreated Dan to consider giving jobs to women on the Trans-Australian.

Dan barely refrained from scoffing. He was proud of what his wife had helped to achieve, winning the women's right to vote, when Australia's American cousins were still bickering about the issue. He smoothed the wayward strands of hair back from her temples. Silver strands now intertwined with the gold. "Louisa, love, when the heat comes in on the Nullarbor, it separates the boys from the men."

"Bah!" Incensed, she raised herself up on one arm.

She didn't realize how tantalizing she was, one bare breast exposed from beneath the bedsheet. Sometimes he wondered if he had done right in telling her the truth of his origins, in revealing that he was a scion of the Livingston-Tremayne dynasty. Yet to have done otherwise was like denying the man he had become. Still, he wanted to keep this new life completely divorced from that of his twin sister.

"I may be an American, Dan Warwick," Louisa said indignantly, "but I know better than that. Women have been enduring the same hardships as men since the colony was founded."

"There are no women in the Nullarbor."

Her eyes became like blue flames. "The aborigine females are living there. They are the Dream Keepers for the next generation of white women, and your daughter will be among its pioneers, Dan Warwick!"

19

1898

One blessing to come out of the financial calamity was a growth of national pride among both workers and employers. A clamor for nationhood arose. It was not aimed at overthrowing British links but rather sought to give Australia a positive status in a part of the world now engaged in war—the Philippines, where Spain was battling the United States.

Reading about that war in *The Sydney Dispatch*, Chevonne became caught up in its heroics. Though not yet sixteen, she had absorbed much of her mother's headstrong and independent nature. As she overheard discussions about the war among her parents' peers, the idea of patriotism became more than a word for her.

So when her father was elected a representative to the most richly endowed assemblage of political ability ever brought together in Australia, she was most eager to accompany him and her mother to Adelaide. With Sydney and Melbourne fiercely competitive, Adelaide was selected as a neutral site for such an event.

There at Adelaide, Dan, along with Ryan Sheridan and representatives from four other colonies, was to act as a framer of a federal constitution. "We plan to establish Australia as a separate, independent country with a unified government," Dan explained to Chevonne. "Our colonies, hopefully, will become states that retain most of their individual powers."

She, her parents, and the faithful Minnie were traveling by a completed portion, the Overland, of the Trans-Australian Railroad. After the first grueling day, Chevonne had become accustomed to the incessant click-clack of the train's wheels and the cinders from the engine's smokestack that blew in through open windows framed by silk moiré curtains.

The March weather was hot and sticky. From their private teak-paneled coach, she could look out upon a countryside that unfolded majestic mountain ranges and treeless plains. Flocks of emus and mobs of kangaroos and their joeys captivated her, city girl that she was.

Occasionally, the dark silhouettes of aborigines

could be seen traversing the bushland afoot. She recalled her strange dream from years before, after she had escaped from the *Elissa*. A dream of aborigines and their spirit Rainbow Serpent. She knew so little of aboriginal beliefs and nothing of Almudj. Only later did she learn that indeed such a spirit existed in the aborigine culture. The dream had stayed with her, a reassurance of her invulnerability to bad things happening to her.

When, at a water stop, perturbed kookaburras erupted from the acacia with raucous guffaws, she was delighted.

She was even more delighted when, making her way with her mother toward the parlor car, she encountered Brendan Tremayne in the narrow passageway. She stopped, mouth open, and stared up at the eighteen-year-old. He was much taller than she remembered. And huskier. He must weigh at least thirteen stone.

His broad shoulders stretched taut the summer serge suit he was wearing. His starched shirt and collar looked uncomfortably hot. His hair was side parted, as was the fashion, but a trifle long. Such a style was labeled, and condemned, a "poet," in the manner of Tennyson.

Her mother was more collected than she. "Brendan Tremayne, isn't it?"

His green-eyed gaze deserted Chevonne long enough to respond to her mother. "Yes, ma'am, I am."

"Is your mother with you?"

"My mother is having dining service in her car. Are you on your way to the parlor car?"

"Yes, we are," Chevonne interjected, ignoring her mother's surprised expression. "Would you like to accompany us?" She wished she had chosen to wear a more sophisticated traveling suit. Because of the heat, she had opted for her light yellow dimity dress with its lace-fringed, elbow-length sleeves. "Or were you intending to read in the parlor coach?" she asked, nodding towards the folded newspaper tucked beneath his arm.

His attention refocused on her, and she felt an inexplicable little thrill. "Really just using an excuse to stretch the legs." His voice, she noticed, was deeper, too. "I'd be happy to join you, if that is acceptable to you, Mrs. Warwick?"

"Of course. Why don't you invite your mother, also?"

He ran a finger inside his high, stiff collar. "She is with a friend."

At once, Chevonne knew who the friend was. All of Sydney knew that the publisher of *The Sydney Dispatch* lived with the Tremayne woman. As one of New South Wales's ten delegates to the convention, Ryan Sheridan would doubtlessly be aboard the train, which accounted for the presence of Annie Tremayne and her son.

Regardless of the public censure, Chevonne liked Brendan's mother. She was real. No pretenses. She said what she thought instead of what was proper.

That occasionally made Chevonne burst out in laughter—an act of impropriety that brought a reproving frown from her mother. A few times, Chevonne suspected her mother of repressing her own laughter, if the tug about her delicately rouged lips was any indication.

High tea was being served in the parlor coach. Three couples and a number of single men were taking tea, talking, or reading. A black-jacketed waiter led Chevonne and her mother to a table graced with brass lamps with rose silk shades.

Chevonne removed her white eyelet glove and was dismayed to see that her hands were shaking. Could Brendan Tremayne have that kind of effect on her? In her memories of their meetings, she could recall a sort of pleasure in his company, but nervousness? No.

By the time he returned, the waiter was serving the tea and crumpets. Brendan seated himself opposite Chevonne and her mother. "Are you staying in Adelaide itself or down at the Bay?"

"At the Bay. Cream?"

"No, thank you," he replied.

Her mother took the porcelain teapot and poured a cup, passing it to Brendan without spilling a drop despite the train's rattling vibration. She smiled. "Mr. Warwick wanted to be in town for convenience' sake, but I threatened him with staging a women's march on the House of Parliament if we had to stay in Adelaide's stuffy old Plaza Hotel."

Brendan chuckled. "My mother's exact sentiments."

Chevonne accepted her cup. The tea sloshed, and it wasn't due to the train's perpetual rocking. "We're lodging at the Macfarlane Hotel."

"We've taken rooms at The Old Gum Tree. Perhaps we'll run into each other."

Her mother turned the conversation to the effort of the colonies to federate, but Chevonne was barely listening. Her attention was centered wholly on Brendan, a man now. A polite, well-bred young man. Along his upper lip was the faint afternoon shadow of a mustache. Did he shave barechested, as did her father? Strange, even though now she knew Dan wasn't her natural father, she never thought of him as anything but that.

". . . as well as the protection of workers from competition from foreign labor," Brendan was saying.

Her eyes watched his lips, long and strongly contoured, form the words. What would it be like to be kissed? To be kissed by Brendan Tremayne? Until now, she had had no interest in the opposite sex. She had been too caught up in her studies and her growing interest in politics, an example set by both her parents.

After tea was over, Brendan accompanied her mother and her back to their coach. When the train lurched unexpectedly, Chevonne stumbled backward and then forward before Brendan's quick arm prevented her from being pitched against the window. His newspaper fluttered to the floor unheeded. Half atop him, she stiffened in his grasp. She saw something flare in his eyes and just as quickly die.

But when she caught her pallid face reflected in the train's window, she knew she had not imagined what she had seen. That same heated yearning was reflected in her eyes.

After the city of Broken Hill the train chugged through the magnificent desert mountain ranges. The Flinders Ranges was a world of colorful cliffs abounding with aboriginal rock painting, granite peaks, folding hills, and plunging gorges.

Chevonne saw little of this. Only one thought held sway in her mind: Brendan Tremayne. He had the build of a man, molded by summers at Dream Time. According to her mother, he had developed an acute business acumen under Annie's tutelage.

Still, Chevonne wondered how she could be so mesmerized by him when she could have her choice of any number of Sydney's young men, who would gladly escort the daughter of the wealthy and well-respected businessman and politician, Dan Warwick.

At last, the train passed through the rich green Barossa Valley and its abundant vineyards and down through the hills of Adelaide, a city of gracious sandstone-colored buildings.

She had hoped to see Brendan again, but, with

the mass of travelers and politicians and their families descending from the steam-hissing train, she was disappointed. Maybe Brendan's mother and Mr. Sheridan had business to attend to in the city proper first.

From the Adelaide station, a horse-drawn tram carried Chevonne, her parents, and Minnie on to the nearby beach resort of Holdfast Bay, called Gleneig by some. Here the first South Australian colonists had landed a mere sixty years before.

The Macfarlane was a quaint hotel of lacy cast-iron ornamentation. Her father had been able to take two rooms, one of which she and Minnie were to share. Their room had red-and-white-striped wallpaper above wainscoted red paint. Minnie was delighted. "Oh, mum, 'tis a grand room, it is."

Her mother shuddered at the decor but delighted in the wrought-iron balcony overlooking the Southern Ocean.

So did Chevonne. She had read *Romeo and Juliet*. The romantic side of her easily recalled the balcony scene, and she knew that she was already older than thirteen-year-old Juliet when the girl fell irrevocably and ineluctably in love with Romeo.

The afternoon was still young, and Chevonne's mother wanted to stroll the jetty first. Her father yielded for the day. "Tomorrow, though, it's work. You and Chevonne will have to occupy yourselves."

"Tomorrow, dear sir," her mother said, tweaking

her husband's handlebar mustache, "I shall be watching the deliberations of the representatives. This is a historic moment that I shall want to tell my grandchildren about."

Chevonne had also looked forward to attending the convention. She considered herself beyond the schoolgirlish behavior of her friends, who seemed mostly concerned with boys these days. The truth was, she knew far more about politics than most adults. She knew that the convention was dealing not just with the individual colonial parliaments versus the commonwealth prerogatives but more so with the Labor Party versus the "bleeding bourgeois hotheads like the Tremaynes," as her father had more than once put it.

but after being held by Brendan in the train passageway, if for only an instant, she no longer cared what the convention was about or what her father said. What might have entertained her twenty-four hours earlier—the antics of an old bellowing bull seal frolicking on the white sands of Holdfast Bay—now left her restless. Her lace-edged yellow chiffon parasol, matching her gored skirt and French gigot-sleeved blouse, twirled and bobbed and dipped in her fidgety grasp.

Her parents noticed her lackluster attitude with puzzlement.

Another twenty-four hours had to pass before her longing was rewarded. With lethargy, she dressed for the trip back to Adelaide and the convention in a yoked skirt and ready-to-made blouse her mother deplored. "It is the fashion of the New Woman," Chevonne reminded her mother.

For modesty's sake, she insisted Chevonne wear short suede pearl gray gloves and a flowerpot toque perched atop a coil of her thick fair hair. "New Women we may be, but we always comport ourselves as ladies, Chevonne."

Dan Warwick had taken the early tram to Adelaide, as he would be doing for the remainder of the convention, and Louisa and Chevonne would come up later in the morning. When they arrived she saw that the stone buildings of Adelaide had a sixteenth-century Renaissance style that appealed to Chevonne. Her mood lightened, especially when she entered Parliament House on North Terrace and saw Brendan among the spectators in the gallery.

Intent on the debate, he leaned forward, chin resting on his fist. Summers at Dream Time had toasted his skin an unfashionable brown, except for the scar he had earned in her defense. His longish hair and his clean-shaven face, as opposed to her father's heavy mustache, captured her imagination.

From experience, she knew him to be brave and bold. His dark good looks beckoned her notice. Even more, he was a young man of mature interests. Like herself, politics fascinated him. His mother's and Mr. Sheridan's involvement in government bureaucracy was his legacy as much as

NSW Traders and the rest of the vast Tremayne holdings.

His mother spotted Louisa and her and hailed them to join her. When Chevonne took the empty seat to Brendan's left, he glanced up. His preoccupied expression lightened, but in the next instant those eyes regarded her with an intensity that shook her innate aplomb.

Years of practiced etiquette enabled her to smile. "How are the debates coming?"

He grimaced. "Slowly. The states' righters are battling those in favor of a strong federal government. At least, the delegates have agreed upon a name for the new federation. The Commonwealth of Australia."

She canted her head and tested the name. "The Commonwealth of Australia. I like that. None of the colonies can be affronted by that."

"States they will be. To appease Melbourne, the capitol is to be located there until one can be built, somewhere between it and Sydney."

She nodded and let her attention return to the delegates on the floor, among them her father, but she still was profoundly aware of the young man at her side. When a recess was announced, he suggested to his mother they adjourn outside.

Annie Tremayne's gaze focused on the young pair. She was outrageously attractive in a parrot green linen suit that emphasized the rich russet shade of her hair. She fingered her jacket's limp yoke collar. "I quite agree. 'Tis hot enough in here for a Turkish bath."

The four made their way outside to stand beneath the portico. An acquaintance, a middle-aged buxom woman, cornered Annie and Louisa to complain of the decision on the federal Parliament's right to levy custom duties. "What source of revenue will be left to the colonial Parliaments, I ask you?"

Chevonne leaned against one of the ten Corinthian columns and languidly fanned herself with her small hat. Little good it did. The convention flag wafted as fitfully from its staff. Perspiration dampened her hose and trickled between her breasts.

Brendan braced a hand on the marble column near her head. In his other hand were his chamois gloves and his straw hat, which fashion arbiters had complained had no class distinction. A year ago it would have been a social crime for any man pretending to fashionable dress to appear in any other than the high silk hat. "A sea breeze would be a welcome respite."

"We walked along the jetty yesterday. I'd rather be there right now."

His eyes brightened. "Have you ever ridden a bicycle? You can rent one at the jetty."

"I've always wanted to ride one. Mama swears she's going to make my father buy a bicycle built for two."

He glanced over at their mothers. "Do you think your mother would mind me teaching you?"

Her mother, perhaps not. Her father, however, would never permit it. Instead of answering directly, she said, "I could meet you at the jetty tomorrow. By the boat harbor."

Guilt gnawed at her the rest of the day. She hadn't lied, she told herself. Still, she felt awful when her mother prepared to return to the Parliament House the next morning and she begged off. "'Tis so hot and stuffy inside. And I am still tired from the trip. Do you mind if I don't go, Mama?"

Her mother leaned down and gave her an investigative kiss on her forehead. "You don't feel feverish. But the trip was arduous." She began to pull off a glove.

Chevonne panicked. "You're going to stay with me?"

Her mother shot her a puzzled glance. "Of course. You're my little girl."

"I'm sixteen, Mama. Not a little girl."

"But just as headstrong," she chided with a smile. "Has to come from your father, not me."

"You've always allowed me more freedom than other mothers give their daughters. And Minnie is here. I will be fine, Mama. I just don't want to go up to Adelaide today."

Her mother hesitated. "Well, I shan't be long. With the tram running every hour, I should be back by teatime. You won't be bored?"

She shook her head. "Not at all. I can always watch the coming and going of the boats." Which was the truth. Just not the complete truth.

With obvious reluctance her mother yielded. She had eagerly awaited the federation deliberations for months now. She was proud of Dan and wanted to be a part of what she was sure would be a momentous event in Australia's history.

Chevonne waited a good half hour before she began dressing. "Minnie, would you fetch that white blouse with the lace jabot for me?"

"You are going out, mum?" Minnie asked, an apprehensive frown on her round face. She had been putting away the clothes from Louisa's trunk.

"Only for a while. Fresh air should help me feel better."

"Mayhaps I should go with you."

Her hands fluttered with her wayward hair. "No, no. I'm just going to sit in the courtyard."

Minnie's mouth twitched with nervousness, but she kept silent and went back to unpacking.

Some of the women who rode the bicycle daringly donned the ladies' cycling dress, a short coat and knickerbockers. Having no such costume, Chevonne chose a divided skirt with a wide wrap that concealed the satin breeches beneath. Still, her ankles would be exposed.

Anchoring a saucy tam-o'-shanter onto her head with hairpins, she shrugged off this flouting of propriety. Was she not a New Woman?

She gave Minnie a peck on her plump cheek. "Ta-ta, Minnie. I'll return soon."

Knickerbockers for the man were, of course, appropriate. Brendan was wearing a pair and a Norfolk jacket. He grinned when he saw her strolling past the men fishing from the wharf. "I can see I have my work cut out for me."

Looking up into those marvelous green eyes, she felt excitement stir. Why? Because it seemed he was forbidden, taboo? "What do you mean?"

He nodded at her divided skirt. "That. But come along. We'll give it the sporting try. Your parents did give their permission, didn't they, Chevonne?"

That close to him, she noticed again the small scar just below one eye. It was a bond between them. Did he realize that? And why didn't he carry a whangee or malacca walking stick, affected by all proper men his age? Did he enjoy riding and golfing? "They didn't object."

On the boardwalk, he rented a bicycle for two from a vendor, who winked encouragingly at her. "You will learn to ride me bicycle in fast time, eh?"

Following Brendan's instructions, she wasn't so sure. Twice, after swinging her leg over the cross bar to mount the unwieldy thing, she nearly toppled over. Only his quick action saved her from falling headlong on the ground.

When he put his hands around her waist to steady her, a giddiness swept over her. "There you go," he said.

She squealed. "Don't let loose of me!"

He chuckled. "I won't. I'm just getting on behind you." The bicycle teetered precariously. "Put your feet on the pedals."

She did. Then, as if supported by a magic carpet, the bicycle moved forward. The breeze ruffled the shorter curls on her forehead. Free. She was free! She laughed. And laughed again. "I love this!"

Behind her, his laughter joined hers. "Much cooler, isn't it?"

It would have been better without such cumbersome clothes. Still, she felt marvelous. Her senses were acute: the smell of fish, the salty tang of the ocean breeze, the scattering sea gulls, her own sweat, and most of all the energy of Brendan, pouring over her.

The tandem bicycle was alive, as alive as the Dreamtime spirits. It dodged lunchtime strollers, who paused to watch and smile and maybe stare at her exposed ankles. It jumped gaps in the boardwalk and danced over loose sand.

She and Brendan pedaled all the way out to where the boardwalk ended and a bumpy brick road meandered along the hard-packed sand. A bewhiskered walrus snored off to one side. Several shanties, mostly fishing huts and seedy pubs, leaned on one another for support.

Further on, where the road began to narrow and the shanties gave way to sand dunes, Brendan said, "We'd best start back."

She was disappointed, but she nodded her assent. However, when he went to steer the bicycle around, she was unprepared and leaned outward in panic. The bicycle wobbled. He tried to counterbalance her weight but the front wheel veered off the brick pavement and plowed into a sand hill.

She screamed. Sight and sound speeded up. Soaring over the handlebars. Sea gulls screeching. Scrub brush. Scratches. Sand in her mouth and nostrils. Skirts tumbled over her legs.

"Chevonne! Chevonne! Are you all right?"

Dazed, she looked up into Brendan's anguished face. "Yes. I . . . think I am."

He wiped the sand from her cheek. "I should have been ready for something like that. I'm so sorry."

She started laughing. "Wasn't it grand? The most exciting thing that's happened to me since you pushed me from the path of the horse."

He grinned. "You're incredible, Chevonne!"

He bent to give her cheek a healing kiss. Merely a light, affectionate kiss. Something else happened. She turned her face fully to him. Their lips met. And lingered. And explored. He took her upturned face between his hands. "I didn't expect this, Chevonne."

Her lips parted. "You were a friend."

"You were a little girl."

"I want to be your girl."

20

1901

     Trains, trams, and ferries carried thousands of people to the great city of Sydney on the morning of January first. At ten that morning, sunlight scattered the overhanging clouds and a southern breeze rustled in to mitigate the awful heat.

Brendan waited at the main entrance to Centennial Park. Chevonne, covering the day's momentous event for *The Sydney Dispatch,* had told him she would meet him at nine-thirty. He consulted his wristwatch, a gift from her to replace his outdated pocket watch.

"It's the latest thing," she had explained, as if he

had been spending his entire life in the outback. As it was, he was indifferent to fashion. He had only recently begun wearing trousers with waist-bands instead of braces and morning coats in place of frock coats.

It was almost ten o'clock. Where was she?

Participants in the parade were already gather-ing: shearers, who were to lead the procession; swarthy Maoris astride great, lean horses; aborig-ines painted with white clay; and dragoons and lancers of Her Majesty's Imperial Troops. In all seventy-five thousand people were expected to turn out for the inauguration of the Common-wealth of Australia.

"Brendan!"

He turned and saw her across the street, her white-gloved hand raised high. She wore a khaki necktie, popular because of the Boer War. Clutched beneath her other arm was her reporter's pad. Her blond hair had been recently marceled and framed her lovely face in waves.

He had to smile. Ever the New Woman.

A horse-drawn omnibus with people clinging to the open doors passed between him and her. Then, skirt in hand, she was shouldering her way through the revelers toward him. As always, her laughing eyes dazzled him.

"Chevonne, darling!" He wrapped his arms around her remarkably tiny waist and lifted her so that her feet dangled below her flounced skirt and her sweet mouth was on a level with his. He ached to kiss it. Even in that crush of merrymakers, though, someone could recognize them. "I thought I had missed you."

Boldly, she kissed him on the cheek, then drew back with a laugh. "You better have missed me, you rake. I read about you escorting Miss Mary Richards to the Boxing Day Ball."

"One of mother's marital machinations. Did the column say how incredibly bored I was? Did it make any mention about the bloke who accompanied you to the send-off of the Sydney-to-Hobart Yacht Race? Lord Brighton's son, wasn't it?"

Her lips made a moue and she wriggled free to straighten her skirts. "He went with me to the harbor to cover the event. Ryan's suggestion."

"Ahh, yes, your erstwhile employer." He took her arm and steered her through a press of shearers finishing the last touches on their float. The rank odor of sheep mixed with that of human sweat filled the oppressive air. "I think he knows about us, Chevonne. It must be the observant newspaperman in him."

"Mother also suspects, I think."

He could feel Chevonne's uneasiness. It was like that for him and her. Had always been. They sensed each others moods and understood without questions or explanations. "You'll soon be old enough to marry and . . ."

She rounded on him. "I'm weary of waiting and pretending, Brendan. I don't care that my father and your mother are on opposite sides of the business and political spectrum. That has nothing to do with us."

He and Chevonne were wiser now. They knew better than to reveal their love to their parents. "If they knew, they would oppose our marriage. I want their blessing, Chevonne. What I feel for you isn't something tawdry. It's beautiful and pure."

A teasing, slightly naughty look crept into her eyes. She was the practical one to complement his romantic nature. "Are you discounting Melbourne?"

He squeezed her hand, in acknowledgement of that shared memory. After the day of their first kiss three years earlier in Adelaide, the convention delegates had adjourned to Sydney, then to Melbourne, the colonial capital of Victoria.

There, while rowing her down the Yarra, they had pledged their love. Beneath a bridge, in the concealing shadows of a canebrake, she had offered herself to him.

God knew, he had wanted her. Badly. The practically bare breast she had lifted from the parting of her corset for his kiss had excited him beyond control. Almost. Since that day, they both had bloomed in the fullness of that love.

Secret meetings, taking advantage of too few ecstatic moments, love only shared but never consummated. How much longer could he wait?

Forever, if he had to. No other woman was like her. Everything that she encountered excited her. She was reckless and free spirited, with a naïveté that amounted to sophistication. Her laughter banished her fears. Intelligent, beautiful, and compassionate was his love. She belonged to him, and he to her.

"Don't tease like that, Chevonne. What has happened or will happen between us was and always will be true and guileless."

Her expression softened. "I know. 'Tis because of that I love you, Brendan Tremayne. You are honest and strong of heart. My noble knight."

At times, he didn't feel that way. Beyond the upright young man, the paragon of English Victorian virtues, lurked something different. The perceptive Chevonne had remarked on it. "I sometimes detect a frightfully strained air to your self-control, Brendan. As though most of your life is lived against the grain of your nature."

"I have only a couple of hours," he said now. "I promised Mother I would speak on her behalf to the Aborigine Art Society in commemoration of this morning."

"Is NSW Traders closed for the holiday?"

He grimaced. "Everyone's off work but me. Mother is joining Ryan for a yacht party."

"We can watch the parade from your office, then?"

He saw the mischievousness in her eyes. "I swear, Chevonne, if you try to seduce me I shall report you to Magistrate Court, whereupon you will receive twenty lashes for solicit—"

She laughed. "You just want to bare my body."

"For mine eyes only and don't you forget it."

He maneuvered them through the people toward the park's exit closest to NSW Traders' offices. A year ago that month, the first case of bubonic plague in the colony had been registered at The Rocks. As an effort to remove the disease-spreading rats, the government had burnt or demolished most of the buildings. NSW Traders' offices had been rebuilt and were now located further up Argyle Street.

The crowd thinned as he neared the three-story building. Its stooped guard, Rankin, was half blind and feeble, too old to prevent a cat from entering much less a burglar. He had been a loyal employee for years and Annie had kept him on after his trembling hands could no longer use a carpenter's plane.

"Your office, Master Tremayne?" he asked, closing the lift's grilled doors.

"Yes, Rankin. Is your family celebrating this morning?"

The balding head bobbed. "Aye, they are. My eldest grandson is in the choir. He'll be singing 'Oh God Our Hope in Ages Past.'"

"A perfect song for Australia's future," Chevonne said with a smile for the old man.

The caged lift jerked to a stop on the third floor. The impenetrable black of the hallways defeated his sight but not his sense of smell. Her clothes were scented with rose petals; her skin with lavender soap. Hers was the fresh light scent that breathed from the hair of healthy children.

Brendan found the hall light and opened the double mahogany doors. Closing them behind him, he drew her into his arms and began kissing her.

"It's been two months, Chevonne," he whispered between feverish kisses. "Two months since I've been able to hold you without fear of bringing your parents' wrath down on your head."

She captured his face between her hands. "Ahh, my love, you talk far too much." She kissed him. Deeply. Taking his breath away. Boldly, she slipped her tongue between his lips.

He gasped and set her from him. "You are trying my willpower, minx." Tunneling his hand through his hair, he crossed the carpeted office to open the window. "Come, darling. The parade will begin soon."

Below, spectators who could find no space closer to the parade route were gathering. The air, heated as it was, nevertheless tempered somewhat his rampant desire.

She came up behind him and encircled his

waist with her arms. Leaning her cheek against his back, she said, "Don't you know I've been in love since the moment I saw you? I was a child then. I am a woman now. Hold me. Oh, hold me, Brendan. Sometimes it scares me, how happy I am."

His resolve evaporated. He turned and caught her in his arms. "Don't say that. We deserve our happiness. We have done wrong to no one."

Yet that nameless fear, that fear that something could go wrong, shot through him like lightning. Burning, searing, disorienting. His kisses were passionate, out of control. His hands had a will of their own. "Chevonne, Chevonne."

She arched her body into his. He could feel her soft breasts against his rib cage. "Brendan, now. Now."

His hands tore at her bolero jacket. He forced her backward until the arm of the settee brought them up short. And even that would not stop his rampaging desire of her. He pressed her into the settee, fell across her, shoved her skirts up above her garters.

He could hear himself grunting, hear her frenzied panting. Yet if she had cried out for him to stop, he did not know if he could have or would have. Too far gone was he in his frantic need to be one with her.

Above her white hose, his hands encountered flesh. Soft flesh. Willing flesh that parted for him. "Oh, God, Chevonne. I can't . . . I can't help myself."

She pulled his face down to hers. "Make me yours, Brendan," she rasped between wet, wild kisses.

"I don't think that is a wise thing to do."

Brendan jerked around. Ryan stood in the doorway, top hat and cane in hand. Brendan sprang upright, shielding Chevonne's near nakedness. "Get out of here! You have no right to—"

"I'm leaving. First, son, I want your promise you won't go through with this."

He could feel his blood beating against his temples. His fists clenched. "This is none of your business, Ryan." Each word was chopped, barely making it past his choked throat.

"I only ask that you will let reason rule the day. Just for today. If you really love Chevonne, is it too much to ask to wait to consummate this love? If this is love, it's love forever, isn't it?"

He hated the reasonable tone of the older man. Yet he knew what Ryan said made sense. His mother's lover had always been fair with him. Almost like a father, but never intrusive. Until now.

"He's right, Brendan." He heard Chevonne behind him, her voice calm and composed. Then she said, "If you wouldn't mind, Mr. Sheridan, I would like to make myself presentable."

With a rueful smile etched below his mustache, Ryan made half bow. "My apologies, Miss War-wick."

After he took his leave, Brendan sat still, while behind him he heard the rustling of Chevonne's skirts. He rubbed the bridge of his nose. "I shouldn't have let things go this far, Chevonne. Not like this. Not hiding. Not in secrecy."

He felt her hand smoothing the hair at his nape. "Patience, my love. Our time will come."

"You and Daniel are both so blinded by your own enmity that you cannot conceive such a thing could happen! But you can't ignore it any-more!"

Annie watched Ryan pace her office. His malacca cane cut the air like a saber. She couldn't remember seeing him so agitated. Wisely, she said nothing, but waited. Sooner or later his tumbling words would make sense.

"My God, Annie, the electrical charges coursing between Brendan and Chevonne are enough to knock a person off his feet."

She tensed. "What?"

He whirled on her, his raven black eyes as sul-phurous as the fumes of hell. "You heard me. You have been so bloody determined to have your own way in everything. Well, I've been a daggy fool."

"You're saying—"

"I am saying that Brendan and your niece have fallen in love." He stalked to the door, paused, and said, "If it's any consolation, I don't think they've consummated their love. Yet."

She sprang to her feet. "Where are you going?"

His smile was thin. "To get drunk. Maybe it would help wipe my love for you from my thoughts and obliterate my misery."

"Drinking won't help."

"'Tis a damned good start."

A little fear beat at her throat. She swallowed it back. She and Ryan had had their differences before. Surely she could figure out a way to bring him around to understanding.

In the meantime, there was Brendan and Chevonne to deal with. Negotiating the intricacies of relationships, she was learning, was much like knitting. A great deal of patience and lightness of hand was needed, while all the while one continually arranged the strands of yarn into a tight, perfect pattern.

For just an instant, she entertained the thought that she was acting like her grandmother. Just as quickly, she dismissed the thought.

She scribbled a note, asking Brendan to meet her for lunch. At this time of day, Brendan would be working in the foreign accounts department, but it was nothing that he couldn't break free from. He was absolutely sound and reliable and had a flair for finances.

She gave the note to her secretary, James. "I am expecting my son for lunch," she told the thin and balding little man. "We'll take it here."

He peered over his spectacles at her. "What would madam prefer for lunch?"

"Send out to Gray's. Something light." She didn't like doing business on a full stomach. "Fruit chutney and rice and parsley soup."

She was pouring tea when Brendan knocked and entered. Tall and ruggedly handsome, he reminded her of her father. And Dan. She gathered her determination.

"Something up, Mum?" He crossed her office and, hitching up his trousers, settled into the chair opposite the settee. "The Ceylon deal going wobbly on us?"

She placed his cup of tea on the low table between them. "No. Raji Darjeeling is cooperating nicely in the trade negotiations. 'Tis something else."

That little knot of fear rose in her throat again. Why should she be afraid of anything? She had handled the most scheming businessmen, successfully negotiated the most formidable deals, survived the ebb and flow of Australia's capricious economy.

And she had survived Nan's machinations. Was this anything different or greater to fear?

She took a sip of her fragrant tea, and the knot vanished. "I have learned that you and Chevonne are seeing each other."

"Is that a question or a statement, Mum?"

She had to give her son credit. He wasn't easily intimidated. "Both."

"Ryan told you?"

Impatience flickered in the veins at her temples. "Does it matter?"

He didn't pick up the tiny porcelain cup. "I'll turn the question on you. 'Does it matter?' Or better, is this something that should be discussed as we would a business deal? I know both you and her father don't approve of us seeing each other, but this is not between you and her father. It is between Chevonne and—"

"This is not about disapproval." Damn it, her cup was sloshing. She set it down. Now that the moment was here, she had forgotten her carefully prepared words. "It's about family. You and Chevonne are family, Brendan. You're cousins."

He stared at her. "What?"

"Daniel and I are brother and sister." Her hands knotted into fists. She hurried on. "I thought Daniel was dead. For years I had detectives searching for him. He had changed his name. The mustache changed his looks. He had left home the runt of the litter and returned with the build of a Greek wrestler.

"Honest to God, Brendan, I didn't know. Not until just before the day of the Great Maritime Strike, the day you saved Chevonne. I realize I should have said something, but I never suspected anything would come of your meeting with her."

Brendan looked heart-struck. The blood had drained from his tanned face. His pain was her pain. What had she and Daniel done in their bitter feud except hurt innocents?

Her son's jaws clenched. "All these years, you've been practicing a bloody deception. If you had been honest from the start, our love would never have been given the chance to bloom. Well, you and your brother battle your own war. I'm off to join one. It certainly makes more sense than the destruction you two have caused!"

After he stalked from the room, Annie's heart didn't seem to be beating. First Ryan. Now her only child. Both turning on her. She had never wanted to hurt anyone, had gone out of her way to take care of her people at NSW Traders. Was active in numerous charities. And yet, she was losing the two people she loved the most.

She buried her face in her hands and wept as she never had.

"I'm sorry, you're not physically fit."

"I'm what?" Brendan stared at the crusty sergeant behind the paper stacked desk. Had the soldier gone batty? Taken a king hit? "I am a boomer of a young man, and you're telling me I am not fit to go off to war in South Africa? Sixteen thousand Australians are fighting the Boer War, and I'm not physically fit?"

The sergeant's color mottled. "You heard me, son. Your mumsy has taken care of this."

Anger burst through Brendan. He had been hoping—no, wanting—to get killed off there in the Transvaal of South Africa. Instead, he was being told he was doomed to healthiness! He almost laughed at the absurdity of it all. Women were working in munitions factories, and he was told he was unfit!

He whirled around, stomped from the British military office, and didn't stop until he reached that of NSW Traders. A startled James began to rise as Brendan shoved open the doors of Annie Tremayne's outer office. "Master Brendan—"

Brendan didn't pause. Instead of lifting the latch he shoved open his mother's door with his shoulder. Such was his force that the frame yielded, and the door swung open with a bang. His mother jumped to her feet. She was wearing a tweed skirt and jacket with a definitely masculine black tie at the neck of her blouse. He felt his fury erupt all over again.

"Wait, Brendan. Please." She came around her desk, her palm raised in supplication.

"I'm tired of being manipulated by you. I'm leaving. I don't know where I'm going, but it's far away from you and NSW Traders."

There were tears in her eyes. "I don't blame you." She bowed her head, and he saw those tears slip over her cheeks. "I've botched everything," she whispered.

He didn't trust her anymore. Yet he had never seen her cry. His legendary mother was said to be as tough as the outback.

"Will you forgive me, Brendan?" Her voice was so quiet he wasn't sure he heard her. "I'm begging you. I was wrong. I'll do whatever you want. Arrange for you to go off and fight the Dutch Boers if that's what you truly want."

This proud woman humbling herself, was this his mother? This new side of her, this never-expressed softness broke down his resentment. His shoulders slumped. "I don't care."

He hadn't slept in two days. He badly needed a way to forget Chevonne. "I'm so bleeding tired."

"Me, too." She passed the back of her hand over her forehead. "I'm so tired of trying to hold it all together. To make it work. To take care of every-one. And everything. I just want to go home. To rest."

Home. Maybe both of them could find rest there at Dream Time. He had been reeling from the knowledge that Chevonne could never be his. The cruelest trick of fate was that they both loved each other. Maybe distance would alleviate his pain. Alleviate his pain, but not destroy his love for Chevonne Warwick.

BOOK THREE

Up jumped the swagman,
Sprang into the billabong,
"You'll never catch me alive," said he.
And his ghost may be heard
As you pass by that billabong,
"Who'll come a-waltzing Matilda with me?"

BOOK THREE

21

1902

Chevonne stared dully at the *The Sydney Dispatch*. Its headline blasted the British behavior in South Africa as morally indefensible.

Lower on the front page, a column noted that NSW Traders was leading the way in social reform by adopting a minimum wage.

Yet another column noted that the new "Telegraph Act of 1901 ensures that no contract is made for carriage of mails on behalf of the Commonwealth unless only white labor is used."

NSW Traders and their fleet of ships would certainly be complying with the act. By immigration restrictions, deportation, and discriminations such as this, a white Australia was definitely being achieved.

Her father would certainly be incensed by this. But she was weary of trying to placate him. In fact, she was almost disgusted with him and this feud with Brendan's mother which had made love between her and Brendan so difficult.

She put down the newspaper and picked up the oft-read, tear-stained letter. A short, terse letter of love and farewell. Though after a year she knew it by heart, her eyes still lingered over the pen strokes of her beloved:

Dear Chevonne,
 This letter is most painful to write. Although I love you more than I ever thought it possible to love another human, that love would be destroyed by what exists between our families. After much soul-searching, I have decided it better to end our affair now rather than watch it die due to the commonplace and to complacency.
                                                            Brendan

So instead, her heart had died. Whatever beat within her chest was simply an organ.

Both she and Brendan had been aware of the enemity between their families. The simple, and obvious, conclusion was that he had tired of her. She had provided temporary amusement. The feud had made it easy for him. The letter had shown him for what he was. Weak. She didn't know where he was and didn't care.

She experienced no pain anymore. Never again, she knew, would she experience joy either. If exist she must, then she would at least make her own choices. Somehow, she would regain her life.

At the knock on the door, she laid the folded newspaper over Brendan's letter. "Yes?"

"Chevonne? It's me."

Her mother. She put on a hearty smile. A hearty smile that her mother would complain was not matched by a hearty appetite. Just yesterday, her mother had chided her about her apathy at meals. "Soon you shall weigh no more than a bird, Chevonne dear. Please do try the Cheshire pudding."

In the year since she had received that letter from Brendan, she had lost almost a stone. Her eyes were dry and huge in sunken sockets. She knew she looked like a walking cadaver, and she didn't care.

"Come in, Mama."

Her mother closed the door behind her and stood wringing her hands. "You are certain this is what you want to do, dear?"

"Yes." She began folding another skirt. She had volunteered as a nurse's aide and was going off to South Africa and the Boer War.

The door's hinges squeaked as it was opened again. Chevonne whirled back, a petticoat she was packing clutched before her. Her father stood just behind her mother. Confusion and anger and agony passed over his face in successive order.

"I can't let you do this foolish thing," he said.

"You can't stop me from going," she whispered to both her mother and father. "You can't keep me under lock and key forever. I'll find a way."

"Oh, God, Chevonne!" her mother cried. "Look at you. You are wasted."

Her father brushed past her mother and crossed to her, taking her stiff, thin, unyielding body in his arms. "Has it come to this? That you hurt so much that you don't care if you are killed?"

The face she turned up to him was tragic. "Yes. Yes, yes!"

"I forbid you to go."

Her laughter was at once hollow and defiant.

"You would risk death because of this Tremayne bastard? He means more to you than the family?"

"The family! The family! It's because of our damned families that this happened. That's the bloody hell of it, and I am sick of our family. I am sick of you and your feuding!"

He set her from him. His expression was hard and unrelenting. "Then don't come back home."

According to legend, the only indigenous folk who inhabited the Transvaal basin were a group from the great Ashanti kingdom. Led by their queen, they had pushed toward the banks of the

Limpopo River, then known as the Crocodile River.

Querying her priest about the hazards of crossing, the queen had been told that all would go well if she offered a sacrifice. She had sacrificed her own son, crying out "Baouli—the child is dead!" Her descendants gave up their warfare and went on to farm the savanna of the Transvaal basin.

Today, descendants of the Baoulis, black-skinned Bantus, worked for the British and Australian troops along the Limpopo banks. Large, loosely woven wicker baskets filled with laundry sat in the shallower water. The river's gray-green current flowed through the baskets and agitated the dirt from the clothing. An ingenious system.

The half-naked Bantu women beat each article of clothing on the rocks with frenzied motions that resembled the Dipri dance of the Bantu that, ironically, invoked harmony within a tribe or society.

The Anglos could certainly make use of the Dipri. Yesterday's battle on the grassy plains beyond had been a disaster for both the Dutch and the British and their allies. The wounded and dead numbered in the thousands among both the British and Australian soldiers. The Australian soldiers, known as Diggers from the 1851 Australian gold rush, were earning a reputation as front-line fighters.

A short distance from the Limpopo River, white, bell-like tents were pitched amidst the thorn trees that sparsely dotted the valley. Weary men rested on cots or slumped against wagon wheels, mess trunks, or whatever support they could find. No breeze tempered the hot afternoon. The white flag of the Eighteenth Field Hospital tent drooped limply.

After yesterday's battle with the Transvaal Boers, Chevonne worked steadily alongside a nurse in a larger tent that served as a hospital. The doctor, a Scottish gent of the Old Guard and a friend of the visiting author, Dr. Conan Doyle, was treating a British lad for a lacerated calf. The leg was in jeopardy, but with help, luck, and prayer the soldier would fight again.

Near the tent flap lay the body of a British gunner smashed by a Boer shell. Flies swarmed around the carcass as it awaited available orderlies to dispose of it. There had been a serious outbreak of the deadly typhoid. Its victims outnumbered the flies, if that was possible.

A young Australian with a stomach wound hovered near death, and it was over him that Chevonne and the nurse labored. He moaned in delirium. Chevonne figured he couldn't be more than nineteen, her age.

His high, flat cheekbones, though no longer ruddy, reminded her of Brendan. At once and automatically, her mind closed a steel door on the image.

The tent's ventilation was poor. The stench was worse. Sweat dripped from both Chevonne's face and that of Maud's, a vinegary old woman who had cursed many a soldier back to health. "The prig could bloody well die if it was left up to those high and mighty farts we call doctors. The Bantus got more sense."

She slapped a gauze pad over the wound to stop the flow. Mechanically, Chevonne began binding the bandage. A field dressing seemed so futile. "So what poultice have you concocted this time without the doctor's knowledge?"

The old woman grinned. She was missing a lower front tooth. Probably more, if Chevonne were to risk peering in that cavernous mouth. "One of the Bantu wenches showed me how to mix a poultice. Kaolin, herbs, and raw eggs should either kill the vermin or the victim."

"Raw eggs?" Chevonne gagged, then swallowed. Strange, she could endure all sorts of horrendous rendings of the human body—an eye hanging from its socket or bloody intestines cradled in the victim's arm—but the thought of raw eggs could turn her stomach.

Not that the fare with the Third Grenadier Guards and the Second Dublin Fusiliers was that magnificent. She suspected that horse meat was on the menu. Certainly cast-iron bread was.

Thinking of Christmas dinners back at home, her imagination ran wild: mutton, pork, duck, plum pudding, currants, wines and spirits. Her mother had brought her own American traditions of Christmas food to the household—roasted turkey, home-cured ham, and preserves. She had even used the Christmas bush in place of the American holly for decoration.

Smiling, Chevonne recalled how appalled her mother was at the Christmas game of snapdragon. Raisins were plucked from a bowl of burning brandy and popped into the mouth. Her father had almost caught his mustache on fire once, and everyone had laughed.

Then her smile faded at another memory, her father's last words to her.

"Are we finished? I really do need some fresh air."

Maud cackled. "Queasy are we now? A grand help ye be. Go on with yeself. I'll tackle cleaning the bloke's privates meself with no help from lusty young lassies. How else can I enjoy what me body is too old to remember?"

Humor, perverted though it might be, was the only way one got through a war. At least, that was Chevonne's judgment of such indiscriminate killing. "If the wound doesn't kill the soldier, Maud, your sexual manipulations will."

Another wicked grin and a delightfully wheezy laugh. "Ahh, but the prig will die happy!"

Chevonne left the tent. The sun was going down. This was the best time of the day. At five thousand feet above sea level the evenings were cool, with a breeze coming down off the highlands to sweep across the veld.

She stood still, feeling the breeze's fingers lift

the damp tendrils around her face. Her stiff cotton blouse was ringed with wet splotches beneath her armpits.

Above her, feathers of white streaked a vivid blue sky. Nearby, flamingoes and long-horned gemsboks gazed warily across at one another from opposite sides of the Limpopo. Farther out, immense silhouettes that could only be elephants trudged single file across the veld.

One might conveniently forget that eight thousand men were camped within cannon shot, if one blocked out the immediate noise and sights.

Nearby, a First Scots Guard major was taking a bath in a tin tub of heated water. His gangly legs hung over its rim. He still wore his khaki helmet with its small colored badge that distinguished the various battalions.

Conical tents were everywhere. On a field where the men usually drilled, officers were playing polo.

The scene was hardly that of the dashing gallantry of the poems about the Great Boer War that Rudyard Kipling was currently penning for the British newspapers.

In front of a covered wagon, British soldiers knelt in preparation for kit inspection. They were oblivious to the flogging of an African tied to a cannon's wagon wheel close by.

Chevonne's stomach churned, and she set off on a fast walk. Troopers in slouch hats and leather leggings rode by to the accompaniment of the creak of saddles and the clanking of swords. Their captain was shouting, "Dress by the left!" and "Bugler!"

She hurried on, past a baggage train and its mounted Gatling gun. The accoutrements of killing were everywhere she looked: revolvers, bayonets, Martini-Metford rifles.

She wandered down to her favorite spot, a bend in the river that had formed a limestone cliff. It was quite a walk from camp, but the hollow shielded one from the view of prying eyes.

The damp sand softened her footsteps. With a weary sigh, she sank to the ground. First her right boot, then the left came off, and her toes squished into the warm, sugary earth. Tucked within her sleeve was a khaki handkerchief, which she withdrew to soak in the water's edge. About her sleeve was an arm band with its Red Cross design.

She used the kerchief to dampen her neck, then closed her eyes and tilted back her head to listen to the soothing lap of the water.

"Cigarette?"

She turned and shielded her eyes with her hand. The sand had silenced the approach of the American mercenary, Thomas Meyers. Transvaal's fabled goldfields had originally lured him to South Africa, but he now acted as a scout for the military since his knowledge of the area was far more detailed than any of their maps. He wore khakis and a slouch hat. A pair of field glasses was suspended from his neck.

"How did you guess?"

"That you wanted a cigarette?"

"No. That I was here."

"My Lady of the Lamp comes here often after you've finished in surgery." He hunkered on one knee a little distance away. He was of average height and of solid build.

She studied the American. She didn't know how old he was, maybe thirty or so, but the weather had take its toll of his face. His skin was burnt, and wrinkles bracketed his light blue eyes. The intense sunlight had bleached his hair. Disillusionment had pleated deep grooves at either side of his mouth.

"I've noticed you watching me, Mr. Meyers. Do I need to be concerned?"

"Thomas." He passed her one of his rolled cigarettes. "There doesn't seem to be much that bothers you. I doubt I could."

"Not with five hundred soldiers within shouting distance." She knew that of late she was so unkempt that she looked like Medusa, but being one of the very few white women, and young at that, bestowed on her incredible beauty in the soldiers' eyes.

She inclined her head and inhaled as he bent and lit her cigarette for her. He was right. There wasn't much that bothered her. Not even the smell of her own sweat.

The man smelled, too. Men smelled different

than women. This was one of the many things she had learned in the numbing span of the last year and a half.

She had matured immeasurably during this time, and had even taken up the disgusting habit of smoking. Her parents would be horrified. She tilted her face to the cotton-puffed evening sky and exhaled slowly. "God, a cigarette can make such a difference between mere existence and creature comfort."

He lit up his own cigarette and without removing it from between his stringent lips, said, "A tankard of beer would work just as well."

A dry smile curved the ends of her mouth. "Know of a nearby pub?"

His eyes narrowed as he peered at her through the haze of his cigarette smoke. "Great one at Kimberly. The fucking Dutch held us pinned in the town for a hundred and twenty three days. The Kings Cross seemed as good a place as any to while away the time and lose the mind in round after round of rum."

"If you get out of all this, what do you plan to do next? Mine the nearby diamond fields?"

He fixed her with those piercing pale blue eyes. His was the unswerving stare of a collector of rare antiques. "Oh, I will get out. My kind always does. We don't let things like morals or ethics stand in our way of surviving. As to what will I do? Follow you."

22

1904

The dress was of white satin, high-necked, with a train. A white lace veil fell well below her knees.

What did it matter? Her love for Brendan was hopeless. Why shouldn't she go ahead and make a life of her own? He had, from what she had heard since her return. He was making Dream Time a model station. He was making it his life.

Only a few selected family friends were to be at her wedding, which was to be held in a small Anglican chapel in a Sydney suburb that coming autumn. Four more months and she would be married.

Brendan had talked of being married in a bush

church. His soul belonged to the outback, among its trees and creeks, whose scent and shade and deep voice had also become a part of his very soul.

Was she?

Chevonne's father would not be among the few somber guests. Had she invited him, she knew he would have refused to come.

She also knew his stubborn refusal to have anything to do with her tore her mother's heart apart. Her mother wanted to unite the two she loved most.

Even Annie Tremayne, not wanting to add any possible dissension, had let Louisa know that, out of respect for the happiness of the bride and groom, she would not attend the wedding.

"I'll take the dress," Chevonne told the modiste, who bobbed her head in pleasure. To provide the dress for the daughter of the influential Dan Warwick was a coup.

Chevonne tilted her head higher as she joined her fiancé for tea later that afternoon at Bridgebain's, a fashionable tea room in the Wooloomooloo section of Sydney. Tom's body did not appear as stocky in his striped frock coat faced with silk. His double-breasted waistcoat of light color and a dark tie marked him as a man of ambitions.

He beamed at her as if she were some incredible beauty. She supposed she was. An austere beauty, her mother had said.

Chevonne had come back from the Boer War tempered by fire. Her inner strength was her beauty. Certainly, her mirror reflected what fashion of the day dictated as beautiful: tall and energetic, in spite of a nineteen-inch waist; youthful skin with the golden glow of health; haunting diamond blue eyes; hair gilded by South Africa's intense sunlight.

She had held out against Tom's low-key persistence. She was certainly aware of the rumors circulating that he was marrying her for her wealth and position. Doubtlessly they had an element of truth.

What had won her in the end was the knowledge that the swaggering Tom Meyers would always be there for her, always steadfast. Steadfast to the point of working only cursorily as a wool factor for several New South Wales sheep stations. He was a grand talker and quick thinker, so when he did negotiate between station owner and commodity markets worldwide, he was quite successful.

On the other hand, she was restless. She had enrolled at the university, but the challenge didn't assuage the emptiness gnawing at her.

Without being aware of it, she was nodding mindlessly at something he was telling her now. All the while, she had barely tasted her tea. Her hand lay lifelessly beside her porcelain cup.

With a tenderness that was not customary for him, he took her hand and kissed the back of it.

"Your flesh is icy. I won't let it stay that way."

She shivered—and realized that she hadn't done so in the thrill of anticipation. Nevertheless, his low laughter repelled her and excited her all at the same time.

Brendan, too, was restless. He had been ever since that moment when his mother had destroyed his dreams, broken his heart.

Oh, he had made a name for himself by revolutionizing the sheep industry. From that day when he had retreated to Dream Time to lick his wounds, he had thrown himself headlong into revamping the sheep station's outdated operation.

During the past two years he had introduced new shearing mechanization and selective breeding. He had finished fencing off one of his runs that covered 250 square kilometers. Where he had had to employ thirteen shepherds and six hutkeepers, he now could manage with six boundary riders after the run had been fenced into paddocks with barbed wire.

He had drilled artesian bores and mounted more windmills. In two of his bores water had surfaced under its own pressure at the boiling point. He had set up refrigerated butcher works at his various runs. This meant that he no longer had to hire drovers to drive his sheep to domestic markets or ports for export.

Yet in all this time, he yearned for more than Dream Time to occupy his enterprising mind.

One thing almost accomplished that, something he had not thought he would be interested in at the tender age of twenty-one, when he had abandoned his interest in relationships, especially those concerning the opposite sex.

Without Chevonne of the laughing eyes, he had no desire.

That was before Lisell entered his life. When first he saw her, he had spared little attention for her. She had arrived with her father, a trained assistant on one of the new mechanized shearing teams. Her father, Hassam Ali, was from Khartoum and had settled in Melbourne, marrying an Irish maid.

The result was the exotic beauty, eighteen-year-old Lisell with dark, sultry eyes, rosy cheeks and pouty lips, and flaming red hair that reminded him of his mother's, though Lisell was smaller in stature and more rounded, more lush, and lacked his mother's quick mind and keen insight.

Lisell Ali did, however, have laughing eyes. And it was that that had captured his attention, however briefly, over the ensuing months. Once, out of curiosity, he had made it a point to talk to her and had discovered both her drollery and her lack of imagination.

"Do you have any interest in furthering your education?" he had asked that first time they talked. A woman's college had just opened in Melbourne.

Lisell's father and several others from the shearing team were busy wielding the clipping machine. It was so loud, with all the pulleys and cords and blades snapping and buzzing, that he had had to repeat his question.

"Lordy, no, Master Brendan." Her smile was captivating. "I never learned how to spell. The teacher kept changing the words."

He tempered his surprise with a smile. "You didn't like school?" They both had to raise their voices in order to be heard.

She stood on tiptoe and put her mouth close to his ear. "Not at all. I cannot read or write, and the teachers won't let me talk."

This time he laughed aloud.

"I can do my sums," she offered. "Me da taught me. But English has come hard for him."

"And your mother?"

"She up and died with consumption back in Ireland. I was taken down with it, too. That's how me da and me came to Australia. To take the cure. The sun, you know."

"Then we'll have to further your education. Our tutor here at Dream Time can teach you the intricacies of spelling, as well as reading and writing."

"Well, thank ye, now." She bussed him on his jaw, smiled saucily, then sashayed away.

Bemused, he watched her brown homespun skirt sway enticingly with her sinuous walk. When he turned back to the shearing, her father was watching him. In those dark eyes, Brendan saw the gleam of profit.

Yes, he would be a miraculous catch for the man's daughter. But he did not plan to be caught, not now or ever.

What he did not count on was the power of sheer sex. For a man of almost twenty-three, he was prime for that explosion of the senses. Other men his age had already discovered that marvelous attraction in their teenage years, but Brendan had restrained himself because of Chevonne.

Lisell inducted him into the exquisite, sustaining pleasures of sex. Oh, he had had those occasional liaisons conducted for physical relief, but he had always come away feeling drained and dissatisfied. Neither he nor his partners had any idea of the joy that came with the art of dallying.

So Lisell learned to spell, and he learned to dally. To take his time, to appreciate the finer aspects of the female body, to communicate through the tongue and fingertips as well as the penis.

They lay in clover that greened the bank of the Wooloomooloo Creek at that part that was shielded from the blistering afternoon sun—and nosy people. Those station people seeking the pleasure of water were not likely to wander in the direction of the clovered bank, where the water ran muddier.

"Brendan, me dearest, ye must not be in such a hurry. 'Tis a grand passion ye have, but ye spend it far too quickly." Absently, Lisell tangled her forefinger in the short, crisp hair whorling at his left nipple.

Eyes closed, his hands were clasped behind his head. The smell of green plants and of lovemaking was in his nostrils. "That's easy enough for you, my lusty wench. You do not have to resurrect a body part in order to experience that grand passion."

He felt her lips close over his flaccid member, and he gave a start, and then relaxed and allowed himself to enjoy her ministrations.

She deserted his hardening flesh for a moment. He heard the impishness in her next words. "See, me lad, it is not that hard to raise the dead."

His hands snaked out to manacle her wrists. "You blaspheme," he growled. Then he tugged her up over him. "Now ride me as a penance."

Her seating was impeccable.

Chevonne's fascination with her unorthodox fiancé eventually waned. Or maybe it was just that she was finally coming to terms with the knowledge that she would never be able to love anyone but Brendan.

Damn his bloody soul.

Why hadn't she seen Tom as a boorish bludger, a man who hadn't wanted common work and who had fallen into bonzer luck by becoming engaged to an heiress?

With great dread, she broke off the engagement. As it turned out, confronting Tom had been incredibly easy. It was amazing what a little money could buy. Even a man's honor. She doubted that Meyers would pop up again. The American's bruised male ego would be unable to admit publicly that a woman had rejected him.

For a while, she tried involving herself in domesticity. With the loyal and vigilant Minnie, she had moved into the tightly packed mass of terrace houses tumbling up and down the steeply sloping streets of Paddington, a fashionable Sydney suburb.

The area had originally been built for aspiring artisans at the turn of the century. Chevonne's house was of 1840s Georgian architecture and required quite a bit of restoration. She soon tired of the project. Bored and fitful, she sought distraction in the one subject that had always attracted her interest. Had not her mother and father and even Annie Tremayne paved the way for her interest in politics?

Naturally, Chevonne chose to run for office. She never did anything halfway.

Naturally, she campaigned for a seat in the state Parliament in her father's opposition party, the Conservative Party.

She began a grass-roots campaign that took her

from one end of the state of New South Wales to the other. An old buckboard and once a cream-colored mule served as her modes of transportation, depending on what the terrain demanded.

For the first time, she was selling herself, her word, her integrity. It was not easy. All that summer and fall and into the new year of 1904, she crisscrossed the Snowy and Blue mountains. She traveled back and forth between the beaches of the Tasman Sea, the plains beyond the Great Dividing Range, and the dry and barren outback. Bushwalking, busy tongues said of her.

She shook hands with the blood-splattered slaughtermen at a meat-packing company.

She went down into the mines at the Zinc Corporation, one of her late grandfather's own mines, with a miner who had paid a high price: three of his relatives killed in the mines.

She shot a game of snooker with a major general at the Imperial Service Club for active and retired military. She was the first woman to flout tradition and enter a gentleman's club.

She lawn bowled with matrons from Newcastle, not only a game but a ritual that required white ducks, dresses, and sun hats.

She helped break horses with a jilleroo and laughed with good humor at her own inadequacy.

She found out a lot about people. Her people. Australians. Unnecessarily modest, they became fierce when prodded. They were a people with appealing candor and directness. The males respected women, certainly, pursued them, even, yet treated them with an almost masculine camaraderie.

Her people were tough, ambitious, visionary, and resilient. She saw these qualities in them and was blind to them in herself.

She found out also that she could not give up her goal to be a politician if she wanted to. She did not want to, of course, but there was a yoke of responsibility that attached itself to her like a tick the minute someone agreed to trust her with their vote.

So no one was astonished when the beauty won a seat in Parliament, least of all her mother and Annie.

At the victory celebration in her small house, she felt outside herself, unable to join in with the gaiety of the people who had campaigned for her. She smiled mechanically as the two dozen other people in her parlor, personal friends and supporters, raised their glasses with chants of "Here, here!"

"Your eyes aren't smiling, Chevonne."

She turned to find her mother at her side. Louisa was a most intuitive woman, and Chevonne had learned that evasion only made her more the fool. As her gaze moved over the revelers, she said in a voice barely above a whisper, "I still love him, Mother."

Her mother didn't have to ask who. She sighed. "I loved Dan, but I don't think he really loved me at the time. But I was lucky. He married me anyway."

Chevonne glanced at her mother. She looked tired. She had worked ceaselessly in her daughter's behalf during the campaign. "I envy your love for each other, Mother. I suppose only the fortunate few are blessed by the gods."

"At the moment, I could gladly thrash Dan for not being here to share your joy—your victory—with us. Why don't you try to reconcile with him, Chevonne? He's had a hard life. He doesn't understand that—"

"Mama, no. Not tonight. Leave be." God, she felt tired. She downed her champagne and held out the flute for a refill. Maybe the nectar of oblivion could make her forget Brendan. But she knew that would never be possible. Not in all her lifetime.

Tongues of flame snapped in the fireplace and kept at bay July's nasty winter wind and sleet. Annie propped her bare feet on the footstool and let the smoke from the cheroot curl from her lips in one continuous spiral. "'Tis a grand pastime you've shown me, Ryan. I should have taken up smoking much sooner."

From his comfortable wing chair opposite the settee where she sat, he gave her one of his slow smiles. His cigar smoke drifted dreamily in the air. "Don't waste time with regrets, Annie. You never have been that sort of person."

"I do more and more now."

"Dwell on the things you've done right."

"Brendan is one of those things. I feel that time and distance have accomplished the healing of his wounded heart. He has earned respect in his own right by revolutionizing the sheep industry. I think he's ready to take full run of the company."

At last, she was truly happy. Almost. If only she could somehow as easily finagle a happy future for Brendan as she had so easily finagled her business deals. But from all she had learned from Nan, one thing stood out the most—you don't try to run other people's lives. Least of all, those you love the most.

Ryan's arrow-straight brows raised. Like his black hair, they, too, were interspersed with gray. "You think that wise? Bringing Brendan back?"

"You don't think he could handle NSW Traders alone? I've kept him posted on every department. He knows the company inside and out. Almost as well as I."

"It wasn't NSW Traders I was talking about. As ever, your mind runs first to business," he chided gently. "I was talking about Chevonne. Putting Brendan at the head of NSW Traders would mean bringing him back to Sydney. He would be bound to cross paths with her."

She managed a shrug. "It has to happen sometime. Only when the two face their situation can they put it behind them."

Annie had more than one reason for relinquishing the tight reins she had kept on NSW Traders over the years. She was beginning to realize that life was passing by her, that she wanted to escape more often to Dream Time.

There was yet another reason: Ryan. She peered at him through the haze of her smoke. A full fourteen years older than her forty-eight, he was not in the best of health. He coughed more often. His step had slowed. His once high Irish color had faded to a grayish pink.

"Marry me, Ryan?"

He paused in lighting his cigar. His eyes narrowed. "What?"

Her pulse beat rapidly in her throat. What if he refused her? "You yourself said not to waste time in regrets. I regret not marrying you when you first asked me. And I'm not going to let that regret continue. I'm going to rectify my mistake. I want you to marry me."

He relit his cigar, then said, "All your adult life you've controlled, Annie. Controlled everything and everyone but me. One thing you can't do is command me to marry you."

Her heart was smote by his casual tone. Her words came out in broken, childlike desperation. "But I love you."

His smile was wry. "I know that. And I love you, too. With every particle of my body. Always have and always will. Till my last breath."

"Then . . ."

"Why won't I marry you?" He placed his cigar on the ashtray. "Because I won't be controlled. They tried to do that to me in Ireland, Annie. That's why I immigrated to Australia. That's what Australia is all about. That's what I am all about. I thought you were smart enough to understand that. I've been waiting, hoping you would some day."

She stubbed out her cheroot in the ashtray. "I do. I do. What would it take to convince you of that?"

"For one, just listen to yourself. Your tone, your words are partially entreating yet partially authoritarian. As if you're still clinging to that vestige of control. Have you become a duplicate of your grandmother?"

She shuddered. "Oh, God, I hope not." Laying her head against a pillow on the settee, she closed her eyes and breathed deeply. "If I change?" Her words were like the sigh of the wind outside.

"As a smith of words, Annie, I know how insubstantial they are. You would have to prove to me your surrender of the need to be in charge. Aye, I want your total surrender."

She watched him through the fringe of her lashes. "What do you mean?"

His grin made him look youthful. "Seduce me. Make love to me. That's a beginning. I'll let you know after that."

She wanted to chuck the pillow at him. Instead, she was caught up in the tension he had established.

Rising from the settee, she crossed the few steps separating her from him and stopped just a hands-breadth from his knees. Slowly, her fingers worked loose each of the myriad buttons running single file down the length of her princess-style tea gown of rich green sateen. The lace flounce at its hem, matching the cascade of lace trimming round the neck, parted to reveal her shapely calves, then long length of thigh.

She was pleased by the flare of Ryan's eyes. "Now what?"

"I think you know," he said, his voice low, his expression almost predatory. "If you don't, you better learn to improvise."

The gown slid all the way to the floor. Ryan's gaze never left her face. She felt unnerved. Gathering her courage, she brazenly sank to her knees before him and began working the buttons of his fly. When his penis sprang free, she bent her head and her mouth over him. His gasp was reward enough.

The taste of him was bittersweet and exciting. Smiling like the sensual feline she had only lately discovered she could be, she looked up at him through her veil of lashes. "Now, sire, will you marry me?"

He captured her face between his hands and leaned to kiss her lips. "I think you may convince me," he whispered. "But further exploration of the situation is in order." He grasped her naked breasts in each of his hands. "Take me to your bed, madam."

23

1909

Guy Fawkes Day, November 5th, was usually warm and beautiful in Australia, but this Guy Fawkes was rainy and muggy. A most miserable day to have a funeral. Or maybe a most appropriate day.

More people than Brendan would have expected attended Louisa Warwick's funeral. Of course, one would expect a large turnout for the wife of a Parliament member. But her active participation in the women's movement had earned her a measure of respect not usually accorded women in that mateship society.

Her interment in the hollowed ground of Mrs.

Macquarie's Point was evidence of this. The place had been an established lookout point since 1810 when Governor Macquarie's wife had a stone chair hewn in the rock at the end of the point, where she would watch for ships entering the harbor.

A perfect resting place for Louisa, Brendan thought. Some nameless female disease was said to have shortened her full life.

He bowed his head in the dismal drizzle, along with the twoscore mourners as the coffin was lowered into the ground. He stood apart from the others, sheltered by a large fig tree. His hands were jammed in his ulster pockets. His homburg dripped with its collection of rain droplets, and his ascot was damper than a Turkish bath towel.

From his isolated viewpoint, he could watch the mourners. His gaze clung to the tall, slender woman nearest the grave. The rain had drenched her black crepe tubular skirt and its lightweight jacket that reached the knees. She looked like one of the lithe, nubile females on an ancient Grecian urn. Her gilt-colored hair was drawn into a clumsy knot at her nape beneath the turned-down brim of her black hat and veil.

On the other side of the cavernous pit, opposite her, stood Dan Warwick. Even taller than his daughter, he still seemed as formidable as he had been when Brendan was but a boy.

Although Nan, Annie, and even he had built an almost impregnable enterprise in NSW Traders,

Dan continued to chip away at it steadily by sponsoring legislative acts and implementing other business tactics aimed at undermining the company.

Meanwhile, Chevonne had earned a reputation as an excellent state politician. Her record showed that three times she had either abstained from voting for or opposed bills that would have legislated acts damaging to the shipping industry. Doubtlessly, her position on this issue inflamed her relationship with her father even further.

Brendan waited until the minister finished praying and the mourners drifted away. Chevonne and her father exchanged a few words, and then he, too, departed for the Model A idling at the side of Mrs. Macquarie Road.

The last of the mourners gawked as his driver, uniformed in goggles and duster, got out and cranked up the automobile imported from America.

This diversion gave Brendan an opportunity he had not counted on: the chance to be alone with Chevonne. If he discounted the presence of his mother and Ryan, now finally married, who were consoling her.

When his mother saw him crossing the grass toward her, she gave a soft cry. "Brendan! I didn't know if you had gotten my message about the funeral time."

He kissed his mother on the cheek. Her eyes were red and teary. "I did." He shook hands with Ryan. "Good afternoon, sir."

Brendan's path rarely crossed that of his mother and Ryan. After she brought him back to Sydney to head up NSW Traders, she and Ryan practically vanished. Either they were off seeking the pastoral pleasures of Dream Time, or they were caught up in social and political reforms that ranged from charity balls to serving soup lines made up of the luckless cobbers down at The Rocks.

At last, he turned to Chevonne. Even though they lived in the same city, they had managed not to see each other, except at a distance.

He could barely see her eyes behind the heavy veil, but he knew they were not those laughing eyes of their youth. From the rumors he had heard, she hadn't laughed in a long time. Not since she had gone off to the Boer War.

"Brought back a bloke that wasn't dinkum, she did. He would have sucked dry her inheritance. A cudger if ever there was one." "Made life hell for her, 'tis said. Seeing other women on the side." "Lucky for her she got rid of the blooming Yank before they said the vows."

It didn't matter that Brendan couldn't see Chevonne's face distinctly. The air between them was still charged. At twenty-seven, he knew there would never be another woman for him. Other women came and went in his life. None would ever be permanent.

"How are you, Chevonne?" he asked quietly. "I know this must be a very difficult day for you."

"Yes." Her lips quivered. How he wanted to kiss them, to hold her, to take care of her. She must be weary. All these years of carrying on, carrying through. If only. If only . . .

His mother and stepfather exchanged communicative glances, said their good-byes, and slipped away.

He took Chevonne's hand. It felt like a natural thing to do. Her hand felt so right in his. "I'm sorry about your mother. I admired her."

"She went so quickly." Her voice was tremulous. "I didn't even get to let her know how much I really loved her."

His own tongue was tied with the love he couldn't express.

With tacit agreement, she and Brendan turned their footsteps toward the lookout. Her sweet scent of lavender and orange blossoms reached him.

"How is your father taking your mother's death? He always seems so stalwart."

"Hard. I think he depended on her more than he realized. She was there for him when he needed to be loved as well as when he needed to vent his wrath at some fool politician. She understood him so well."

"How is it between you two? You and your father?"

"He has never been fully able to open himself to others, to let down the wall he has built. But the morning Mama died, he sent for me, asked me to help him pick out the dress for her burial. I think he wants to reestablish our relationship, albeit a wary one."

They stopped at the overlook. The surf thundered below. Beyond, the Tasman Sea was lost in the fog. "I want that, too, Chevonne. I want to reestablish our relationship."

Her hand trembled in his. She didn't speak, and he couldn't see her expression. He lifted her veil and smoothed it back over the brim of her hat. *Oh, God, those marvelous eyes.* They glistened now. "Maybe not like before. But I need you in my life. I need you as my friend."

She nodded. Her lips quivered. "Me, too."

He squashed the gut-wrenching temptation to kiss her. It was the hardest thing he had ever had to do. Instead, he tore the veil from her hat in one rip. Her mouth opened in surprise, and he stuffed the netting in her free hand. "Don't ever hide your eyes from me. Shall we go back now?"

For one horrible moment, he thought, nay feared, she was going to throw her arms around him. All his control would have vanished. All hope of sanity, salvation, heaven, would have been dashed. Then she nodded again, withdrew her hand from his, and turned her steps back to the waiting carriage in a brisk walk.

He lay in bed that night, wanting her as he had never wanted her before. The promise of the girl had found realization in the woman. Why had he been allowed to sample the heavenly fruit, then been denied all taste of it forever afterward?

His hands curled into the sheets. Sweating, he rose and walked naked to the window to open it. Rain pelted his body, cooling only its exterior. Inside, a wildfire raged. What was he to do with the rest of his life?

He closed the window and turned back to his bed. Yet he found himself pacing the confines of his bedroom, his thoughts keeping time with his feet. Short, staccato steps. Short, staccato thoughts.

He loved Chevonne. Therefore, her best interests had to come first. She could never be his in this world. But he could see that what he did do didn't make her unhappy. What the hell could he do, damn it? Leave her alone. Stay busy. Work.

Work he did. From that moment on, he devoted himself entirely to directing NSW Traders' interests, a lonely but rewarding task. Besides replacing his iron-clad ships with steel, strong and lighter than iron, he floated the Broken Ridge Steel Works for a percentage of the company. The first open hearth steel in New South Wales was poured that year.

His biggest accomplishment was inspired by that afternoon at Louisa's funeral, when the mourners had stopped to gawk at Dan's Model T. Imported from America.

Why import?

Brendan set out to negotiate a fifty-fifty deal with the Americans and established the Chevrolet-Tremayne Automobile Works. The automotive assembly line was the first of its kind in Australia.

Brendan was hailed as a young industrial genius. And probably damned by Dan Warwick.

All Brendan's mental and physical fatigue, however, didn't keep him from seeing Chevonne's face in every woman. He yearned for her ever . . . his yearning as old as her absence but each moment new.

24

1914

 Moira MacInnes was a young socialite and Chevonne's good friend and political supporter. Sensual, attractive, intelligent, Moira also was blessed with the ability to focus intense attention on whatever project interested her at the moment.

When Brendan realized that he was the present object of her interest, the discovery was mildly pleasing to his male vanity. That and nothing more.

The vivacious brunette was hostessing a ball to raise funds for Chevonne's bid for reelection, this time for a seat in the new Liberal Party. Over two hundred of Sydney's most prominent citizens had been invited to the fund raiser held at the Queen

Victoria Building, built in the style of a Byzantine palace a decade earlier.

Naturally, as one of the more prominent citizens, he had received one of the engraved invitations. The fact that he was also Australia's most eligible bachelor doubtlessly added immeasurably to Moira's warm greeting in the receiving line.

When he came to Chevonne in the receiving line, he felt only a numbness. For too many years, he had reminded himself that she was his cousin. That that was all she could ever be to him.

Dressed in pearl gray beaded satin, with a décolletage low off the shoulders, and long, pale pink gloves, she appeared ethereal. Her golden hair was swept up off her neck in a cascade of ringlets.

He bowed low over her gloved hand and moved along the receiving line to her escort, a sandy-haired man with pale gray eyes. The Scots poet laureate, Bruce McClenden, wore a smirk that irritated Brendan, and he didn't think his irritation really had that much to do with the fact that he was said to be courting Chevonne.

Later, in the sea of bodies, Chevonne passed near him. Like a wave, they crested together for a magical moment. He managed to drop a careless kiss on her cheek. "Hello, Chevonne."

Their gazes locked. She smiled. A polite smile. "Hello, Brendan."

He ached to kiss that white neck that held her

head at such a regal angle. Kiss that slender, grace-ful column where her rapidly beating pulse betrayed her awareness of him.

Then she was whisked away again into another circle of admirers. But that careless kiss had ignited the sleeping flames of his unrequited passion.

McClenden cornered him later, pressing a glass of wine on him. "Red Renella from the famous vineyards south of Adelaide on the Fleurieu Penin-sula. You Australians go all out here, Tremayne. Nothing imported. Not even French wine. No, sir. Chevonne believes in protecting your national interests."

"I commend her." He downed the wine in one gulp. Fortunately, McClenden was soon tugged away by someone else.

"Not fond of the Scottish chap, are you?" Moira asked later, handing him another glass from the tray of a passing waiter.

Brendan raised a brow. "I was that obvious?"

She laughed. She had perfect white teeth. Her almond-shaped brown eyes were daring. "No. McClenden has that effect on everyone. What Chevonne sees in the bloke amazes us."

He finished the wine. "Chemistry, maybe." He signaled for another glass from a nearby waiter. He was drinking far too much, he knew. What did it matter? What did anything matter?

Her eyes sparkled. "Ahh, yes. Chemistry. That inexplicable tug of the passions."

He barely tasted the wine. "Tug? How about combustion? Explosion strong enough to destruct any chemistry lab?"

She laughed. Her lips were wet with wine. "The way you make it sound, I can almost understand how chemistry could drive one to abandon all propriety for the chance to experience a passion beyond the commonplace. That rare passion that involves all the senses, that is so consuming that all else is forgotten."

Her words, huskily spoken, aroused him, but it was in search of Chevonne that his gaze turned.

She was deep in conversation with an elderly man, Joseph Chamberlain. He was the British Secretary of State for the Commonwealth.

Brendan excused himself to Moira, saying, "I would like to bend Chevonne's ear on the need to encourage foreign capitalists to continue investing in Australia."

He had to give Moira due credit. She smiled serenely. "If Chevonne is elected and the Liberals win an absolute majority in the House and Senate, you can count on her full support—as long as native industry is protected against European, American, and Asiatic competition."

It wasn't protective tariffs or foreign capital he wanted to discuss with Chevonne. By the time he reached her side, she was conversing with a high court judge. Brendan simply said, "I have a message for you," and leaned down to whisper, "Come with me."

She didn't ask where. She never glanced to see if anyone was watching or considered what anyone may have thought. She turned back to the judge and said, "Something has come up. Will you please excuse me?"

Without touching, they both left the ballroom. Outside in the hall, he took her gloved hand. "You know what I want?"

Her black-fringed eyes were inordinately large. "Yes."

He drew her down the gaslit hallway. The building had not yet been refurbished with electric lights. Women complained that the electric ones were not as flattering to the skin. He thought Chevonne's looked incredibly lovely.

Together they ascended the carpeted staircase to a floor of suites used as offices. His commodities broker occupied one. Had none of the dozen doors been unlocked, Brendan would have broken one down. Nothing was going to stop him now.

The first one he tried yielded. Gaslight from the hall filtered into the darkened office. Bypassing the desk and credenza, he went directly to the balcony doors off the main office and opened them. The fresh November air did not restore his senses, but rather excited them.

He turned and, pulling Chevonne along with him out onto the wrought-iron balcony, caught her up against him. He inhaled her scent. It flowed throughout his body, heating his blood, clouding his judgment. Only her. There existed only her. "Only you." He didn't realize he was murmuring the phrase as he covered her upturned face in kisses.

His fingers tore loose her sun-streaked tresses and they spilled over her naked shoulders. His lips followed her locks, bestowing kisses on her shoulders and that portion of her breasts exposed by her square décolletage.

She clasped his head to her. Her fingers tunneled through his hair. "Oh, God, Brendan, it's been awful, this wanting of you."

His fingers, fumbling with the urgency of all those years of restraint, unhooked the buttons down her back. Her dress, then her corset, gave way, and he crushed her against him, but her hands pushed him away. His words came out in a groan. "Chevonne, don't. Don't deny—"

Then he realized her hands had crept between him and her and were frenziedly loosening the buttons of his waistcoat. Somehow a tangle of clothing pooled their feet. They sank to their knees. The night air closed around their entwined bodies. The darkness cloaked them. They became one, wrapped in the mystery of the night. He filling her, she sheathing him.

He could feel himself peaking rapidly, and he forced himself to slow down his pace. He nuzzled her soft breasts until her nipples thrust against his tongue. But Chevonne's hot kisses, her arching hips, and her tight body gave him no respite.

When at last fulfillment came, first for him, then for her, their mutual tears cleansed them of all past pain.

Too soon, the night air dried their tears and chased away the fog of alcohol. Clearheaded, he stared at her, aghast. He was jerked back to reality. Had he gone insane? He began dressing her, pulling her gown up over her shoulders, groping at the hooks.

"What are you doing?" she whispered.

He could hear the frantic note in her voice, and said, "We can't let this happen again! Nothing good can come of this night, Chevonne. You can only be hurt by this."

"I don't care about me!" Her hands clutched his shoulders. "I care about us! Don't do this, Brendan. Together, we're greater than anything that could hurt us."

He knew now he should have told her the truth long ago. The real reason behind his flight from her. Perhaps guilt over his continuing incestuous thoughts had kept him silent. He was so confused about his feelings for her that he didn't know anymore what was his highest truth.

He caught her face between his hands. "Don't you understand that you have your career to think about? You have a responsibility to the people. And I have a responsibility to NSW Traders."

She swallowed and turned away. "I understand." Her voice was empty of feeling. As was his heart.

*   *   *

Chevonne stared down at her belly. Flat enough. Nothing to indicate that she carried Brendan's seed. Pleasure and panic surged through her at the same time, overwhelming her.

She knew Bruce would marry her if she gave him even the slightest hint that she wasn't averse to the idea. But how could she give up Brendan, despite his callousness?

How could she settle for lukewarm affection when she knew there was such a thing as grand passion? But perhaps she was lucky that she knew. It only came once. Nothing guaranteed that it would last forever.

That morning she told Minnie that she was having Bruce to dinner and instructed her to serve turbot prepared the old-fashioned way with scallops in a cream-and-dry-vermouth-flavored Mornay sauce.

The wine was poured liberally. She wore an off-the-shoulder gown. Often, she bent toward Bruce, exposing her cleavage. Often, she laughed at his self-centered stories. Stories that were elaborated on, that painted him in a glowing light.

"You are really a great looker, you know that, Chevonne?" His eyes half closed. She knew he was mentally undressing her.

She thought she was going to be sick. Her turbot lay on her gold-rimmed plate, untouched. Her smile felt fake, almost macabre. She lowered her voice to a husky purr. "You excite me when you look at me like that, Bruce."

His pale eyes flared. Then his brows lowered in confusion. "I've been looking at you like that since the moment I saw you standing outside the Old Royal Pub down at Five Ways."

Five Ways was a mass meeting of streets in Paddington, not far from her office across from the Victoria Barracks on Oxford Street. Bruce had had the temerity to approach her and ask her to tea. That was when they had first met.

Her fingertips brushed up and down the valley created by her corseted breasts. "Lately, I haven't felt that I excited you."

His eyes locked on her fingers' motions, he tossed down the remnants of his wineglass. His third or fourth this evening. "You haven't exactly acted like you wanted me to bed you."

To bed me? This was a poet noted for his lyricism? She swallowed her rage. Her lids lowered demurely. "I've been so caught up in campaigning for reelection. . . ."

He pushed back his chair and rose unsteadily. His grin stretched like that of a gargoyle. "I'm gonna spread your legs and make you feel like you've never felt before."

She didn't doubt that.

She knew then she couldn't go through with the deception. She couldn't let him defile her.

*　　*　　*

Over the next few weeks, Brendan flung himself
into a courtship with Moira MacInnes. For the past
year, she had been openly flirting with him at the
Royal Regatta, the Mardi Gras, the Arts Festival.
So, he thought, *Hell, why not?*

He began squiring her around Sydney. Their
names became linked in the newspapers' social
columns. Occasionally, his eye scanned the column,
then, without interest, moved on.

It was assumed that he had bedded the young
divorcée. In truth, his apathy extended even to the
sexual realm. He knew that his lack of interest puzzled the sensuous brunette, but he really couldn't
bring himself to feel aroused by all her ploys.

When Chevonne was reelected to her seat in
Parliament, he dutifully escorted Moira to the
victory celebration. He steeled himself for his first
meeting with Chevonne since their tryst four
months earlier.

He was shocked. Chevonne, who should have
been elated, looked wan. No, ill. Like a faded gar-
denia, her skin had lost its creamy color and
turned sallow. Her eyes and hair were lackluster.
Compared to Moira's vibrant beauty, Chevonne
could have been a walking corpse.

"The campaign has been most rigorous for
Chevonne," Moira murmured. "She looks fagged
tonight." She smiled up at him. "I've been so busy

with you, I hadn't noticed Chevonne's health. I really must tell her to take better care of herself."

That protective side of his nature burst through. As a boy, had he not saved Chevonne from the runaway horse? At this moment, he loved her more than he ever had before. Later, he held her hand a little too long and his eyes stared down into her eyes. "Chevonne, can I talk to you later? Alone?"

She shook her head. "No." Her smile was polite. "There are so many loose ends to tie up, what with the campaign and election."

He could only move on.

That night, he told Moira he would not be seeing her again.

"It's Chevonne, isn't it? You're in love with her. So be it." She fingered his ascot. "I'm still available for you, Brendan beloved."

Moira was glowing with health and vitality, even in her disappointment. Why couldn't he care for her? Because he could not block out Chevonne's anguished face.

When he made no response, Moira pouted. "At least, spare me my pride. Take me to your house and let me spend the night."

"Why? What would that serve?"

She shrugged her lovely shoulders. "People talk. Let them think what they will."

So, he was to be a gem in her crown. What people thought didn't bother him. "Have it as you want, Moira."

He installed her in a guest bedroom that night. As for himself, he was unable to sleep. He dressed early, before the sun had risen, as was his habit, and went downstairs.

"G'day, sir," the butler said and set a cup of tea before him and a folded newspaper.

Almost desultorily, Brendan glanced at the headlines. His eyes widened as he read. Germany had declared war on Russia and France, and in return Great Britain had promptly declared war on Germany.

The Australian Parliament was calling for volunteers to make up an expeditionary force of twenty thousand men promised to Great Britain. The Australian Imperial Forces were to be formed immediately.

Chevonne had to have known last night of the frightful news. That must explain her haggard appearance.

So, it appeared as if a war of worldwide proportions was beginning. He assessed what this war effort would involve. He knew he would commit NSW Traders' steamships to transport men and horses and equipment to battlefields on the other side of the world.

Wearily, he climbed the stairs. He felt old, although he was only thirty-two.

In the guest room, Moira was awake and stretching lazily. Her breasts were full, her brown nipples pouty. Mother Earth breasts. She held out her arms. "Come, my strong stallion. Let me ride you."

"It's time for you to leave. I have a lot to attend to this morning."

She rose, naked, and crossed to him. Lightly, she kissed his lips. Then he heard her soft laugh, her whispered, "You know, I just learned yesterday that your mother ousted my grandfather from NSW Traders board of directors. Small world, isn't it?"

His blood chilled.

25

1915

    Volunteers for what was being called the Great War trained at Liverpool, near Sydney. By the end of October of 1914, NSW Traders had provided twenty-six transports carrying Australian soldiers and ten carrying New Zealanders.

The transports gathered in the deep waters of King George's Sound on the south coast of Western Australia. On November 1, under the escort of British and Australian warships, the latter built in NSW Traders' shipyards, the convoy steamed out onto the high seas bound for the Middle East. En route, the Australian cruiser *Sydney* engaged and sank the German raider *Emden* at the Coco Islands.

Dan didn't know whether to rejoice or mourn. The *Sydney* had also been a NSW Trader vessel. Brendan Tremayne was hailed as Australia's most prominent citizen and patriot.

Forever that Tremayne name to haunt me, Dan thought.

He picked up the newspaper and began reading about the war again. Even though Phillips Enterprises had agreed to the Crown's request to produce uniforms and weapons for the war effort, he had never been pleased about the ethics of this war. Or any war. He had almost lost his daughter to the Boer War. He had almost lost his daughter, period. Now he had her back.

Nursing an infected tooth, he turned the page, searching for something else of interest. Anything to distract him from his sore jaw, anything to distract him from the occasional moans coming from the upstairs bedroom.

He was a stranger in this Paddington house. He was virtually a stranger to the young woman upstairs, who labored to deliver his grandchild.

At least that fool of a Scotsman was gone. A scandal, some said, since Chevonne was large with child. Chevonne wasn't saying who the father was, and Dan wasn't asking.

A scream tore him from his reverie. The newspaper dropped from his hands. He took the steps two at a time. Midway up the staircase, a wail came. He stopped, trembling. His grandchild.

More slowly, he climbed the remaining steps. He felt old indeed.

Minnie met him outside Chevonne's bedroom. In childbirthing, the bedroom door was as impassable to the male as a harem gate. "'Tis a strapping granddaughter ye have," the wizened old woman said. "Colleen, ye daughter said to call her."

"Chevonne? How is Chevonne?"

"It was a tough one for her. A fighter she is. I'm going back inside. The doctor says that you can see your granddaughter and daughter later."

Later was almost too late.

During the night, as Dan dozed in a chair, the doctor awoke him. His balding head was covered with perspiration. "Mr. Warwick. 'Tis your daughter."

Instantly, he was awake. Fear slithered down his spine.

"She's not recovering as I had hoped."

He brushed past the old doctor and headed for the stairs.

"The birthing was too much for her," the old doctor called out. "She's asking for you."

Dan shoved open the door. Chevonne lay in bed. Little sounds like a kitten's mewl issued from her dry, cracked lips. Her eyes were partially opened.

He must have made a sound, because she said, "Papa?" It sounded more like a croak.

"I'm here, Chevonne."

"The baby? She is all right?"

"Colleen is fine." In truth, he had not been able to bring himself to look at the infant. Minnie was in the nursery with the howling baby.

"You must love her."

He took his daughter's hand. It was so thin. And so cold. "Of course I will."

"No. No matter what. Love her. She is Brendan's child, too. I want him, Papa. I want to see him before I die."

The hair on his nape stood up. "Die? You're not going to die. Do you hear me? You're not going to die!"

"Please. I want Brendan."

He was surprised to find he was weeping. His tears were dropping on his and his daughter's clasped hands. "Chevonne, don't give up like this. You can live. Will it so!"

"I . . . want . . . Brendan." With each word her voice seemed to lose power. Her demand was a faint litany in his ears.

"You can't die! You're all I have left!"

"You . . . have . . . Colleen."

Anger surged through him. "She's not you. She's Brendan's child! It's Brendan's lust that is killing you, damn it! This incest is all his fault!"

"Incest . . . what are you . . . talking about?"

He bowed his head. He had been carrying this secret, and this feud far too long. And look at the heartache it had brought him. "Brendan is your first cousin. His mother and I are twins."

For a moment, Chevonne stared at him with wide eyes. Then she began to laugh. A hollow laugh. "Oh, God! Oh, God!" Her laughter turned maniacal.

"Stop it!" he commanded. He was scared.

At once, she stopped. She fixed him with a piercing gaze. "You must learn . . . learn to forgive, Papa. If we are to have any peace. Any chance of happiness. Now listen to me. I am not your natural daughter. Mother loved you . . . from the first."

She paused to draw a weak breath. "But she was already carrying me. You must forgive her . . . forgive Annie . . . and forgive yourself."

Stunned, he stared at his daughter. She would always be his daughter, despite this revelation. In an instant that seemed his lifetime, he realized the enormity of his sin: his unwillingness to try and understand Annie, his arrogant belief that he was above mistakes, his determination to carry his past hurts with him like a shield that would prevent new ones.

"I'll find Brendan. I promise that. Only promise me you will live."

The baby was sleeping peacefully, swathed securely in the flannel blanket. Dan reached down and touched the curling black fuzz of hair. She was so tiny. He could see the blue veins in her hand that was no larger than a farthing.

"Colleen," he whispered. Testing the name. Yes, a suitable name for this precious gift of life.

At that exact moment, he knew he would never be able to die in peace unless he could eradicate his need for revenge, his bitterness, and come to terms with Annie and Brendan.

Where his proud sister had learned to humble herself for her child, he had not. It was time he changed that. He had lost too many loved ones. Nana, Louisa, Frank. He must not let his pride and bitterness ruin any more lives.

With the step of a man twenty years younger, he returned to his bedroom and began dressing. He would go to Brendan Tremayne this very morning. Tell him what Chevonne had said. Tell him about his daughter Colleen. And beg his forgiveness.

That decision made, Dan fully appreciated that agony and pleasure that his grandmother and parents and, yes, Annie, saw in the land, in Australia. Colleen and her generation were its fruit, its salvation.

The hour was still early, only half past seven, when he descended from his Model T and lifted the brass knocker of the door on Elizabeth Bay. A startled servant, an old man, opened the door. "I'm here to see Mr. Tremayne," Dan said. Eagerness to set things right made him impatient.

"Mr. Tremayne, sir? Why, he joined the Anzacs and shipped out last November."

*   *   *

Brendan was learning a lot about trench warfare since joining the Anzacs, that special corps of Australian and New Zealand troops. The Anzacs had established a reputation for outstanding bravery, but the trenches certainly weren't the place to demonstrate such overrated glory.

A network of trenches could stretch as much as 950 kilometers across Europe. In some places, less than 100 meters separated opposing lines. Between those lines of trenches lay no-man's-land.

"Over the top!" a British battlefront commander would shout.

He and other Diggers, Australian soldiers, and Poms, their British counterparts, would climb out of the trenches and dash across no-man's-land.

Armed with fixed bayonet, Brendan would fling grenades, struggle through barbed-wire entanglements, and skirt gaping shell holes. Around him, other soldiers dropped like flies, picked off by machine-gun fire.

He supposed that was the glory part. The real courage was for the other part of trench warfare. The trenches had connected lines so that troops and supplies could be moved to and from the front. Rain filled the dugouts with water and mud, and rats swarmed through the vermin-infested trenches.

Those conditions in the trenches had to account for why he had volunteered for an engagement that was being kept top secret. That and the fact that he really didn't care about personal safety or survival or anything anymore. Remorse had driven him beyond caring. How could he had given in to his lust like some rutting animal? Chevonne deserved better than that.

Then again, maybe he had volunteered for this particular assignment because of the decadent pleasures available after training hours were over.

The Anzac forces were being trained at a camp near Cairo. When not practicing maneuvers, the Australian and New Zealand soldiers pursued pleasures in the cafés and dives of Cairo.

Brendan picked the lowest dives he could find, which wasn't hard to do in that war year of 1915. His favorite spot for debauchery was in the Old City of Cairo, with its crenellated roofs and ancient minarets. Lanterns lit crooked, narrow streets, and veiled women sat like hens in bead-curtained doorways.

The den of delight he selected was far back in a warren of dirty and dark alleys. In that dimly lit place, one reeled from the onslaught of the senses: hashish smoke, strange lutes thrumming off-key melodies, and a stench that was incredible, which told him he was still alive. His senses still reacted, if not his heart.

So when the Anzacs were informed on April first that all leave had been canceled, he didn't feel nervous or frightened. He felt absolutely nothing.

The British general staff had conceived of a plan

to weaken Turkey by forcing a passage through the Dardanelles and bombarding Constantinople. It was a plan for romantics, a plan for those who believed a rich prize outweighed suffering, cruelty, and losses.

Which was what the Anzacs faced if they stormed Gallipoli, the peninsula overlooking the Dardanelles waterway. The heights of Gallipoli were steep and defended by a well-equipped force trained to a fighting edge by the German military adviser to Turkey.

The night of the twenty-fourth of April was exceptionally clear. Had Brendan been back home, he would have been able to see the Southern Cross, that arrangement of stars visible in the Southern Hemisphere and for which the Australian flag had been designed.

Before dawn he and the rest of his advance party rowed for the shore in small boats that kept getting swept farther down shore by the tide, away from the designated spot that was a gradual incline, to an area where the slope was steep and forbidding.

"The command's got to be crazy as loons," a private next to him breathed in the dark of the predawn.

"No worry, chaps," another soldier said. "We can carry the day."

Brendan wasn't so sure. Still, when the boats were landed and an officer commanded, "Over the top!" he followed orders. With the rest of his troop, he stormed the heights of the rugged promontory, singing and shouting.

As they scaled the cliffs, Turkish fire mowed down hundreds around him. Still he pressed on, against tremendous odds, in spite of incessant rifle fire, and bombardment from concealed positions.

He felt a burst of pain in his thigh. Another in his shoulder. He shouted his determination. He battled forward fiercely and valiantly, Chevonne's laughing eyes beckoning him, beckoning him to keep his dreams.

Annie stared at the newspaper article with tears in her rheumy eyes. Her mind couldn't comprehend such a ghastly number. Nearly eight thousand Australians had been killed in the attempt to take the Dardanelles. In the reports filtering back to Australia, Brendan's name was lumped among the dead or missing in action.

Her attention was intruded upon by a popping, rumbling noise. Dropping the newspaper on her reading table, she went to the door herself. Ryan, with the help of a cane, walked in from the breakfast room to join her on the veranda. "What the—"

Because of the shortage of petrol in wartime, few people could afford the luxury of operating an automobile. Yet a Model T motored slowly up the mulberry-lined drive of her Elizabeth Bay home.

To her dismay, Dan alit, carrying a covered basket. As her twin brother drew near, much nearer, she could see that his face was lined with the years of heartache.

"You've triumphed after all, Dan," she said quietly when he walked through the door desolately. She blinked back her tears. "There is no reason for New South Wales Traders to stay in business."

"I think there is," he said softly. His veined hand tugged back the flannel cover on the basket. "Brendan and Chevonne's daughter. Our granddaughter, Annie."

"Oh, my God! Ryan!" She turned to clutch the shoulder of the one man who had been her source of love, comfort, hope over the years.

He put his arm around her waist. "Come into the drawing room, Dan. Rather than a cup of hot tea, I'd say a strong shot of bourbon is in order."

To explain the muddle of the baby's birth and how Chevonne was actually not Dan's biological daughter was easier than to ask forgiveness. While Annie, tears of delight in her eyes, held her granddaughter, Dan stumbled through words that should have been easy for an articulate politician such as he.

"I looked for the worst in people, instead of the best. I don't know if you can ever find it in your heart to forgive me, Annie, but I'd like to start healing our relationship by making a peace offering."

She looked up at him, slightly puzzled. "There's

no need for such a thing, Daniel. I'm as much at fault. I shouldn't have—"

"Annie, I'm trying to tell you something. That as a legislator, I sometimes have more pull than even the powerful Annie Tremayne. At least, when it comes to politics."

He leaned forward on the settee. "I've located Brendan! He's in a field hospital outside Cairo. Rather banged up but with all his limbs intact. With some string pulling, I've managed to have him shipped home."

Chevonne sat in the small garden of her home in Paddington. Reclining in the chaise lounge, she tilted her face to the June sun and soaked up its winter light. She tried to imagine the light filtering through her flesh to warm her dormant heart.

Her father had promised . . .

She clung to that promise, the only real light in her life, discounting Colleen. But as much as she adored her daughter, the baby could not be what Brendan had been to her.

She heard a rustling in the dead leaves littering the yard, but she did not bother to open her eyes. The squirrels were busier than ever this year.

The light brush of lips across her own startled her. Her eyes snapped open. Bending over her was her beloved. She blinked, not trusting what she was seeing—those green eyes like fires, consuming her. "Brendan!"

He knelt beside her, gathering her in his arms. Arms that wore the chevrons of a sergeant on their sleeves. Her cheeks were wet, and she wasn't certain whether the tears were hers or his. "Darling. Darling, Chevonne." His voice cracked like the leaves underfoot.

She began raining wild, fierce, passionate kisses all over his face. "Oh, God, I must be dreaming!" she gasped.

Catching her face between his hands, he stopped her foray of famished kisses and gazed down at her with a love in his eyes that was a hundred times brighter than the Southern Cross, so much more warming than the June sunlight. "No, my dear Chevonne, our dream has been kept."

Bibliography

Arden, Harvey. "Journey into Dreamtime." *National Geographic*, January 1991. 2–39.

Clark, Charles M. *A History of Australia*. Melbourne: Melbourne University Press, 1971.

Clark, Manning. *Short History of Australia*. New York: NAL, 1963

Danl, Joe. *Thornbird Country*. New York: Warner Books, 1983.

Eaton, Clement. *The Growth of Southern Civilization*. New York: Harper & Row, 1961.

Garrett, Wilbert E. "Australia, A Bicentennial Down Under." *National Geographic*, February 1988. 157–294.

Holmes, Ann. "Elissa, the Saving of a Queen." *Museum & Arts*, April 1992.

Hughes, Robert. *The Fatal Shore: The Epic of Australia's Founding*. New York: Random House, 1988.